THE HARP AND THE SEA

Lou Sylvre
Anne Barwell

A NineStar Press Publication

www.ninestarpress.com

The Harp and the Sea

Printed in the USA

Print ISBN: 978-1-64890-062-4

First Edition, July, 2020

Also available in eBook, ISBN: 978-1-64890-061-7

For those who have fought, and continue to fight, for the people they love.

A Note from the Authors

Although this story is a work of fiction, we've set it against a backdrop of real-world places and historical events. While the locations you'll read about do exist, and there certainly was a Jacobean rising in Scotland in the 1740s, the story we've created is a romantic fantasy. We authors may have taken a few liberties because...well, there's magic!

'Tis believ'd that this harp which I wake now for thee

Was a siren of old who sung under the sea.

—Thomas Moore, *The Origin of the Harp*

Part One

Chapter One

1605 the Scottish Border Marches

Robert Ker of Cessford, Lord Roxburgh wielded nearly autonomous power at the turn of the 17th century as Warden of the Scottish Middle March. Often called the Debatable Lands, the Border Marches had rough and fluid application of law. A violent nature and loyalty to kin and ally were all the tools Cessford needed to enforce his judgements. His position made him a powerful man, and though he owed allegiance to Scott of Buccleuch, he marched mostly to his own drummer.

But in the year of Our Lord 1603, King James VI of Scotland became also James I of England, and set about unifying the two countries into Great Britain. His "pacification" of the Border Marches in truth meant abolishing the office of Warden, renaming all the Marches the Middle Shires, and killing enough Borderers to make the rest bend the knee. Having lost autonomy, Ker wormed and weaselled his way into the king's courts at Whitehall and Edinburgh and commenced warring on the people of the March without mercy as a way to impress the monarch.

*

On a rain-soaked day in autumn, 1605, the rough men who served Ker of Cessford and King James Stuart shoved Robbie Elliot into a damp prison cell beneath Hermitage—a stark and haunted castle located almost dead centre in the Middle March, a place Robbie had once called home. When he heard the heavy oaken door thunk shut behind him, rattling the rusty iron chains and window bars, he fell to his knees in the filthy straw that lay scattered over the stone floor. He and a half-dozen others had been force-marched sixteen miles from Hawick, bound, handled rough, and prodded with sticks. Now Robbie tried in vain to find a few square inches of his body that didn't cry out in pain.

"There's water, Robbie." The weak, high-pitched male voice came from the darkest corner of the cell, and it gave Robbie a start for he'd thought himself alone. "In the barrel there," the man continued. "It's clean enough."

Robbie's legs obeyed him after only a brief argument, and he stood and walked to the barrel. Dust and chaff floated on the top, but when he dipped the single iron ladle and brought the water to his lips, it had no foul smell. "I've had far worse," Robbie said, and then drank.

When he'd slaked his thirst enough, he turned to his cellmate, who'd stepped out of the shadows. "How'd you come to be here, Keithen?"

"Same as you, I'd wager. I'd heard the warden's men were on the march, and I meant to hide at my old da's holding, east of Kelso. But I was caught no more than ten miles from Hermitage castle and strung along with five others—including your stepbrother Jem. We'd thought we'd go no further than the gallows on the hill, but they brought us here."

"Jem? He's here?"

"Alas, Robbie, he was a lucky one, for he'll never see these cells. He fell on the trail, and the warden's man kicked his head a mite hard. Snapped his neck."

Robbie piled up some straw and sat, slumping back against the wall, his own head pounding as if he'd been the one kicked. Keithen, who tended to prattle on most of the time, stayed blessedly silent until Robbie spoke up a few minutes later. "Yes, probably lucky to die then, quick like that. Do you ken why they brought us here? What they're planning for us?"

A sudden rattle of heavy keys beyond the door interrupted the prisoners' conversation, and a single, crusted pot was pushed inside, its contents warm enough to steam in the perpetual cold of the below-ground keep.

Keithen said, "Porridge, or what passes for it," and then got up and lumbered stiffly to fetch the pot.

Robbie realised all at once that his insides had gone so hollow he'd be happy to fill them with a brick if it was all he had, and he wasted no time. Given no utensils, the two men scooped the thick, sticky oatmeal with their hands, minding neither the slight burn nor extra flavour of the dirt and blood on their own skin. By the time they finished, Robbie had forgotten his last question entirely until Keithen answered it.

"I heard a couple English talking yesterday—their voices come down clearly through the shaft, just there." He pointed at a corner of the ceiling, a black, empty rectangle amid the grey stone. "They said we'll be marched to Carlisle, and wicked James himself, the king, travels there too. They'll hang us all at once—for his entertainment."

Robbie said nothing for a long while, his mind focused instead on whether he could find a way to die sooner rather than give the king his satisfaction. He could think of nothing short of refusing water or smashing his head against the stones, and he knew he wouldn't do either. Although small in stature, he'd proven himself brave in battle when he was no more than fourteen, and he'd borne his wounds as well as any man. *But courage has its limits,* he thought, *and the pain of drying to dust from the inside out or smashing my own skull is beyond mine.*

At last he said, "Well, Keithen, some comfort. At least we'll die among our own, and not alone."

*

The distance from Hermitage to Carlisle measured a bit over thirty miles. The trip took three days, due to the need to move more than a hundred prisoners, most of them weak or lame. On the surface, the journey seemed a bit kinder than the forced march from Hawick. If a man fell and couldn't rise to walk again, the guards tossed him onto the cart, rather than kill him or leave him to die, but that wasn't compassion. They made no secret of their orders to bring as many as possible to Carlisle alive, for that castle's lord meant to make a grand spectacle of the mass hanging.

Carlisle's dungeon stank of offal and sweat accumulated through centuries of cruelty. When Robbie stumbled into the broad room with Keithen and a score of others, he first thought perhaps his sanity had fled, for some of the stone had a crimson colour that made him think of raw wounds, and all manner of eerie images had been carved by prisoners into the walls. The smell of damp made him think next of his thirst, but when he looked around, he saw no water barrel such as at Hermitage.

Then an old man—who looked much like Robbie imagined Death would appear—rose feebly and stumbled to a spot on the wall where water oozed from the stone, stuck out his swollen tongue, and licked away the droplets. Silence fell on the crowd of new arrivals as they watched the man, but a guard looking on from outside the iron bars of the door laughed.

"No need for you to lick the stones, Reivers, for the king is here, the gallows are ready, and the hangin' is set for dawn."

Robbie guessed dawn had arrived when he heard the rattle of keys moving cell to cell down the aisle. Many of the captive men began to pray, a few to weep, but this wasn't the final call, not yet. When the door swung open to the room, six guards, heavily armed and armoured, entered the cell and lined the prisoners up against the long back wall, then four more guards entered with a soft, waxy-looking man cloaked in fur and wearing cloth of gold and royal purple.

"His Majesty!"

The shout came from a man alongside the foremost guard, rather a pretty fellow, Robbie thought. The prisoners all bowed after a few received blows, and Robbie didn't see any point in doing otherwise, so he made the least bow he thought he could get away with. When he straightened he felt the king's eyes burning into him, so he turned and met the man's gaze. James but said nothing, only cocking his head to the side as if studying a rare bird.

Still, no one could have been more surprised than Robbie when the king addressed him. "Your name?"

"Robert Elliot."

King James raised his eyes again, and one of the guards took a threatening step towards him, the butt of his sword raised, so Robbie added, "Your Majesty."

A fleeting but cruel smile crossed the king's lips. "Elliot? You *are* a Reiver, then?"

"Yes...Your Majesty. By birth."

"Birth..." The king raised his right brow and turned his head slightly so it seemed he examined Robbie with that one large brown eye. His smile became a smirk. "You are young, though. Have you gone a-reiving?"

"I'm twenty-two years old come the new year, Majesty. And yes, I have ridden out with my clansmen."

"Ah! But you have another trade?"

Keithen spoke up—quite bravely as he had not been addressed—"Your Majesty, Robbie is a bard, a piper, and has a sweet touch indeed on the strings of the harp."

Robbie's fingers twitched of their own accord at the mention of the instrument he so missed, but he said nothing. The king, too, stayed silent, and no one in that dungeon room moved—or even breathed, it seemed.

Finally, James nodded. "I see. I've a notion to hear you play, Robert Elliot." He turned to his guards. "Take him. Feed him, clean him well, and bring him to me."

The door clanged shut behind the king and his men, and all Robbie's fellow prisoners moved away from him, crowding themselves in the far corner to give him berth. Some few cast him a pitying look, as if his fate to go before the king was worse than theirs, to hang. And Robbie felt inclined to agree. Keithen came to sit next to him on the straw pallet against the wall, and Robbie turned to him, angry.

"Why'd you tell him that, man? Why did you betray me?"

Keithen twisted his lips into something like a smile. The expression made him look mildly contrite, but he didn't apologise. He whispered, "Robbie, are you forgetting that the first time you marched out to fight when you were fourteen, I took you under my wing and taught you to soldier? Do you not understand how thoroughly I know you?"

Robbie was afraid he knew what the older man was getting at. "Of course I remember, Keithen. If it hadn't been for you, I'd have died in the very first clash. But say what you're getting at, straight out."

"Lad, you have a great gift with the harp and song. You're not a Reiver true; your only crime against the king is your birth into the Elliot clan. You're young, and you should have your life ahead. It's not my words that are going to buy you a chance at it. I know how you are, Robbie, about men—not women. You don't hide it well. The king, they say he's like you in that. It's your person, then, and perhaps your songs, that might spare you hanging. My words just gave him the excuse he needed to separate you out from the rest of us—who are certainly damned."

Keithen shook his head and blew out an exasperated breath, then concluded, "Live if you can, Robbie. Live for all of us."

*

Robbie had followed the guard sent to fetch him up to a small room one level up from the dungeon cell. He'd eaten the food he found on a rough table there, having no qualms about filling his belly at the Keeper of Carlisle's expense. Not food from the nobles' table, clearly, but solid fare—mutton stew and dark, heavy bread. Likely what the servants ate. He had both water and dark ale to drink, and by the time he pushed away his bowl, his belly felt packed fuller than it had in months. After the meal, two women came in—one young, one old, both coarse—bearing pitchers, lye soap, and thick cloths. Two men followed bearing a round oaken tub filled with water warm enough to steam.

"Sithee," said the younger of the two women in the cadence of Highland speech. "If the king is no' happy wi' the job we do cleanin' and dressin' ye, he'll be punishin' us. Please, mon, strip and step into the tub!"

They scrubbed every inch of Robbie's skin to the point he felt too raw to wear clothes, but he donned the shirt, breeks, and stockings they'd brought for him, and put the slippers on his feet. The clothes were of finer cloth than any he'd worn since he'd fled the king's 'pacification' with his cousins a year ago to hide in the caves at Glenshee, the centuries-ago Elliot clan home in the Highlands. He spent only a single thought wishing he'd never come home. He had more immediate concerns. As he dressed, he argued with himself.

I could get used to a full belly and soft slippers.
Sure, and you know what you'll have to do for it.
Perhaps James is looking for a good bard?
Don't be daft, Robbie Elliot.
It doesn't matter, really, does it? For I'll no more sing for him than serve him in bed.
And so you'll hang, then, Rob, after all.

"I will," Robbie said aloud into the now empty chamber, and then sighed. "But I'll hang with a full belly, and that's something."

*

The sun was about an hour past dawn when Robbie was taken up to the castle proper. It hurt his eyes, and it gave him a start; the hanging had been slated for dawn—why hadn't he felt anything when so many kinsmen died?

But when he was marched into the king's solar, he saw out the broad windows the gallows lined up on the greensward, each with a Borderer standing beside it with a guard—he wasn't to miss the hanging after all. Something sharp twisted inside Robbie's belly, and he clenched his teeth to keep tears from forming. He didn't entirely understand his own reaction. He didn't love most of these men. Many had been cruel to him because they knew him, knew what he was and who he was likely to lie with. But they were kin, even those of rival families, and if Borderers were rough and hard and sometimes lawless, they'd been pushed into it by the avarice of royalty, nobility, and church. "They're only men," he whispered, not thinking.

"Be silent," one of James's men said, then pushed Robbie forward in front of the king, knocking him to his knees.

"Robert Elliot," James said. "You will watch this spectacle with us so that you can make a song of it. You'll sing it at our celebration this night."

Robbie wanted to refuse, but he couldn't find breath. The king snapped his fingers and pointed to a corner, and the guard all but dragged him there, facing a tall window. Robbie looked outside. Directly across, Keithen was being led to the rope. Startled, he drew a sharp breath and turned his face away—and that was when he saw Melisandre, Lady Talwyn, the Witch of the Hermitage, standing a short distance away facing the gallows.

She chanted and drew her hands through the air in sweeping gestures, and when she finished on a last loud syllable, Robbie thought—just for a moment—that he saw a curtain of gold light drop over the windows. The witch turned to the king and bowed, though not deeply. "Your Majesty," she said. "It's done."

"Good," James said from his chair. "The last thing we need, in this world full of demons and dark things, is to suffer a barrage of curses from dying Borderers. You are certain none can penetrate the shield you have set?"

"Yes, sire."

"Go then and collect your reward from Carlisle's treasury. But know this, if you have tricked us, if any curse touches us this night or if we ever find out you borrow your magic from the Devil and not from the Holy Spirit as you claim, you will burn."

As Melisandre left, she slid her eyes sideways to meet Robbie's puzzled gaze for just a moment. As she passed, Robbie could have sworn that in his mind he heard her say, "Not a word, Robbie Elliot. You do not know me!" He knew it for a warning.

Robbie watched his kin hang, and by some gift of ancient gods, he didn't flinch, neither looked away nor cried out. He watched, but not for the king. He stood witness for the Borderers whose lives were so brutally, so unjustly wasted that day. And while he did not envy them, he did think that his lot, to bear this knowledge and live, might be the worse fate.

When that was over, the king ordered him to take off his shirt. Robbie refused, and the king's men ripped it off.

The king told Robbie to sing. He refused, and at a signal from James, a guard struck him open handed until he couldn't stop a cry of pain.

The king asked, "Do you know why we brought you here, Robert Elliot?"

Robbie didn't answer.

The king's voice grew husky, and he shifted in his chair. "You seem extraordinary, compared to the worthless souls we hung today. Beautiful, in fact. If you will come to us willingly, Robbie. If you will perhaps sing and play for us, and grant our other wishes, you will live— perhaps a long life. Perhaps in luxury, with all your wants and needs fulfilled."

The king waited, but Robbie gave no reply, so he spoke again, this time with a tone of anger. "What do you answer, Robert Elliot."

"No," Robbie said, and let his disgust and defiance show on his face. "No, Your Majesty. I'd rather die than lie with you, or even sing at your command."

"Ah," said James and sighed—a genuinely sad sound. "Well, then you shall."

James Stuart clapped his hands, and the guards marched Robbie away.

Chapter Two

Robbie was taken away from the king's solar by a different route than the one he'd taken to get there, a darker way, musty and damp. He tried to convince himself he was ready to die, but his heart beat so hard and fast he could hear it echo in the narrow stone corridor. Just when he thought they couldn't be far from the gallows, one of the guards forced a reeking cloth over his face. He breathed in once—and knew nothing at all after that.

When he recovered consciousness, he lay on damp grass surrounded by starved-looking trees—an ancient yew and elders heavy with overripe, rotting red berries. Among the vegetation, a stone cabin squatted crookedly with a light shining out from under the door and a plume of smoke rising from the chimney. A river rushed noisily by in the near distance. Most likely the Eden, Robbie thought, as he couldn't have been unconscious overlong.

He struggled to his feet, still slightly dizzy, and looked around. He could see no one, but then a woman's voice came from the dark under the trees. "I arranged your escape, Robbie Elliot. You are here because I've purposed it."

"Lady Talwyn?" The voice was clear and musical, and Robbie knew it well, for Melisandre, Lady Talwyn bore the sobriquet 'Witch of Hermitage Castle.' Robbie had known her from childhood, as did all Armstrongs and Elliots who lived in that dark castle or under its shadow.

She stepped forth, her face bearing its famous and deceptive smile. "When I saw you in the king's presence, I knew what he wished, and I knew you would not accede. Thus, I knew you would be condemned, so I paid a few good men to bring you to me instead."

"But the Stuart will certainly know I haven't been hung!"

"No. I arranged a ruse as well."

Something about that statement licked at Robbie's conscience, but he didn't pursue it. He had other questions, and he couldn't bring himself to believe this was even happening, much less that he would remain safe in these circumstances. "Why would you do this thing for me, Lady?"

"I have reasons—more than one. We will speak of them later. For now, I will tell you only this. You have a touch of magic in you, though you've only used it for the beauty of your song. We are kin, of a distant sort, and I believe you can be of use." She laughed suddenly, merrily, and shook her head. "But there is compassion in my heart as well, Robbie, and I know you are tired, and sore, and frightened, and more than anything, hungry. Come in. Dine and take your ease in my home, such as it is."

Robbie did go in and found comfort there that night and for the following week, even finding the witch decent company, though he knew she was not as she seemed; her age and appearance remained disguised by glamour spells. She wanted to apprentice him, for her efforts to teach her son, whom she called Fargy and clearly did love, had come to naught. He simply couldn't learn the complicated things she was trying to pass on.

"The boy has no more magic in his spirit than he has a head for numbers," she said.

Robbie might have run away at his first chance, but his first night there, she brought out his harp.

"I had some men retrieve this for you. It was in the weather overnight and likely needs tuning, but I hope you'll play for Fargy and me."

Robbie never thought once of saying no. When he saw his harp, he simply rejoiced, and within the hour, he knew the bliss of being lost in his song. Melisandre and Fargy loved hearing him play and sing, but he didn't do it for them; he did it to ease his own tired soul.

He learned a few things from her in the days he stayed with Lady Talwyn—he found her everyday spells came easily—but he knew they were only simple things, and not even true magic. He could ward the front door. He could encourage the coals to flame. He could call a bird—but he'd done that before simply by singing a quiet song or playing his harp.

All the while, Robbie was aware of Fargy's growing infatuation with him—all sorts of smiles and touches, and seeking Robbie out when he meant to be alone. Robbie wasn't interested, couldn't be, for though the witch's son was tall and strong and very fine to look at, he thought like a child. Robbie knew he'd be using Fargy wrong if he took the favours he seemed to want to offer.

His uneasiness began to build by the fourth day. The matter of Fargy niggled away at him, and something else hovered in the back of his mind. Not even his harp could set him at ease. He couldn't quite make sense of the Melisandre rescue, but more than that, he felt lost in his own mind, as if he couldn't quite pick up the thoughts he wanted.

On the seventh day, he knew he had to get away for a time to clear his thinking. He set out not long after dawn while the witch was at her altar making prayers to the old gods with twigs and blood and a bowl of water for Clíodhna, her favourite. Out in the fresh morning, he breathed deep and walked on, following a narrow path to the banks of the River Eden. There, standing on a high knoll, he thought he could see gulls over Solway Firth, though it was a long way off.

The breeze coming through crisp and clean cleared his mind, and he sat down on a solitary stone to think things through. He focused foremost on questions as to why the witch had paid his way out of James Stuart's grasp, but he found no answer. He wondered how the king could have been so easily fooled, and he recalled what Lady Talwyn had said that day.

"I've arranged a ruse."

*

When Robbie returned to Melisandre's cottage, the peat fire in the hearth felt warm and homey, tea and cheese and biscuits satisfied his hunger, and a dreamy feeling came over him. Fargy came in from outdoors, bringing an oddly fresh smell of autumn leaves with him, and sat in the rocker, pulling it close to where Robbie had stretched out on his pallet. Too drowsy to put distance between them, Robbie ignored Fargy's starry-eyed gazing and closed his own eyes. He must have slept, for when he woke to Melisandre's voice, the light that came in through the west window lay low and slanted and yellow gold, and the shadows had grown long.

"Robbie," the witch called. And when Robbie sat up, she added, "It's time for you to choose."

His thoughts confused, Robbie sent her a questioning look.

"Will you stay and apprentice with me, or no? You may never have great power with magic, but what magic is in you flows easily. I can teach you many things."

"I must choose. You can teach me." Robbie said, and it wasn't a question. He merely repeated what Lady Talwyn said, feeling that was what he was supposed to do.

"You must choose, Robbie. You'll stay with me."

Robbie was about to affirm that he would, though his thoughts continued to seem strangely askew. But at that moment, a skein of geese flew low overhead, calling out to one another, making a raucous noise with their harsh voices. The sound roused Robbie, shook him free of the drowse he now guessed the witch had laid over him. He went out through the door to stand in the yard.

He took in the sight of the place, and it was as if he'd never seen it before. Worn thin patches of sod, chicken feathers and rotting entrails, fallen stones and rusted pots. The cabin slouching down and leaning, filth caked on the threshold and window casings. Melisandre followed him out, and Robbie's gaze pierced her glamour, revealing to him her wizened skin, sunken eyes, and matted, filthy hair.

Her voice cracked and scraped over Robbie's brain. "Ah! You see me true, do you, Robbie? Well, no matter. I can return you to peace with our home, with me. You can live out your life—a long one—in beauty. There's no shame in a glamour. Everybody pretends their lives are prettier than they truly are." Her voice sweetened, and she walked towards him, her hand held out in front of her as if to cast something on him again.

"Don't come closer, Lady Talwyn." He had no way to predict whether she would heed him, but she did. In his moment of clarity, he remembered the question he'd intended to confront her with as soon as he returned from his morning wandering. "Tell me, what did you mean when you said you arranged a ruse so the Stuart wouldn't know I'd not been hanged? And before you answer, Lady, please remember: though I'm young yet, I'm not a fool."

Melisandre turned away from him, and when she turned back, she'd restored her glamour, though their surroundings remained disgusting. She stood quietly for a moment, a frustrated—or perhaps chagrined—smirk on her lips. "Very well, then. Perhaps you have more magic in you than I thought. But you said you're no fool, and if that's true, you will choose the path I've laid for you despite any displeasure. What I arranged, you see, is for another to die in your place."

Robbie's jaw went slack. "Who?"

"It was nobody in particular. I had Fargy find a man who looked a bit like you, and I traded him to the guards with their payment when they brought you."

"That's...horrible, Lady Talwyn."

"Do you think? More horrible than allowing *you* to die? Did *you* commit some great crime against James Stuart?"

"Yes," Robbie answered her first question. "It is more horrible."

"Well, at times it's necessary to do such things. Come back inside. The evening has grown chill."

"No, Melisandre. I'll not follow you inside, and I'll not take the path you've laid for me."

She had reached the door now, and she stood on the threshold as she turned back to face him once again. "One more thing you should consider before I take that 'no' as final. You have learned far too many things I'd prefer to keep hidden. If you will not stay with me, all my efforts to save your skin will have been in vain." She waited a moment, brows arched. "Do you see?"

Before Robbie could answer, Fargy ran towards his mother—beautiful and simple as ever—and fell on his knees before her. Clenching the hem of her dress, he cried, "Mother, no! Please do not kill Robbie! I love him! Please?"

Tears were streaming down Fargy's face, and he kept crying "no, no, no" while his mother bent to embrace him and attempted to soothe him. Finally he broke free, ran to Robbie, and grabbed his hands. "Robbie, please. Please stay! So Mother won't have to kill you. I love you, Robbie! Maybe you love me too?"

The crying continued, and it was all Robbie could do to break the man's good heart, but he must. "No. No!" He repeated it more firmly and pulled his hands from Fargy's grasp. "I don't love you, Fargy, and I won't. I can see that your mother truly does care for you, though." Lady Talwyn had begun to silently cry over her son's distress. "Still, I can't stay."

Fargy let out a howl of despair so awful Robbie's heart skipped.

Lady Talwyn embraced her son again. "Quiet, now," she said. "All right, I won't kill Robbie."

Still sobbing, Fargy choked out, "Promise, Mother?"

"Yes, I promise. Now go inside and make me some tea."

After her son was inside and out of earshot, the witch turned to Robbie. "I suppose it would have killed you to say to him that you loved him? He's a beautiful man, Fargy is."

"But I don't! How could I? He's a child, in his mind. And I'll not be false with him any more than I was false with the king."

"Ah! So you're holding out for true love, is it?"

Robbie said nothing.

After a silence, Lady Talwyn nodded. "Well, gather the few things you have. We will go to the river at nightfall. Fargy will carry your harp for you. I've a small boat. I'll set you on your way. Do not think of running, Robbie. I'll not kill you, but see, I can't let you live in this place now, if you're not safe under my roof. If the king's men find you, we'll both live our last hours in Carlisle's thirsty dungeon."

Robbie thought for a minute, lips pursed, then slowly nodded.

"Do I have your word you'll not break away? If not, I'll bind you, and I won't be kind about it."

"Yes, Lady. You have my word."

For the rest of the afternoon and on into evening, while Fargy and Robbie ate a supper of stew and bread, the witch stayed in the small room where she kept all her books and ingredients. Her mumblings seeped through the intervening wall, the low sound a source of distress for Robbie. He fought the urge to bolt, but Fargy could hold him, and would, and Melisandre would make good on her threat.

Finally, when he thought he could bear his unease no longer, she came out into the cabin's living space, flushed and slightly breathless.

She refused the bowl of stew Fargy held out for her. "We'll go now."

Once they left the cabin yard and came under starlight, Robbie felt a sudden need to get away, certain the witch's plan didn't involve a simple bon voyage. But how could he run when his beloved harp was secure in Fargy's thick-muscled arms?

Perhaps Melisandre heard his thoughts, or guessed them, for she repeated, "I'll bind you, Robbie, and I won't be kind. Follow along."

He trudged ahead in the darkness for some time before he realised she likely had already put a binding on him. She'd tied him magically to his harp. As time passed he became less and less able to think of anything else. He stared at the harp, focused solely on its gleaming wood and curves. Fargy became all but invisible carrying it.

They arrived at the River Eden and went down to a place where a shallow bank slowed the waters. A small cobble lay half-beached there, and Fargy placed the harp in it as his mother instructed. Melisandre told Fargy to go back home. Though he protested, he went.

Robbie stepped into the boat on his own—but he thought possibly not by his volition. Seated, he hugged the harp to his chest.

"Give me the key, Robbie."

No thought of disobedience entered Robbie's mind. He bent to the harp's base and opened the small slot there, removed the tuning key, and passed it to the witch. He puzzled only fleetingly about why she wanted it, or how he would tune the harp without it. Still he sighed in relief when she placed the key in a box, snapped it shut and whispered a word to seal it, then set it near him in the boat.

"Ironwood," she said, "of a kind that grows only on the Isle of Man, and only rarely there. When it falls into the water, it won't float on the surface, but neither will it sink and stay on the bottom. Instead, it will drag along, in tow of any current that catches it." She laid bundles of several herbs in the boat. Robbie wondered about them, and he wondered why he didn't care more about what was happening to him. Only mildly interested in the witch's doings, he asked no questions.

"Now," she commanded, "sit whilst I prepare your soul so that Clíodhna will cradle you as you descend, and you may indeed live. You wanted a chance at true love? You shall have it. You shall perhaps have it over and over again, but...well. Never mind."

She placed both her hands on Robbie's head, and something warm entered and expanded inside his skull. "I've made for you a spell, Robbie. Perhaps my very finest work. It may be a kind of blessing, but I'm sure it will seem a curse. I lay my hands on your head to prepare you. Now, whatever I speak, you will remember."

She told him about the elements of the magic: the harp and its key, the sea and Robbie's soul. And then she began to chant, and the signs she wove with her hands hung in the air and burned:

> This harp I curse to hold your mind, this boat
>   to hold your breath.
> The sea will receive your soul, suspend it
>   'twixt life and death.
> So ye shall wait for the call of a woeful and
>   broken heart,
> Wakened ye'll strive to kindle love, to coax the
>   flame to start.
> If love slips through your fingers like water
>   ye'll follow it back to the sea.
>
> To Clíodhna go ye, of the murky deep
> To wander waves in darkling sleep
> 'til three times sings the harp
> And three times spills the blood

And need like a candle flames
And sparks the key beneath the flood

And two hearts shall in rapture tell
That love does come to break this spell.

Twice she chanted it, and when she commenced a third repeat, she raised her hands towards the boat, and it pushed away. As she spoke the last lines, Robbie felt the river take the boat in its grasp. He'd long since lost sight of her and her shore when he smelled the salty tang of Solway Firth and heard gulls crying overhead and all around.

Just at pearly dawn, the firth gave way to ocean. Robbie noted with mild interest that water had begun to pool around his bare feet in the bottom of the cobble. He paid it no mind, for he understood that there was no undoing this plight.

He waited content, hearing the wind's music on the harp strings and the rhythmic lapping of the sea.

Chapter Three

Glenfinnan, 1744

Ian MacDonald walked briskly, in part because of the cold, and in part because he'd never been one for putting off a confrontation. If that was what this was. If his uncle, the Laird Alistair, had something he wished to discuss, it was better to get it over with. Ian well remembered the last conversation they'd had that had started with Alistair's 'request' for Ian to meet with him. Although it was an exchange he'd prefer to forget, he wouldn't back down from another.

He'd done nothing wrong. Not now, not recently, and—he still vowed—not ever. What he'd had with Angus wasn't wrong, but the way Angus had reacted had left Ian with a determination never to be put in that situation again. He'd been brought up to stand up for whom and what he believed in. Angus apparently hadn't. Unless the man had been lying to Ian the entire time they'd...

Ian's steps faltered. Angus had been scared, that was all. And, Ian thought bitterly, Angus apparently hadn't believed what they'd had was worth fighting for. And if Angus hadn't, why should Ian?

The past was the past and needed to stay there. He'd keep his head down and follow orders, just like he had for the last two years. Besides, he hadn't seen anyone since who'd taken his interest as Angus had done.

He wasn't likely to either.

The past was the past. And Ian was where he was meant to be. The warmth from the hall ahead beckoned. Ian sped up his steps again and rapped on the main door before entering.

"You wanted to see me, sir?" Ian asked after he'd taken the seat by the fire his uncle indicated. He warmed his hands over the flames, thankful for the excuse to be inside. It was cold out and would most likely snow by nightfall.

"Aye, lad, I did." Alistair MacDonald studied Ian intently for a few moments. He was a quiet man by nature but wise, and when he spoke, the people of his clan listened. "You're a good lad, and I'm verra fond of you."

"I know ye are, Uncle." Ian was fond of his uncle too. The man was like a second father to him but had always been very careful to be seen not to favour his nephew. Needless to say, people still talked, especially about the seemingly blind eye their laird had turned in regard to Ian's 'preferences.' In a small community it was near impossible to hide anything, despite Ian's intentions to keep private things private. He'd never been good at hiding his feelings.

"This is why what I'm about to ask of you is verra difficult for me, although you're the person best suited for the task." Alistair sounded so serious that Ian looked at him in surprise, and with some concern. He'd only heard this tone on very few occasions, and it had only been directed towards him once. Once had been more than enough.

"Have I done something wrong?" he asked, holding his head up high. "That Campbell devil deserved what he got. You said so yourself at the time." Ian frowned. "I haven't done anything I shouldn't, Uncle. I swear." He'd mostly kept to himself since the incident with Campbell a few months back, although he'd been tempted to hunt the man down and finish him off after what he'd done.

"I know you haven't, lad." Alistair handed Ian a cup of ale, which he took but didn't drink. "I know it's not been easy for you, but ye made the right decision in leaving him well alone, and often those are the hardest." He took a sip from his own cup and then put it down on the floor by his chair. "People still talk, and they don't forget."

"Aye, don't I know it," Ian said, keeping his voice even.

He'd seen the way some of the older women looked at him, and although they didn't say anything to his face, he'd heard the talk about how he'd never shown interest in any of the local lassies. Nothing went on in their village without those old women knowing. Some of them thought *they* ran the village, rather than the laird, but Alistair had never challenged them on it. He probably had enough sense not to.

"I'm putting it behind me. I promised ye that, and I'm a man of my word."

What was this about? Alistair seemed to be hedging around whatever it was he needed to say, and that wasn't like him.

"I know ye are." Alistair met Ian's gaze. Ian returned it without flinching. "Although you've done nothing wrong, if this plan is to succeed, people must believe you have."

"If what plan is to succeed? Uncle, what is it ye would have me do?" Ian didn't like the sound of this. Surely, his uncle wouldn't expect him to do something dishonest? Ian might be loyal, both to his clan and to the Jacobite cause, which he knew his uncle supported, but there were some lines he would not cross.

"I have pledged our support to the Bonnie Prince as ye well know." Alistair took a drink of ale. He nodded towards the cup Ian held, indicating he should drink, but Ian shook his head. He wanted a clear head so he could follow whatever it was his uncle was about to say. "When the prince reaches Scotland, he will need money to raise an army and take back the throne that is rightfully his."

"Aye, he will." Ian still didn't see what any of this had to do with him. Surely his uncle did not expect him to steal for the cause? No one on the laird's holdings could be called rich. They had enough provisions put aside for the coming winter so no one would starve, and their animals would be well cared for, but there was nothing extra. Nothing left that could be traded to fetch money for the cause.

"Are you a loyal Jacobite, Ian?" Alistair asked. "Will ye do what I bid, no questions asked, no matter the consequences to yourself in doing so?"

Ian hesitated for a moment. He really didn't like the sound of it, but in the finish, there was only one answer he could give. "Aye, sir, I am, and I will."

"Good lad." Alistair smiled, but there was sadness in his eyes. "As I've said, the only way this will work is if people think you've done something wrong." He put down his tankard. "We have been trusted to guard a great treasure. It needs to be kept safe and well hidden."

"It's for the prince? You want me to guard this treasure until it's needed?

"Aye." Alistair nodded. "I have a place for ye to keep it safe, but only you and I will know of it. It is also important that no one knows of your part in this. If you disappear, questions will be asked, especially as you've made it clear you have no wish to leave Glenfinnan."

The beginning of their conversation made more sense now. "You're banishing me," Ian said slowly. "After everything that happened with Angus, and your decision to let me stay, you want people to believe I would still betray you? Surely there's got to be another way!"

"There isn't." Alistair got up from his chair and stared into the glowing embers of the fire. "I'm not doing this lightly. If I tasked anyone else with this, there would be too many questions asked."

"I wouldn't betray ye."

"No, you wouldn't." Alistair turned away from the fire. "I trust ye, but you've been caught once doin' somethin' most people think you shouldn't have. It's not unbelievable you would again."

Ian bit his lip. "Uncle, the thing ye refer to caused no one harm, and my taking up a *friendship* is a far cry from betraying my laird, my cause, and my people. Do ye honestly believe I'd do that?"

"Nae." Alistair placed one hand on Ian's shoulder. "But your clansmen need to think ye would. We can't risk anyone going after you, either for vengeance or out of concern. I will tell them tomorrow that it is already done. Stealing from your laird is not only a serious crime, but a betrayal of trust. The story will be that I had no choice but to act immediately as soon as I caught you in the act. It is a harsh punishment, but better for everyone concerned."

Alistair was right. No one questioned the ruling of the laird or would insult him by asking questions as to the nature of Ian's crime. The implication that Ian had stolen from the laird, from his blood kin and beloved uncle, would be enough, especially given the stories already told of him. Of his being caught in a compromising position with another man.

"Can my mam and da know?" Deep down, Ian already knew the answer, but he needed to ask anyway. He hoped the question didn't sound childish. Despite Alistair's trust in him, Ian always felt much younger than his twenty-five years when he was in his uncle's presence.

"Nae." Alistair cleared his throat. "I'm sorry, Ian." He reached inside the leather sporran that hung below the belt buckle of his kilt and drew out a small envelope. "Keep this on your person at all times. It is a letter in my hand, clearing you from wrongdoing. It states that you are on clan business with my blessing but does not go into the specifics of that business. Only use it if you have to, but ensure you do if it comes down to it." He smiled a little and leaned over to ruffle Ian's hair as he had when Ian was a child. "You've grown into a good man, nephew. I'm verra proud of you."

"Thank ye, Uncle." Ian would miss his uncle. A chill was beginning to settle in his gut, a fear that he might never see him again. "When do I leave and where are ye sending me?"

"Collect your belongings as quickly as possible. You leave tonight. There is a boat waiting for you on the shores of Loch Shiel a short distance from here." Alistair handed Ian the envelope.

Ian tucked it inside his sporran and nodded. "At the part of the shoreline where the sea meets the sky?" It was a fanciful description for a place where his uncle had taken him when he was younger. They'd never used the phrase in front of anyone else.

"Aye. The man you'll meet there can be trusted. He'll take ye to—"

Ian held his finger to his lips, signalling silence. He listened carefully. Yes! There it was again. The telltale creak of the floorboard just outside the door. He reached for his dirk and crept silently towards the sound.

Alistair nodded, then jerked his head towards the door. He'd heard it too. "He'll show ye everything ye need to know," he continued as though their conversation hadn't been interrupted.

"You can rely on me, Uncle." Ian heard rustling, just for an instant, and barely there but still unmistakable, especially for an experienced hunter.

He kicked open the door, hard and without warning. The man behind it went flying, and Ian was on top of him as soon as he hit the ground.

His opponent kicked and fought, managing to punch Ian in the face. He brought up one hand. In it was a knife. He slashed at Ian, drawing blood. Ian slammed his knee against the man's wrist. The weapon dropped onto the floor. The eavesdropper brought his other hand up to land another punch, but Ian ducked and grabbed him, pinning his arms to his sides. Ian let go and pulled him up by his hair before he had the chance to move. Ian held his dirk to his prisoner's throat. How much had he heard?

His captive's breathing was heavy, ragged. Ian dragged his dirk over his opponent's throat. A tiny trickle of blood welled up from the wound.

"Who sent ye?" Ian hissed. "Give me one good reason why I shouldn't just kill you." Ian put more pressure on the blade. The man froze and stopped struggling. He closed his eyes.

"Ian! Stop!" Alistair stood over both of them. "We'll learn more if he's kept alive."

"Aye, Uncle. Let me alone with him. I'll find out who he's working for." Ian lowered his dirk, but he kept a firm grip on his captive, turning his head to get a better look at him. Ian didn't condone torture, but his captive didn't need to know that. He opened his eyes and glared at Ian. He was dark haired, with eyes to match.

"Domnall Macintosh!" Ian realised why the man looked familiar. "Is this how ye repay the laird's hospitality? I should slit your throat for your treachery."

Macintosh had stumbled into their village during a storm, seeking shelter little more than a month ago. He'd offered to stay and help with the hunting as a way of showing his thanks.

Aye, he'd showed his thanks, to be sure. More like his true colours. The bastard!

"Douglas! Jamie!" Alistair raised his voice and within moments two men were running towards them. "Take 'im," he ordered. "Find out how much he knows. I will join you shortly."

Douglas and Jamie MacDonald were brothers and Alistair's personal guard. They'd worked for and with him for over twenty years. Ian knew both men well. He'd have been surprised that Macintosh had managed to get past them, but the secret way into the hall was only known to a trusted few, so it usually wasn't guarded. How had Macintosh discovered it?

"Aye, sir." Douglas twisted the intruder's arms behind his back once Ian had relinquished his hold. He gave Ian a quick smile and nod of approval. Douglas had taught Ian how to hold his own in a fight and helped him hone his skills.

"They know the true story behind my banishment?" Ian asked Alistair once they were alone once more.

"Aye, they do." Alistair raised an eyebrow. "That doesn't surprise ye, lad?"

"No." Ian had phrased it as a question, but it was just confirmation of something he'd already guessed. "I trust Douglas and Jamie with my life. And yours."

Alistair smiled grimly. "They'll find out whatever Macintosh knows, and how much he overheard. If he doesn't know what we need, he might well be useful in other ways. I suspect it was no accident that he found his way to us when he did."

"You'll trade him?"

"Aye, if there's something worth trading him for."

It was more than the man deserved, but Ian would respect whatever decision Alistair made on the matter.

Ian frowned, his memory returning to their interrupted conversation. "Where are you sending me?"

"To Skye." Alistair pulled Ian into a rough embrace. "We've spent enough time with words. I wish you Godspeed, Ian."

Skye? He was going to Skye? Oh, good Lord. He'd heard stories of that place, of its dangers and isolation. Ian swallowed. How long would it be before he saw any of his own people again?

Ian returned the embrace, ignoring the tears that threatened to well. His hand stung where the knife had drawn blood. He'd tend to the wound later if needed. The blood was staunched. That was all that mattered for now.

He glanced at the door. He might be a loner but there were still people he would miss. Not just his parents and his cousin, Kirstin, but others. Good people, kinsmen and friends like Jamie and Douglas. There would be no one he knew on Skye, and he'd need to stay away from its few inhabitants. He'd be alone. Craving the company of people, wishing he could watch them from a distance as he did now.

"You can rely on me, Uncle."

"I know I can, and I know what I ask." The laird's voice sounded suspiciously choked. "I will send for ye when it is time."

Chapter Four

Skye, February 1745

Ian loved looking out at the sea. He'd never really been one for it before, but he'd learned quickly since arriving on Skye the only way he was going to survive the experience was to work out a rhythm for his day and try to stick to it. Only trouble was, he'd never been much for routine either.

He kicked at a piece of driftwood on the snow-covered Camas Daraich Beach. It broke with a dull crunch, falling in pieces not far from his feet. He trudged towards it, his boots leaving their mark in the light smattering of white beneath them. Ian bent and picked up a piece of the branch. It was rotten. He let it drop to the ground before reconsidering and retrieving it. It would do for the fire, if nothing else. That was one of the reasons he came here, after all, wasn't it? To collect wood for the fire.

He'd need the fire tonight. It was cold, the chill of it seeping into his bones.

"Gawd, I sound like an auld man," he muttered. "And I'm talking to myself. Again." Still, it was better to give in to a bit of craziness than the loneliness threatening to overwhelm him if he let it.

The first month had been the hardest. Ian had sworn he'd go crazy, being on his own. He'd come down here and yelled at the sea several times, needing to hear the sound of a voice, although it was only his own. He hadn't said anything he shouldn't, though. The secret he carried was not one to be shared. No matter how lonely he felt. His uncle—his laird—had tasked him with an important mission. Ian reminded himself of that each morning, and it was his final thought before he drifted off to sleep each night.

The nights were the worst, when the loneliness tried to reach for him, to swallow him whole. The dreams that came with his feelings of isolation weren't only because of his current situation. Those had started after Angus. They hadn't spent any nights together, for Angus was too scared of their relationship being discovered to risk it, but they'd both drifted off for a bit after lovemaking. Ian had woken in Angus's arms, half sleepy, his head on Angus's chest, listening to the steady thump of his heart, and feeling his lover's breath caressing his hair.

Those were the dreams that plagued him now when he slept. Not dreams, but memories, although with the way they had faded over time, they might as well be the former. Sometimes Ian woke with a start, certain he felt strong arms around him, but the murmured "I love you" wasn't Angus. Had never been Angus. In all the months they'd been together, Angus had never spoken those words, even going as far as placing a finger over Ian's lips when he'd started to whisper them. Even now, Ian rubbed one hand absently over his heart with the memory. He'd loved Angus, of that he was certain, or at least he'd thought so for the short time they'd been close. But had Angus ever loved him?

Ian had begged Alistair not to reveal Angus's identity, to let what many would see as a transgression be solely Ian's. Alistair hadn't agreed—Ian hadn't acted on his own.

But Alistair had finally given in to Ian's request to take the blame. They were not to see each other again, and Angus was to return to his life as it was before, to take on the responsibilities—and the wife—his father had chosen for him. Angus had thanked Alistair for his leniency, and left quickly without even a backwards glance for Ian or voicing his concern for Ian's fate.

It was not the reaction of a man who loved another. And certainly not what Ian would have done if their situation were reversed.

The shadow of what they'd had still hung over Ian. He doubted Angus had ever given it a second thought. He'd walked away from Ian, free to live his life, and as far as Ian knew, that was what he'd done. His wife was a pretty lassie, and a few months into their marriage already heavy with child.

Time was a strange thing. So were memories. Ian wasn't sure of any of it anymore. The more distance he put between the present and the past, the more he questioned what he'd felt for Angus. Or what their relationship had truly been.

An infatuation? Or a friendship which had crossed a line it never should have. It was often a thin one between friendship and love. Alistair had told Ian after Angus left that he was young, confused, and he'd mistaken his feelings for Angus for something that could never be. One day, he'd said, Ian would find a young lassie, and he'd know. True love, real love, was unmistakable, and when he did find it, he should hang on to it with both hands and never let it go.

True love? Ian snorted. His fingers curled around the stone he'd picked up from the side of the track leading to the beach. It was still in his sporran, one of several he'd collected on his walk that morning. He threw it as hard and far as he could. It skidded along the water, once, twice, then three times before sinking without a trace into the white-crested waves.

He watched it disappear with some degree of satisfaction. Throwing stones wasn't the most ideal way of working of his frustrations, but damn it all, it felt good and was a better option than slamming his fist against a wall.

Wait. What was that?

Ian strode to the shore's edge, the freezing water lapping at his boots. He strained his eyes and peered across the sea towards the Isle of Rum. A glint of metal caught his eye, just briefly before it was gone, but there long enough to know he hadn't imagined it the first time he'd seen it. The day was clear day, despite the cold, and the sun still bright enough to give him warning that a boat approached.

His hand went to his dirk, silently cursing he'd left his sword back at the cottage. Friend or foe? If it was foe, why hadn't Fergus sent a warning? A distant cousin, he, like Ian, had a mission from their laird. While Ian guarded the treasure, Fergus acted as lookout. Any sign of an intruder and Fergus was meant to light a beacon, a sign that someone was approaching. From his position at the Point of Sleat, he had a good view of not only Sleat—where Ian was living—but any routes an intruder might take to get there.

It might be nothing, but Ian couldn't afford to take that chance. The treasure was well hidden. Only Ian knew its location. He'd deliberately buried it well away from the cottage he'd come to think of as home, and he'd die before revealing his secret. He was a Scot, and loyal to not only his laird and his clan, but also to his king. Not the man currently sitting on the throne, but his true king. James, or rather his son Charles, who would rule once his father abdicated. His people had been under the thumb of the English for too long. It was well past time for the rightful king to reclaim his throne. The uprising thirty years ago had failed. This one would not.

At least it wouldn't if Ian had anything to do with it. When the prince arrived to lead the fight, he'd need resources, and the jewels Ian had hidden were an important part of that.

Another glance out towards the waves did not yield anything helpful. He needed to find somewhere he could hide, but would also provide a decent view of the beach. Ian was no coward. Still, one man going up against several was foolish. While he'd give his life for the cause, throwing it away for nothing would not achieve anything.

At the very least, he needed to get off the beach. If he'd managed to get a glimpse of these intruders, *they* might have seen *him*. He strode briskly towards the rocky terrain at the edge of the beach and headed for higher ground, where he'd get a better view.

The track was muddy, the slush of new snow mixing with dirt making it difficult to get a good grip underfoot. Despite that, Ian kept up his pace, but he was breathing heavily by the time he'd put a good distance between himself and the beach.

He strained his eyes, just able to make out the small ship anchored offshore. A smaller speck was heading away from it—a reasonable size boat being rowed towards the beach where he'd been half an hour before.

This would do. He didn't need to reach the point— Fergus would already be keeping watch from there—just find a place where he could keep an eye on the unwelcome visitors without being seen himself. Too far away and he wouldn't learn anything.

Knowing his enemy was important. Jamie had taught him that. A fight was not won on brute strength and skill. Anticipating an opponent's next move was not always easy, especially if up against someone unknown. Ian also needed to bury his emotions, especially his anger. Going into a fight angry was a sure path to losing one.

He'd let someone get away before because of it. Let his anger cloud his judgement and turned his back when he shouldn't have. He'd learned his lesson and was lucky he hadn't lost his life.

It seemed to take an age before the boat reached shore. Ian shrugged his shoulders, trying to rid himself of the stiffness in his upper back. There were half a dozen men in the boat. Their leader waited until they were on shore before joining them. There was something familiar about the man. Ian edged closer in order to get a better look.

His foot slipped in the mud. He grabbed at a tree branch to steady himself, cursing under his breath. So much for staying hidden. The last thing he needed was for his presence to be noticed.

Ian stilled, perspiration dripping down the back of his neck despite the cold, but luck seemed to be on his side, for once. Once he was sure it was safe, he silently crept closer to the men. An inner voice whispered to him that he should have stayed where he was, further up the hill. But his curiosity was piqued now. He knew this man. He was sure he did. But who was he?

"Search the area," the man said. He was heavyset, with dark hair. "I want the bastard found. Him and that treasure he's guarding." He spoke loudly, his voice carrying in the wind.

Hamish Campbell.

Ian's breath hitched. He'd know that voice anywhere. What the hell was Campbell doing on Skye?

Campbell glanced towards the treeline where Ian was hiding, his mouth turned up in a sneer, but he didn't appear to see Ian. His eyes were as dark as Ian remembered. Black like his soul.

"He can't be trusted, Uncle."

Ian had spoken those words to Alistair months ago. He'd known Campbell couldn't be trusted the first time they'd met. Alistair, however, was determined not to judge one man on the actions of others of his clan, but this particular Campbell was a slimy devil. He'd wormed his way into their community, and not just that, he'd set his sights on Ian's beloved cousin, Kirstin.

Campbell waited until his men had moved away a distance before beginning his own search. He walked with a limp, Ian noted with some satisfaction. Without thinking, he reached for his dirk. It was a shame he'd only managed to wound the bastard.

"She's a pretty one, your lassie," Campbell had said. "But she's not yours, Ian. She needs someone who will look after her, give her what she really wants. I figure that makes her mine." He'd worn that sneer then too. Ian had wanted nothing more than to wipe it from Campbell's face.

Kirstin had backed into a corner, her skirts held tightly around her. She was pale, her red locks dark against the pallor of her skin, her eyes wide with fear. "I'm not anyone's lassie," she'd hissed, but there was none of her usual fire in her words.

That was what had scared—angered—Ian more. That whatever Campbell had already done to her had left her like this. Ian and Kirstin had been close since they were bairns. They'd grown up together. Yet, he'd never seen her like this. She was brave, and spoke her mind. Just like she'd done when she'd found out Alistair knew about Ian and Angus. She'd gone to Alistair on Ian's behalf. Ian was mortified when he found out. But whatever she'd said to him, Ian was sure it was one of the reasons the laird—Kirstin's father—had shown leniency towards both men.

"Bastard," Ian muttered. "What are ye wanting now?"

Did he know Ian was on Skye? Only Ian, the laird, and few others were supposed to know of Ian's task, and Ian trusted all of them implicitly. But wait. What about Macintosh? Alistair wouldn't have traded him—he would never let go of someone who might have knowledge of the treasure, and of Skye, and he'd never been one to be lied to. He could sense a lie a mile off. That only left one alternative. Macintosh must have escaped and taken the information to whomever he was working for.

Campbell's order to his men had sounded personal. Could Macintosh have been in Glenfinnan on Campbell's orders? It made sense. Campbell knew the village well enough and had built the trust needed to find out about the entrance into the hall. He hated Ian as much as Ian hated him. Ian might have stuck his dirk in the bastard, but Campbell had deserved it, and more. A moment's distraction when Kirstin had run for help was all it had taken for the fight to turn in Campbell's favour. Pain had exploded in the back of Ian's head. He cried out and tried to lunge at Campbell, but all Ian knew before he was swallowed up by darkness was his enemy cursing him to hell. When he regained consciousness, Campbell was gone, and Ian was lying on a bloodied floor, his fingers wrapped around the sharp edge of the dirk he'd plunged into Campbell's leg.

Ian still had the scars.

And he knew Campbell wasn't finished with him yet.

Campbell had been interrupted when Kirstin arrived with help. It was the only reason Ian was still alive.

Wasn't it? Alistair's reasoning that Campbell made the choice to run—instead of taking the risk he'd be captured or killed—made sense, but Ian wasn't so sure. It would have only taken a moment for Campbell to kill him or leave him for dead. Campbell was a petty man who wasn't used to losing a treasure he'd decided was his for the taking. He'd told Kirstin as much.

He'd lost her because of Ian's intervention. He damn well would be losing his treasure this time too.

"MacDonald?" Campbell yelled across the sand as he closed the distance between them. "I know you're there, and I know ye can hear me."

Campbell was bluffing. He had to be. Ian held his breath, not daring to move. Campbell was coming straight for him.

Ian could take him down. He knew he could. But it wasn't just Campbell he would be fighting this time. The man had others with him. Others who would be on top of Ian as soon as they realised their leader was in trouble.

Killing Campbell wasn't worth risking the treasure. As much as Ian was tempted to answer, and do away with the bastard right there and then, he'd made an oath to Alistair. Not just to Alistair, but to the cause.

Ian bit his lip, forced himself not to answer.

Campbell halted his steps, coming to stand mere feet from Ian's hiding place. Surely he couldn't know where Ian was?

But when Campbell spoke again, it was still loudly. "That's right, lad. Keep hiding like the coward you are. Ye didn't best me the last time we met. Ye won't this time either." He smiled. A shiver ran down Ian's spine. "Skye's not that big. We'll find ye, wherever ye are, although my guess is it's not far from here." Campbell shrugged. "It's a shame the auld man wouldn't talk. Still, he had his chance. Just as you'll have yours."

The auld man? Ian silently drew his dirk.

That explained the lack of a warning beacon. Fergus must have been captured...or...Ian swallowed. He'd worry about Fergus later. Being distracted by his concern for the older man wouldn't do either of them any good now.

Ian's cottage wasn't far from the beach. Once they found it, they'd have him. At least he'd had the presence of mind to hide the sword, even if he'd been too foolish to keep it with him.

Campbell kept talking. He'd always liked the sound of his own voice. "I haven't forgotten your inference the last time we met, MacDonald. Don't make me regret letting you live. Pretty lassie, your cousin." He chuckled. "I've been thinking about renewing my interest in her. She'll need to learn her place though."

Ian bit his lip again, this time so hard he tasted blood. The bastard was bluffing. Anything to get a rise out of Ian, to make him lose his temper. Kirstin was safe. If anyone came near her again... Alistair had one of his men watching her. He wouldn't let anything happen to his daughter.

Not after what Campbell had done last time.

But Alistair had been too late then. If Ian hadn't been passing by... It was pure chance he'd heard something as he walked by Kirstin's room, and known she should have been there alone.

Ian tightened his grip on the dirk, his knuckles white.

"Hamish!" One of Campbell's men ran towards him. He was dark like Campbell, and of a similar build.

"Niall. Did you find something?" The way they spoke to each other gave the impression the two were kinsmen, or at least friends, rather than one in the employ of the other.

"A cottage further inland. About ten minutes from here."

"Empty?"

"Aye, although there's definitely someone living there. I've left two of the men searching it. If there's some clue to be found, they'll find it." Niall placed a hand on Campbell's shoulder. "You're certain MacDonald is here?"

"Aye, that I am, Niall." Campbell nodded slowly. "Once we find him, I'm sure he can be convinced to lead us to the treasure. He has no right to it; the so-called cause be damned. It will be ours for the taking."

"And if we don't find him?"

Campbell shrugged. "If not this time, we will the next. I've seen enough of the man to know he's loyal to a fault. If he's been tasked to protect this treasure, he'll not leave it, no matter the cost to himself. I've waited this long, what's a while longer? Give him time. He'll slip up, and we'll have him. He can't hide forever."

"We could leave a couple of men behind to keep watch," Niall suggested.

"Nae. That will be something he'll expect. There's no point in sacrificing any of the men, and he'd kill them to keep his secret." Campbell stared out to sea, and shifted his weight off his bad leg. "Or they'd kill him, and I don't want that. At least not yet. Ian MacDonald and I need some time to get reacquainted first. I owe him, and I'm a man who repays a debt."

"Aye, that ye are, Hamish." Niall nodded towards the trail leading away from the beach. "Do ye want to take a look at the cottage yourself?"

"Nae, if there's anything there, the men will find it." Campbell lowered his voice to a whisper. Ian had to strain to hear it. "I don't want to miss our appointment this evening. If the men don't find anything, we'll come back another time. Give him a chance to lower his guard again, and then we'll have him. I have time, and patience, especially for something worth waiting for. There are plenty of nooks and crannies to hide in. Trying to search them all today is a waste of time. There are other things that need my attention first."

"That's not what you—"

Campbell grabbed Niall's arm. "Ssh, man," he hissed. "He doesn't need to ken that."

Campbell glanced around before letting go. He brushed sand from his coat and continued speaking in a much calmer manner as though his recent outburst hadn't happened. "Go fetch the men, and we'll be on our way. There's nothing more to be done here today."

What was Campbell up to? Ian watched Niall leave the beach and waited several minutes before slipping away himself. There was no point in keeping an eye on Campbell, as it was doubtful he'd reveal anything about his plans, especially if he thought Ian might overhear. Ian thought it unlikely Campbell knew just how close his prey really was. He was a sneaky one, and Ian wouldn't put it past him.

He'd *said* he wouldn't leave any men behind, but that didn't mean he wouldn't, so Ian had no intention of going back to the cottage for a few days. He'd catch whatever he needed for food, but first he needed to find Fergus.

Whatever the risk, he was a good friend, and loyal to the clan and the cause.

But what if he was already too late?

Even if he was, Ian still had to know what had happened to Fergus and whether he could still act as lookout. But for now, his priority was finding Fergus, in case he was injured and needed help.

It was a slow climb to the Point of Sleat, more so than usual as Ian kept a careful eye out for any of Campbell's men. Usually, he enjoyed the walk through the heather-covered moorland, but there was too much urgency to be had in it today. There was no sign of Fergus anywhere, and the further Ian trekked, the more the feeling of dread grew in him. Finally, he reached the rocky outcrop, which meant he was close to the point, and the spot where he and Fergus had agreed would be a good place to light a signal fire.

Ian gritted his teeth and kept moving. He didn't dare stop to catch his breath. "Where are ye, man?" he muttered, finally reaching his destination. He peered into the distance, straining his eyes, but there was nothing. Had Campbell been bluffing? No, he wasn't one to do that, and he'd known about Fergus. Perhaps they'd taken him with them? Ian felt his hopes lift for an instant. If they had, Fergus might be still alive.

A patch of red caught his eye, but he wasn't close enough to see clearly. He sped up, clambering over rocks as quickly as he could.

"Oh no, oh, Lord, no."

The red he'd seen wasn't Fergus's kerchief as he'd hoped, but something else. Fergus lay in a crumpled heap on the ground, his eyes wide and unseeing. Ian dropped to his knees beside the body of the man he'd briefly called friend.

Fergus's throat had been cut. By Campbell's men no doubt.

"Damn ye, Campbell. Damn ye to hell." The wind tugged at Ian's hair, and his eyes pinpricked with tears. He hadn't known Fergus that well, but no one deserved to die like this. At least no good man.

Ian's expression hardened. If Campbell returned, Ian would be waiting for him. He'd allowed Campbell to crawl away from a fight once. He wouldn't again. Aye, when Campbell returned, Ian would be waiting, and this time, he'd see to it that their meeting would have a very different outcome. Death was too good an end for everything Campbell had done, but it would have to do.

Ian would make sure of it.

Part Two

Chapter Five

Skye, June 1745

Ian woke with a start, his dirk already in his hand before his eyes were properly open. He glanced around, unable to shake the feeling that something was wrong, although if asked what or why he couldn't explain it...

The harp was gone!

Memories of the evening before flooded his mind. He'd walked by the beach as he usually did, checking that all was well and there was nothing there that wasn't supposed to be. Since his run-in with Campbell and his men, he'd made a point of keeping an eye on the area at least twice a day. The harp had caught his eye, the tip of the old wood caught on the white crest of a wave, not quite submerged, or belonging.

It had taken but a moment for Ian to make the decision to rescue the thing. Part of him identified with it, he suspected. It had been so long since he'd felt he belonged. Sure, this was an important task he'd been given, but it was so lonely, especially since Fergus had died. It wasn't as though he and the old man had conversed much, but Ian had taken some comfort in the knowledge he wasn't completely alone. When his uncle had bestowed the task upon him, it was understood he'd keep to himself and not have much to do with the locals.

It was safer for both him and what he guarded as it didn't take much for stories to travel and find the wrong ears.

He still regretted not having had the chance to tell his parents the truth behind his banishment. His parents might not have approved of their son's relationship with another man, but they hadn't turned their backs on him for it. However, it hadn't stopped his mam from telling him it wasn't natural. A fine young strapping lad such as himself should get himself a pretty girl and settle down.

Months spent in only his own company hadn't stopped him wishing for what he didn't have, and what he truly wanted. On a cold night, those dreams were both a comfort and a curse.

A firm thigh. A muscular arm. The scent of someone unmistakably masculine.

"Aye, because that's going to happen," he'd muttered as he waded out from shore to recover whatever it was stuck out there, neither a part of the sea nor the land.

The water was freezing, but he'd expected that. He'd shivered, but it wasn't from the cold. One firm yank and the harp was in his arms. His breath hitched, his imagination caught in the same way the instrument had been trapped by the seaweed, a green slimy rope holding it to its watery prison.

The harp was still beautiful, despite the state of it. Once ashore, Ian allowed himself to run his callused fingers over it, marvelling at the smoothness of the wood. Amazingly, the strings were still intact. He plucked at one, and then another, wincing at the following cacophony. It needed a good tuning, but he didn't possess the knowledge. He had no clue what song it should play, just the strong feeling it was missing something—that like him, it wasn't complete.

His thoughts snapped forward to the present, his attention taken by the slightly open door of his stone cottage. He'd shut it the night before, he was sure of it.

Ian's eyes narrowed. Some thieving bastard had been in his home while he slept! Fully awake now, he grabbed his sword and its sheath as he stomped out of the cottage, intent on capturing the culprit and at the very least giving him or her a piece of his mind.

At least it wasn't Campbell or one of his men. If it had been, Ian would know it by now. Campbell wouldn't have let him sleep but more likely held a knife to his throat and ensured his waking was a painful one.

"Not very clever for a thief, are ye?"

The tracks leading from just outside the door were clear as day, the red rays of the rising sun highlighting them as clearly as though the thief had left a sign-posted trail for Ian to follow. He didn't need any further invitation. The harp needed to be kept safe, though if asked he wouldn't have been able to say why. Still, he had to find it.

The footsteps led him to a clearing some distance from the cottage. A man sat huddled on the ground, clutching the harp to his breast. He seemed lost, afraid, yet for some reason very familiar.

Ian forgot to breathe for a moment, lost in the sight before him. The man was slim and blond, with long hair stretching down to almost his arse. He stared at Ian, his green eyes the colour of the deep sea. Neither of them moved.

And then the harp began to sing.

*

The sun finally rose, and Robbie Elliot felt its warm finger skim along his pale skin, seeking his bones to warm them. Every time this moment had repeated itself throughout his long life, for just that blink of time, his existence seemed worthwhile. To feel the sun caress and kiss his skin, to see it spark gold off the knotty locks of hair that hung before his eyes, this one feeling made his heaven. It would pass too soon, but for that instant, everything was perfect.

He looked out at the olivine sea. He loved her, gave thanks to her for the gifts she had given. She was his mother, but she gave with a cold breast.

Heavy footsteps approached; it would be the Highlander who'd been asleep in his cottage when Robbie snuck in to retrieve the harp. The man would be afraid of witchcraft, once he saw Robbie sitting before the harp, legs stretched on either side, leaning over the arc of its neck as if it were an ailing lover.

Robbie hadn't made it to land yet from his most recent stint at sea when the ruddy Highlander had lifted the harp from the foam at the edge of shore, but he'd been aware. Even before Robbie left the surf and stepped on dry sand, he'd sensed the man who'd touched his harp and felt he'd known him a lifetime.

And the feeling had woken him quickly, completely, mind and body, had pulled him towards the beach as if he were a fish on a line. He didn't fight it. For the first time in so many that he'd lost count, a *man* had found the harp! It was a man who'd been drawn to the magic, who'd touched it and touched Robbie, though he—this Highlander who'd found the harp—had no way to know what he'd done. Drawing his first harsh breath of air as he rose from the sea, Robbie had felt such hope that it stung his eyes.

Voice raspy from long disuse, he'd whispered to himself, or perhaps to the sea. "Can it be at last? Can this be the completion of the magic?"

For all he had tried, he had not been able to make the harp sing with any of the women he and the harp had met—be they ladies or housemaids, whether they wanted him or not. And he knew why. He was, despite everything, the same Robbie Elliot he'd always been, and they were women. How could that work?

Now, sneaking a glance as the finder approached him across the meadow, Robbie thought, *But this is truly a man. A ruddy, huge Highlander, kilt-clad and bearing a hand-and-a-half sword across his back.*

When the man found the harp, Robbie had still been roaming far out among the waves. But despite the distance, with all the senses of the sea at his disposal, he'd seen and heard with his mind's eye—and no less clearly. The great bear of a man had hefted the sodden wood of the harp in one massive hand—a hand that Robbie could feel as if it grasped his own flesh—and carried the wounded thing to shore, whistling off-key some song of the Highlands.

And now the Highlander stepped into the glade where Robbie sat in the sun with the harp before him as if ready to coax a tune from her broken strings and warped neck. He strode across the sunlit ground, the red flush on his face and neck betraying his anger, his eyes on the harp, intent.

But when at last the tall, red-headed Scot raised his eyes to meet Robbie's... Oh, wonder!

The harp began to sing.

*

The music called to Ian, touched him. It seemed to caress him inside. Ian bit down on his lip to stop himself moaning aloud. It took hold of him, and he was caught by its sweet melancholy, a melody that stopped all too soon, its song incomplete, much like Ian himself.

He seemed to know the tune, or rather it knew him, yet he'd never heard it before in his life.

Then, just as suddenly, it was gone.

He took a step forward, shaking himself mentally, trying to clear the fog from his mind. The man before him glanced away, his grip still firm on the harp. Probably a good thing, as Ian wasn't sure he could have broken the gaze between them. To his embarrassment, his cock hardened under his sporran. He shifted his weight from one foot to the other, trying to centre himself, and ignore his reaction.

First the song, then the man. What kind of witchcraft was this?

"It sang," Ian whispered, half to himself. But how was that possible? Its strings might be still there, but apart from the couple he'd plucked when he'd found it, most had come away from the instrument. They flowed loosely from it like strands of seaweed, or hair.

"Aye," said the man. He grinned. "You heard it too, then?"

"Aye, that I did." Ian swallowed, forcing himself to focus. By all that was good, this man was beautiful, more so this close. What he wouldn't give to run his fingers through that long blond hair, if only to brush the locks from his face.

Another step forward, and he shivered.

Whatever this feeling was, he couldn't give in to it, however much it called to him. He was on Skye for a reason. The task was an important one for the cause. His clan depended on him; he'd taken an oath to see it through no matter what. He would not betray that trust.

Ian came back to himself with a start. He drew his sword. "Who are ye, lad, and what's your business here?"

"I beg your pardon, sir, I mean no harm. You found my harp, and for that, I thank you."

The man spoke softly, but Ian heard his words clearly. His voice was deeper than Ian expected. This was no lad, but a full-grown man, probably not much younger than Ian.

"Your harp?" Ian cocked an eyebrow. "I think not. It's an auld thing, of the sea." His eyes narrowed. "I'm thinking ye stole it from my cottage, stole it while I slept!"

"It is of the sea, aye," the man said, "but I swear I'm telling the truth when I say it's mine." He didn't loosen his grip on the thing. "I'm Robbie. Robbie Elliot. Are you the chieftain of those who dwell here?"

Ian couldn't help but laugh at the idea. He sheathed his sword, hoping he wasn't making a mistake in doing so. His gut told him Robbie wasn't a threat.

"A chieftain? Nae, lad, I'm but a loyal clansman." He inclined his head in greeting. "My name is Ian MacDonald, and this isle is my home, at least for now."

"What is this place?" Robbie loosened one arm from the harp and gestured at their surroundings.

"Ye don't know?" Ian peered at Robbie again. He wore plain-coloured breeks; his loose shirt was sprinkled with sand, the grains glistening in the sun. A piece of seaweed had threaded itself through his hair, the green peeking through the thick strands taunting him. It would be so easy to pull those locks free, to watch them flow unfettered down Robbie's back.

Ian clenched one fist. Damn it. That had been his downfall with Angus too. Ian had a weakness for hair, for the feel of it, and Angus had a black mass of it. Thick like Robbie's, but not as long. Ian looked lower, to the thick blond curls below Robbie's collarbone. His cock twitched.

"No." Robbie shrugged. "As I said, the harp is of the sea, so I've no clue. I was hoping you'd tell me. That, and the year, and what brings you here."

Was something wrong with Robbie's wits? It was a strange question to be sure, but still one Ian figured he'd answer. After all, it had been asked in the first place.

"We're on the Isle of Skye, and it is the year of Our Lord seventeen hundred and forty-five." Ian watched Robbie's face for a reaction.

"Forty-five," Robbie repeated, almost to himself. He shook his head. "I'd lost track, more than I realised. My gratitude, sir." He stared up at Ian, his gaze unflinching. "What are you meaning to do with me, then?"

"Do with ye?" Ian stared back. "I'll have to think on that one." He gestured for Robbie to stand. "We can't stay here, that's for sure. We'll go back to my cottage, and I'll decide on the way."

Robbie's presence complicated things somewhat. Common sense told Ian he should deal with the problem right then and there on the beach. What was he thinking taking Robbie back to the cottage? He could hear his uncle's voice in his head, telling him to run this stranger through. One clean thrust of his sword and Robbie would cease to be a problem. The cause was the important thing; Ian wasn't supposed to lose sight of why he was here, and why he couldn't be allowed to fail.

For all he knew this could be a trap set by that bastard Campbell. A tempting one, given that Robbie was the embodiment of everything Ian had wanted these past months. But surely Campbell didn't know where Ian's preferences lay? No one was supposed to, Alistair had seen to that, but even so, it didn't stop the gossip. And gossip had a way of travelling far beyond where it should.

"Do you have any soup or stew?" Robbie shook sand from his clothing, that damn harp secure under his arm. He clung to it as though it was an extension of himself, yet for some reason Ian couldn't explain, he could have sworn it looked like the two of them belonged together.

"Maybe," Ian said cautiously. It wasn't enough that Robbie had taken the harp, but now he wanted to partake of Ian's food as well. "Are ye hungry, lad?"

"Maybe." Robbie grinned. "It feels like I haven't eaten in years." He paused for a moment before adding, "Sir."

"My name's Ian, Robbie," Ian corrected him gently. "I'm no chieftain, just a clansman doing his duty. I've already told ye that."

"Aye, sir...Ian, so you have."

"Ye already know the way. Walk slowly in front of me and don't stop until we reach the cottage. Don't think about running. I'll catch ye if you do."

"I wasn't planning to run." Robbie grew quiet after that, and the rest of their journey was undertaken in silence, for which Ian was glad.

His mind made up for the quietness of the lad in front of him, arguing for and against what should be his next course of action. Aye, he knew the importance of keeping the treasure safe, and his instructions to keep to himself and not let anyone know of its whereabouts.

Upon pain of death, his uncle had said, repeating the words of their chieftain. They had to be prepared, if not to fight, then to at least be in a position to offer support of some kind to the man who could become their future king.

Despite his conviction to follow those orders, Ian had never been one to kill a man in cold blood if there was no need for it. He'd defend himself, and fight in battle, but his gut told him Robbie wasn't his enemy, nor was he one of the clan's.

As Ian rested his hand briefly on the hilt of his sword, he thanked God that he'd hadn't reacted without thinking and killed a potential enemy. Still, he couldn't stop his imagination from showing him an image of Robbie struck dead. Ian's footsteps faltered at the vision of Robbie sprawled on the trail, limbs sticking out at unnatural angles, clutching the harp in lifeless arms, his surprise captured forever in his eyes as part of his death mask.

Ian swallowed, dropping his hand from the sword hilt to his side, and picked up the pace again before Robbie could realise he'd lagged behind. He couldn't kill the lad, not like that. Robbie meant no harm to the cause, or at least had shown no sign of doing so. There'd been something odd about the way he asked the questions about where and when they were. A flicker in his eyes—of confusion, then relief—hadn't been there long, but Ian still noticed it.

Just as he'd noticed Robbie hide the fear in his eyes before he glanced away. Robbie might give the impression of being in good cheer for the most part, but there was another darker emotion lurking not far beneath.

Ian had always had a gut feeling about people, an uncanny sense of whether they were to be trusted or not. It had held him in good stead in the past, and trying to ignore it only led to grief.

A hard body stopped Ian in his tracks when he walked straight into it. His dirk was in his hand in an instant. He backed off hurriedly, warily glancing around, cursing himself for allowing his mind to wander. "What is it?"

"We're here, so I stopped." Robbie shrugged. "I didn't think I needed to tell you. After all, you told me not to run, and you'd have to be paying attention to notice if I did."

"I was paying attention," Ian muttered, not happy about being caught out. He returned his dirk to its sheath at the top of his stocking. Distraction wasn't something that happened to him when he had a task to perform, at least not to this degree. That harp and its witchcraft must be doing something to him. "Come inside, and I'll see about fixing both of us some porridge."

While Robbie stood looking around the long, narrow interior of the cot, Ian stoked the fire.

"Come sit down here where it's warm. Ye look like you've been cold so long ye wore out the shivers. And take off that soaked shirt. I'll loan ye my spare."

Robbie seemed to find it hard to believe that Ian—or anyone—would be taking care of him. "Does all this—the fire and the food and all—does it mean you've decided what to do with me?"

"Aye, I have." It might be a mistake, but he'd trust his gut this time round. Whether it be witchcraft or not, for now, he'd take a chance with Robbie and hope he was right. He could change his stance later if he wasn't. "For now, I'm taking ye captive, but if ye do anything to make me regret that decision, that will change."

Robbie stared at him, his expression suggesting he had no clue as to the implications of Ian's decision.

"I won't kill ye, and I'll keep ye safe," Ian elaborated. "I won't do ye harm, unless ye give me good reason to."

The smile Robbie gave in response lit up his face. God, he was a fine-looking man. "Thank you, Ian. I promise I won't betray your trust."

*

Robbie heard the sounds coming from the forest first, before the big Highlander did, and he supposed it was the frightened look on his own face that alerted Ian and, it was to be hoped, told him that the party coming through the woods, weapons and armour clanking, had nothing at all to do with Robbie. The timing—these others approaching the cottage just as the two of them arrived—was unlucky coincidence.

"Scared, are ye, lad?"

Ian whispered the question, but obviously he didn't want an answer. Robbie nearly laughed inside when Ian illustrated his frustration with a champion eye roll.

"This day has gone horribly amiss, Robbie. I'm tempted to blame you, but I like to think I'm a fair man. Sit here quiet. I'm going to see who's coming up here looking for trouble. And that's a point I should make. Whatever I tell you, you'll do it, or you'll be later wishing you had."

"You don't have to threaten me, Ian, sir!" Robbie was about to add that he'd do anything he could to stay with Ian and follow him. At least until he could learn whether indeed the magic—the harp and the sea—could at last be soothed with Ian's touch, just as Robbie's fears were quieted against all logic every time Ian looked him in the eye.

When Ian put his big, callused hand over Robbie's mouth, just the gentlest touch, Robbie thought, *I don't think I'd mind overmuch if he were to soothe more than the magic.* Desire stirred in Robbie in a way he hadn't felt in...well, he didn't know, because he didn't know how long he'd been out in the sea...

But now is not the time—

Ian interrupted Robbie's thoughts with a low growl. "It isn't a threat, man. I never make threats. Sit quiet, aye?"

He didn't wait for an answer, but crept off into the thicket behind the cottage without making a sound. Robbie found Ian's stealth amazing for such a brawny man. But then, if he'd grown up in the coastal forests, he would have learned to run them in near silence. A matter of survival.

Ian moved swiftly when he came back, and said not a word before he hefted Robbie—as if he weighed nothing at all—and slung him over his shoulder. He stepped away, moving towards the trail that passed behind the cottage. Panic struck Robbie so hard in the gut he thought he'd heave if he'd eaten anytime in the last century. He forced himself not to cry out, not wanting to bring the attention of the men coming up the draw, closer now. He pulled Ian's thick red braid, slapped at his back, but it was as though the man was impervious.

So he gave the thick muscle between Ian's shoulder blade and his spine a good, hard, bite.

Ian flinched, made a sound in his throat, and went three more strides, veering towards the cold back wall of the cottage. He slid Robbie off his shoulder and slammed him none too gently against the whitewashed stone.

"What do ye think you're doing, then?" His eyes honed in on Robbie, his gaze so intense it seemed there was no distance at all. "You know I've agreed to make ye captive, in lieu of killing ye. Ye know that means I must see to your keep and your safety. Those men coming closer up the path are no friends. They'll hurt ye if I leave you. Unless ye know them. *Do* ye know them?"

Robbie read confusion in Ian's gaze, or bewilderment, maybe even...hurt. "No! Ian! Wait, I'm sorry. It's just I canna leave without the harp!"

"The harp! That broken, warped, waterlogged pile of old sticks and broken strings?"

"Yes," Robbie nodded. "That's the one."

"Don't give me cheek, and don't call me daft, Robbie. That harp is worthless and feckin' heavy. Ye'll come quiet with me now—I'll carry you so you won't be crashing through the brush all noisy. They're getting far too close for comfort."

"Sir, I promise, if you let me hold the harp, you will not feel its weight at all."

Chapter Six

The harp might have been light, but Robbie was heavier than he looked. After making sure their pursuers were a safe distance behind them, Ian put Robbie down.

"Stay put," he hissed. "I'll return to ye; I promise."

While he hated leaving Robbie, even for a few minutes, Ian wasn't about to run blindly without knowing who these men were. Suspicions were not fact, and if it was Campbell or his men, they already knew where the cottage was, and they'd be after Ian and the treasure. However, that wouldn't mean Robbie was safe. Ian had made a promise to keep him from harm, and Campbell was just as likely to use Robbie to ensure Ian's cooperation if he suspected they knew each other. They hadn't known each other long, but it wouldn't matter, and Ian was not about to see Robbie hurt on his account.

He crept back the way he and Robbie had come, taking care not to get too close to the cottage. Damn that Campbell picking this day to decide to return, but Ian had known it was only a matter of time.

The voices were still too far away to make out what they were saying. Ian crouched and strained his senses. The wind was on his side, and he was able to decipher a couple of words. Although they weren't in context, he recognised "MacDonald" and "jewels," and the one who had spoken them. Not Campbell but another voice Ian wouldn't forget in a hurry—Niall, who had conversed with Campbell on the beach that day.

He heard breathing behind him, and a hand touched his shoulder. He spun, dirk in hand. Annoyance, tinged with fear, quickly followed his initial relief when he saw who it was. "I told ye to stay put!"

Robbie jumped back, nearly losing his footing, the harp cradled in his arms. "I'm sorry. I thought you might need some help," he whispered. "I couldn't just stay there and do nothing." He tilted his head to the side, listening, his complexion pale.

"They're not good men." Ian kept his voice low and hoped they wouldn't be overheard. He dragged Robbie back to his feet. "Stay behind me, and no arguments. When I tell you to do something, do it." As much as he wanted to throw Robbie over his shoulder again, he figured it was more important to have the freedom of movement to draw either his sword or his dirk in a hurry. "And if they sound like they're catching up with us, ye run as though the devil himself is after ye, and ye dinna stop."

"I'm not leaving you, Ian—" Robbie began to protest.

Ian shook his head. "This isn't your fight, and I'll not have you hurt because of it." He put his fingers to his lips, signalling Robbie to be quiet.

Robbie's eyes widened, but thankfully, this time he did as he was told. He followed Ian's lead and ducked again into a crouch.

The hairs on the back of Ian's neck stood on end. His gut clenched. Campbell and his men didn't scare him, but the thought of that bastard getting his hands on Robbie did. Ian already felt driven to protect him. There was something about Robbie, an instinct Ian couldn't ignore, similar to knowing he'd needed to rescue Robbie's harp from the sea. He shivered, remembering how he felt when the thing had sung.

Finally, he gestured to Robbie that it was safe for them to move. Campbell's men had gone in the opposite direction back towards the beach.

But where was Campbell himself? Ian was tempted to see if he could discover Campbell's plan, so at least he'd know what he was up against. But he dismissed the thought as a foolish one. Better to get as far away as possible and hide for a few days. Decision made, he knew without a doubt where to head. It wasn't one of his favourite places on Skye, especially with the stories told about it, but it would give him a good view of the bay and, as such, at least some advantage.

"I hope that harp is as light as you claim," he warned, "for ye'll be lugging it a while. Where we're heading is a good five miles north of Armadale."

"It's not just a claim, it's the truth," Robbie confirmed.

Rather indignantly, Ian thought, at the idea Ian still might not believe him. He didn't seem to recognise the name Armadale, which was odd, as it was a MacDonald stronghold. So far, Robbie's reactions seemed to confirm he wasn't spying for Campbell as he didn't know anything of Ian's mission—a relief as Ian wanted to be able to trust him.

"Good." Ian smiled. "Keep up and stay quiet. If ye can't keep up, ye'll let me know, and we'll rest awhile."

"I'll keep up," Robbie said. "I'll not be a burden to you."

"You're no burden," Ian murmured. "Give me the harp if it does get too heavy, aye?" he added as an afterthought. He'd already turned his back on Robbie, half because they needed to be on their way and had wasted too much time already, but also because he didn't want to see Robbie's expression once he realised, despite his protestations about the harp, Ian still didn't quite believe him.

To his credit, Robbie stayed silent for the next couple of hours, although lack of conversation didn't make Ian any the less intensely aware of the fact that he wasn't alone. Ian kept up a demanding pace, determined to get as far away from their possible pursuers as quickly as possible.

Once they reached the small river at the final stretch of their journey, Ian signalled for Robbie to stop. "Rest here a moment, and drink." The day wasn't a warm one, but Ian had worked up a sweat. "You've done well."

"Better than you expected?" There was a twinkle in Robbie's eye. "I told you I'd keep up." He knelt by the stream and put the harp down carefully on the bank beside him. "Although, I did wonder if you didn't believe me about that either."

Ian cupped his hands and drank deeply from the stream before replying. He wasn't about to lie about it. "Perhaps not," he admitted. "But I'm still getting to know ye. I can only make assumptions on appearances, but..." How to put this without insulting the lad?

"But?" Robbie followed Ian's lead and drank from the stream, and then splashed his face and hair with water. The droplets clung to his skin, one lingering on the tip of his nose.

Ian was surprised how badly he wanted to reach over and brush it off with his finger, or better, with his tongue.

He bent and dipped his head briefly into the water and then shook himself dry, the shock of the cold water forcing him to focus. Ian's desire for other men had already gotten him into trouble. He'd not let it happen again.

"But?" Robbie repeated, but his voice sounded hoarse.

Ian looked up in surprise. Robbie was staring at him, his tongue outlining his lips before he swallowed and looked away.

Ian cleared his throat. "There's much more to ye than ye appear, Robbie," he said softly. He wiped his hands on his kilt, using the motion not only to dry them but to collect his thoughts.

"How much further?" Robbie collected his precious harp, tucking it under his arm again, and stood. He didn't comment on what Ian had just said.

Ian wasn't sure whether to be relieved by that, or whether it was merely a reprieve. Robbie might be keeping secrets, but then so was Ian.

"We're nearly there." Ian pointed upstream. "We keep to the path we're on until we reach a grassy slope. Take care as you climb. There are sheer drops on two sides."

Robbie peered into the distance. "I can see something, up high, perched on the edge of the cliff." He frowned. "Is it a castle? Are they friendly? Won't they ask questions?" His grip tightened on the harp.

"Aye, it's a castle. *Caisteal Chamuis*." Ian used the Gaelic for it, rather than the other name by which it was known: Knock Castle. "It's long abandoned, but it's owned by the MacDonalds, and it's safe."

"Are you in trouble, Ian?" Robbie's attention returned to Ian. He was watching him with an intensity that made Ian flinch and want to turn away.

"We'll be safe here," Ian repeated. "We can stay overnight and head back to the cottage tomorrow. That will give Campbell time to get bored or give up."

"Do you think he'll find what he's looking for?"

The question took Ian by surprise. His brow furrowed. "What makes ye think he's looking for something?" What had urged Robbie to ask? Surely he couldn't know about the treasure?

Robbie shrugged. "Just a feeling, Ian. Nothing more."

"A feeling. Right."

"Aye," Robbie said. "I'm sorry. I don't know how else to describe it." There was a strange timbre to his voice when he spoke. "The kind of feeling that's important and shouldn't be ignored."

"Aye," Ian said absently. He knew about those, but he doubted Robbie was referring to the same thing he was. Could the lad have some kind of sixth sense? He hoped not, especially considering the stories that were told about the location where they'd be spending the night. Ian might have a healthy respect for the old stories, but it didn't mean he had to like them. Truth be told, they scared him, but he wasn't about to admit that to anyone. He'd been teased enough as a child about it.

Robbie was still watching him, but it wasn't just curiosity. There was concern in his expression too.

"It's fine. There's nothing there for him to find, either at the cottage or near it." The treasure was well hidden and a good distance away. Ian wasn't foolish enough to lead Campbell away from his home and straight towards where he had buried it.

Robbie nodded but didn't reply. Instead, he followed Ian in silence for the rest of their journey, until they were almost at the castle.

"Was this a fort?" he asked.

"The auld stories say there was one here before the MacLeods built the castle three hundred years ago."

Despite his reservations about the place, Ian couldn't help but be drawn to it all the same. Even abandoned, it stood guard above the rocky headland of Knock Bay. Some of the castle walls had originally been constructed at the same time as the old keep that had stood there before it. The bulky walls would give him and Robbie some protection if Campbell did find them and attack.

"Dun Thoravaig, it was called, according to the stories my da told me."

"How long has it been abandoned?"

Ian had to think about that one. "My granda talked about the MacDonalds living here. He came to a gathering once when he was a young man, probably about our age. They left for Armadale not long after." He wished he'd seen the castle in its full glory. It struck him as rather sad now. Deserted and almost forgotten apart from a few of the older members of their clan, and only kept alive by the stories, and its ghosts.

Robbie placed one hand on the bulky stone wall. "If we're going to stay, we should find food first. Better to do it now." He grinned at Ian. "And if we have to fight, it's better on a full stomach, aye?"

Ian's stomach growled at the reminder. He'd been so focused on getting them both away from Campbell he'd forgotten his missed breakfast. "How are ye at hunting?" Not only had he missed breakfast, but it was now almost time for supper.

Robbie laughed. "We don't need to go looking for food when it's running right by us." He pointed to the stream. "Did you not see the trout in the burn? I'll catch us some supper. We'll not go hungry."

"We have nothing to catch them with," Ian pointed out.

"We have our hands." Robbie seemed puzzled by Ian's comment. He handed Ian the harp and headed back down the slope towards the stream. Ian followed closely behind, not wanting to lose sight of Robbie.

By the time he caught up with him, Robbie was already wading into the shallows of the stream. Ian watched him, curious. His grandfather had talked about catching fish in the old way, but he'd never seen it done.

Robbie put his finger to his lips, warning Ian to be quiet, but didn't seem to notice Ian's nodded response. He was already focused on the water. He stood there completely still and quiet, and then slowly bent and dipped his hands into the water. A dark shape swam upstream, but from the shore, Ian couldn't see it clearly.

Robbie's hands clenched closed, and he gave a triumphant yell. He straightened, a wriggling trout captured in his grasp. He looked up at Ian and grinned again. "Supper," he said, climbing back onto the bank, his prize firmly in his hands. "Thank you for taking care of the harp."

"I wasn't about to let it go, especially with how important it is to you." Despite his protestations about Robbie lugging the thing, Ian had to admit he couldn't leave it behind in good conscience either. He hadn't thought twice about taking it, although he didn't know why Robbie thought it hardly weighed a thing. Being made of wood and waterlogged, the harp was every bit as heavy as Ian expected it to be.

The smile Robbie gave him made Ian blush slightly. Lord, he was a beautiful man, especially when he smiled like that. It stirred something deep within Ian, a yearning for a missing piece of himself he'd never thought he had any chance of finding. He turned away quickly before Robbie could see his reaction.

"We need something to go with it," Robbie said. The fish had stopped wriggling. It was a decent size and would feed them well. "I thought I saw mushrooms as we approached the castle."

"Aye, I remember my granda talking about there being a garden of sorts near where the kitchens used to be. Perhaps there are still some wild plants growing from what remains of it." Ian knew how to tend a garden and what to look for. His ma had taught him, partly to keep him occupied while his da and uncle were away hunting. He'd wanted to go with them and couldn't until he was older. She said it was the only way she got any peace.

It didn't take long to find what they were looking for, and Ian was delighted to dig up some tasty roots, as well as some edible greens. He noticed Robbie watching him, and couldn't help but laugh at his surprise.

"I can look after myself, Robbie. I wasn't fixing to starve; no point if I did, is there?" Having what they needed, Ian nodded in the direction of the castle. "I think we're safe here for now. I'll build us a fire inside the old wall of the keep, perhaps in the castle itself. We'll need shelter for the night, and some protection from the wind."

"We haven't been followed?" Robbie seemed to relax a little although he'd phrased it as a question.

"I don't think so. If they'd figured out where we'd gone, they'd be here by now." He stood and stretched. "Come on, let's get the fire started. It's cold. The trouble with having a decent lookout up here is that there's not much protection either. We should get out of the wind, and have our meal while we still can."

After finding a suitable place to settle for the night, Ian soon had a fire going. The light was already dying. "Clean the fish and set it cooking, lad. I won't be long."

"Where are you going?" Robbie didn't sound concerned, more curious than anything.

He trusts me. Ian hoped it wasn't a mistake on Robbie's part. Despite having escaped Campbell's men so far, he knew in his gut it didn't mean the danger was over. "The ground is hard. I'm going to collect us some bedding so we can get a good night's sleep."

*

Ian leaned back, resting his head against the coarse wall. It was rough against the back of his neck, but he felt contented and relaxed. By the time he'd come back with some cleavers and grass for their bedding, Robbie had plank roasted their supper, and had not only collected cold water to wash it down with, but had made some tea from the wild herbs growing nearby.

Outside, the wind howled. Ian had made the right decision to light the fire inside the castle itself. There was rain in the air, and he preferred to sleep where it was dry. He'd spent nights in the rain, wrapped in a blanket, and had no desire to do so again anytime soon.

There was a loud crash outside. Ian jumped, glanced around nervously, and took a long drink of his tea. He listened again, but the noise didn't repeat, although he could hear scuffling. He doubted it was rats—the sound wasn't right for the little buggers, and they tended to be where they could forage for food. There was nothing here for them.

"It's just the wind," he mumbled, wrapping his fingers around his bowl of tea.

Robbie had found some bowls in what was left of the kitchens, which had been abandoned like the rest of the castle. They worked well for the tea they'd brewed from mint Ian found in the garden. Ian was thankful for the hot drink.

"You're thinking it might be something else?" Robbie asked. He rested his head on his knees, his arms clenched around them for warmth. It was chilly despite the fire.

"No," said Ian firmly. He heard the scuffling noise again, but further away this time. "Probably not." He lowered his voice. "Ye know this castle is supposed to be haunted?"

Robbie's eyes widened. "Haunted? Do you know by whom?"

"Aye." Ian took another sip of tea before continuing. It wouldn't hurt to tell Robbie about the ghosts. Talking about them might help his own nervousness, and take his mind off that bloody noise. It was getting on Ian's nerves, sending shivers through him that were nothing to do with the cold.

"According to the stories, there are two ghosties who haunt the castle."

"Have you seen either of them?"

"Nae, but my granda thought he saw something once." Ian shrugged. "My gran told him it was the drink. He never did tell anyone exactly what it was he saw though." That wasn't exactly true but his granda had made him swear never to tell anyone, and Ian kept his promises, even if the old man had been dead these past ten years.

"Maybe he did see something," Robbie said thoughtfully. "Ghosts appear to those who are meant to see them for whatever reason."

"As long as I'm not meant to see one, that's fine."

Ian had promised to tell Robbie about the ghosts, so the sooner he got it over with the better. Now he was about to talk about them, the knot in his stomach grew tighter. He swallowed, tasting the bile that rose in his throat, and quickly took another sip of tea. It did nothing to rid him of the sour taste in his mouth. He didn't like thinking about the things. They weren't natural and, as such, weren't something he was sure he could take on and win if they decided he and Robbie shouldn't be there. Why had he been foolish enough to think it might help his nervousness? If anything, it was making it worse.

"Not all magic is bad, Ian," Robbie said softly. "And not everyone who practises it is evil." A shadow fell over his face. "Although some are, and it's not always easy to tell until it's too late."

"Is that what ye think these ghosties are? Some kind of magic?" Ian hadn't thought of associating them with magic. The idea did nothing to calm him. In fact, more the opposite. Magic made him just as nervous as ghosts. He preferred foes he could see, and knowing what he was up against. At least with a man, he could run his sword through the bastard or take him down in a fist fight.

"I don't know. Sometimes things are just what they are, and there's nothing we can do about it."

Robbie gave Ian a smile, a shy one this time. It was very endearing, and Ian felt a slow warmth spread through him. He ducked his head so Robbie wouldn't see his flushed cheeks.

"Tell me about the ghosts?" Robbie asked.

"There's supposed to be two of them. One's a Green Lady, a *gruagach*. She's associated with the fortunes of the family who occupy the castle. She's happy if good news will come, and weeps if there is to be bad news."

"So what happens to her if the castle is abandoned?" Robbie shook his head. "I think it's sad she has no one now. It must be lonely for her."

Ian hadn't thought about it like that. "Aye, I suppose. Maybe she hopes someone will come one day and give her some company again?" It was a little too close to his own situation, and he had to admit he was enjoying Robbie's company, especially tonight in this place. The lad was intelligent and had an interesting way of looking at things.

"I hope she does get some company again. Being alone is not something I'd wish on anyone, especially not for several lifetimes." There was more than wistfulness in Robbie's voice. He sounded so sad, so desolate, that Ian wanted to reach out, wrap his arms around Robbie and offer him comfort.

"I wouldn't wish it on anyone either." Unsure as to how Robbie would react, and not wanting to scare him, Ian stayed where he was and stared into the fire. The flames seemed to dance this way and that, forming faces in the red light he couldn't quite make out.

"You said there was more than one ghost?" Robbie broke the silence, finally. He wore an expression of concern when Ian looked up at him.

Ian plastered on a smile, wanting to lighten the situation. He'd become lost in his own demons for a moment. It was unfair to drag Robbie into that. "Aye. A *glaistig*. That's a spirit who looks after livestock, although there's not much of that here at present. There would have been years ago though."

"Perhaps he ventures further afield?" Robbie suggested. "I wonder what happens to spirits whose original purpose no longer exists. Do they find a new purpose or just fade away?"

"I'd like to think they find a new purpose." Ian didn't want to think about those sad souls simply fading away.

"Aye, I like that idea." Robbie warmed his hands over the flames. He listened, cocking his head to one side. "What's that noise? Can you hear it?"

Ian shook his head. "We're alone. There's nothing—"

The shrill chattering made him jump. He dropped his bowl, spilling the remains of his tea onto the ground. He leapt to his feet, dirk in hand, and glanced around warily.

It sounded again, and this time, Ian recognised it for what it was: a merlin. He sat down again quickly, rather red-faced.

Robbie laughed. "That's no ghost, Ian. It's flesh and blood same as us, despite the name of the bird."

Ian scowled at him, but it was difficult to be upset for long with seeing that twinkle in Robbie's eyes again. He sheathed his dirk. "The bloody thing gave me one hell of a fright, it did." His mouth twitched, and he couldn't help but chuckle. "Aye, I think you're right about there being nothing magical about it despite its name."

The fire was beginning to die down. He debated building it up again but decided against it. Instead, he got up and began to lay the bedding he'd collected earlier. It was going to be a chilly night.

Robbie watched him. He seemed unsure, as though he wasn't certain what he should be doing. Ian didn't ask him to help with the bedding. There was no need as it wouldn't take long, and Robbie might as well enjoy what was left of the fire.

Ian turned back to the task at hand, pausing when Robbie started whistling. It was a tune Ian knew well. He'd heard it sung many times. For now, he was content to listen rather than join in, although he couldn't help but sing the lyrics in his mind.

The fray began at Otterburn, between the night and the day.

The bedding complete, Ian took off his cloak and kilt. They had no blankets, so those would have to do. Robbie had stopped whistling, and the only sound was the crackling of the fire. The lad would freeze sitting over there. There was only one thing for it. Ian took a deep breath. He could do this. They needed to keep warm. There was no point in surviving this far only to let the cold finish them off.

"Come to bed now, Robbie." Ian lay down on the bedding, shuffling over to the far side by the wall to make room for both of them. "It's going to be cold when the fire burns down."

*

Robbie held his gaze firm on the coal root of the flames. True, he enjoyed the fire's dance, but more to the point, he avoided watching Ian disrobe, preparing for bed. He stole a few glances, of course, admiring again the man's hard, wild beauty. The moment reminded him of times long past when he'd gone with some clansmen to raid or hunt, wanting to marvel openly at the finest of his cousins but rightly wary of the danger.

His nervousness here with Ian had a bit of a different flavour. He knew with certainty that Ian had a love of men, but no idea whether he was accustomed to yielding to the desire.

Even if he is, what if he doesn't want me?

"Come to bed now, Robbie."

Robbie shivered at the sound of those words, though Ian's voice was no more rough and magnetic than usual. A tide of panic-fuelled energy surged through him, and heat rose in his cheeks. He turned away, hating his telltale blush and hiding his equally heated, hardening cock behind the oversized shirt he'd borrowed from Ian. He'd never see another place he wanted to be more than right there next to Ian on that bed of cleavers, straw, and mugwort.

But not yet, he thought, hearing the sound of the distant sea draw close and clear in his mind. *It isn't time.*

As much as Robbie wanted to let his body have everything it clearly asked for, he took control. Growing up in the Borders, a boy like him learned quickly to quash all evidence of his desire for men. He'd had more practice at it than he ever wanted, and if that wasn't enough, he possessed the strong will of a born Reiver too. He could keep his cock from causing trouble.

Even if that wasn't what he wanted at all.

"Robbie," Ian said, and he sounded less braw and more annoyed this time. "Come to bed, man! It's growing colder by the minute, fire or no."

Robbie sighed and lay down as gracefully as he could manage on the makeshift pallet. Instantly, he felt the cold sift over his skin. Ian had been right: no way could they have been able to trust their lives to sleep without making use of every bit of warmth available—including the heat coming off their bodies. Ian held the cloak up so Robbie could slip in beneath it, then pulled it up over his shoulders.

Ian shifted until they both lay on their backs, touching all along their arms, hips, and legs. To Robbie's surprise, he began to fall asleep only seconds later, feeling the rocking of the sea in the counterpoint of his breath under Ian's. But Ian had begun singing, and though Ian's wasn't a singer's voice, the slow bass notes of his range vibrated low in his muscled chest. Robbie felt the song roll out almost as much as he heard it. He recognised the song as the one he himself had been whistling earlier, by the fire. "The Battle of Otterburn," a Border song about a long-ago Border battle. A song already centuries old when Robbie was born. That Ian even knew it came as a bit of a surprise, *but songs, they travel like wind.*

No love song, that's certain. Robbie had to stifle a laugh at the thought. But the melody and the poetry of the lyric—beautiful. He listened quietly through battle and yielding and funeral biers, but for the last three sad verses, he joined his voice to Ian's, a clear octave above.

> The fray began at Otterburn,
> Between the night and the day;
> There the Douglas lost his life,
> And the Percy was led away.
>
> Then there was a Scottish prisoner taken,
> Sir Hugh Montgomery was his name;
> For sooth, as I say to you,
> He brought Percy home again.
>
> Now let us all for the Percy pray
> To Jesu most of might,
> To bring his soul to the bliss of heaven,
> For he was a gentle knight.

At the last, a fast, broken chord sounded from the harp, lying a bit more than an arm's length away on its own bed of hard earth. The harmony lingered in their rough shelter, and Robbie didn't breathe again until it faded beyond the reach of his ears.

After, he lay silent until his heart calmed, then turned his head just enough to see Ian's face in a sliver of moonlight. Catching up his courage, he asked, "Did you hear it, Ian?"

"Aye, man. I did."

Silent, Robbie watched as Ian's expression slackened in sleep, the rise and fall of his breath becoming slow and even. When he was certain the big, beautiful Highlander slept soundly, Robbie whispered his hope to the dark.

"That's twice," he said. "The harp has sounded twice." He allowed himself the smallest smile and drifted to sleep on an encouraging thought.

As signs go, it seems a good one.

Chapter Seven

After being away for a day, hiding from the intruders—Campbells, Ian had said, though he hadn't explained—they came back to a cold cottage in which the damp had already settled. First things first, Robbie shredded tinder and laid the kindling while Ian, whose long, strong arms could carry quite a bit more, went out to fetch logs for the fire.

Once it was burning, the blaze was such a comfort Robbie could have been tempted to sit before it and soak up heat, but as always, much awaited doing. The work would warm him just as thoroughly; there would be time for sitting later. Ian went back out to bring in Bessie the cow, milk her so they'd have butter and cream as they needed, and make sure nothing wild had stolen a chicken while they'd been gone.

The mutton stew had kept fine over the cool night in the iron pot, and when the fire had created hot coals, Robbie set it on the hook in the fireplace to heat for dinner. Then he set about tidying the cottage—sweeping the hard earthen floor, beating the dust from the hide that served as a hearth rug, shaking the blankets to rid them of bugs. He'd just finished those tasks when he saw something scurry over the small table Ian used as a writing desk. It was a mouse, and though it proved too quick and canny for him to catch, he managed to chase it out of the cottage.

Shaking his head but smiling at how well the chase had warmed him up, Robbie went back to pick up the pages the creature had scattered in its haste to escape.

He had no intention to read Ian's private letters, but both his eye and his mind were too quick to stop. Surprised, concerned, and a bit confused by the words written above what he was sure was a MacDonald seal, he was about to read it again, but the sound of Ian's footstep outside the cot brought him back to his senses. Hastily, he returned the papers to what he thought was their proper order and resolved to forget what he'd seen, if he could.

By the time Ian stepped inside, Robbie was ladling stew from the pot, its rich aroma tantalising as they seated themselves with bowls, spoons, and hard crusts of bread. Once their appetites had been sated, they sat wrapped in sheepskin near the fire in Ian's two rough chairs, waiting for the tea to brew. Few words passed between them, the quiet feeling strangely peaceful to Robbie, yet uneasy at the same time—until Ian broke it.

"You're an Elliot, you said. A Borderer? A Reiver?" Ian's question came from out of fire-lit silence.

Though Ian's face showed no more than placid interest, a prickle of hair rose on Robbie's arms, as if he sensed a threat just around the corner. He tried to stay calm when he answered, but he struggled a bit.

"Yes, sir. We were Reivers, then...when... But we still remembered where we came from in the Highlands, and why we took to patrolling the Borders in the first place."

"Ye did, aye?"

Ian's eyes focused sharply on Robbie's face at that moment—so sharp Robbie imagined he could feel them like nails hot from the forge. Robbie forced himself to hold his gaze steady in return, but not without effort. Relief washed over him when Ian sighed deeply, muttered a soft "ach, aye," and rose to stoke the hearth fire. As Ian pushed and prodded with the iron poker, a fountain of sparks lit his face, and Robbie thought he saw a great sadness lying heavily over his features.

Finally, Ian stepped out of the door of the cosy blackhouse into the gale outside, which was blowing so hard the stones weighting the thatch on the roof were knocking against one another—a strangely musical counterpoint to the rainfall and moaning wind. Robbie was left wondering whether to worry that Ian had decided to be rid of him after all, or perhaps to worry that whatever troubled Ian would lead him into danger in the dark storm. But when the brawny Highlander returned perhaps a quarter-hour later, he seemed undamaged, indeed refreshed, and his gentle expression didn't carry any threat.

"So then, Robbie lad," Ian said. "I remember a bit of what I learned about the Highland Elliot, too. Why don't you tell me some of your story, and we'll see whether the versions match, with all the centuries and agony standing between."

Robbie poured tea for them both, letting the fragrant steam bathe his face. As he passed Ian a mug and sat down, he answered his question simply.

"It was Robert the Bruce who sent us to the Borders, after the treachery of others threatened Scotland. We guarded the Marches for generations, for Scotland's benefit, before things changed."

Ian muttered, "Aye, and I suppose it's not right to blame you for the reiving that undoubtedly ended a century before you were born." He chuckled. "But you confuse me. Mayhap that's the reason I'm wary."

Robbie ducked his head to one side, a silent apology for what he was about to say. He hoped it wouldn't shatter the peace, but he couldn't lie, and a lie it would certainly be if he didn't say it. He drew in a deep breath, and took his chance.

"No, listen. I was. That is...when I was born at Hermitage, we Elliots held it. We had pride of our name, but we...that is, many men of our clan...indeed, we were Reivers. And mercenaries, and enforcers—rustled the cattle, kidnapped men, made the farmers pay for protection."

"Nonsense!" Ian's outburst came with an angry red face, but his brow furled in what looked like confusion coupled with hurt. "What would make you spout such daft lies? James, sixth king of the name, put a stop to reiving and brought the debatable lands under his hand more than a century past!"

"Yes."

"Aye? So?"

"Ian, please believe this. I do not deceive you. I did live when the Elliot was a Reiver clan. And although I myself suffered under James's attention to the Borders, I did not know he'd succeeded in his conversion of the Marches until the third time I...came ashore."

Ian fumed and sputtered, gave a mighty—and frightening—cry. Then he let his head drop in his hands, covering his eyes, and when he lifted them again, his face held something akin to disgust. "No more, then, man. It's true I see nae deceit in ye—ye believe what you say. Let it lie, for I refuse to hear it."

Robbie stopped to consider possible consequences before he spoke; they might be rather drastic, he knew. But in the end, the same core of honesty that made him spite the king and the witch all those decades past made him speak. "But you deceive, Ian."

"What's that?"

"You deceive. I...saw the letter from your cousin, the laird."

Ian reacted, and the raw force of it frightened him for just an instant before annoyance overtook fear.

"No," he said. "Do not assume. You left it out on the desk, and I don't think you can blame me for letting it catch my eye when I saw the laird's seal at the bottom. The story you told me about banishment is a distraction. You do not have to tell me your truth—I am the captive after all—"

Ian laughed—actually laughed! "Oh, are ye now? I wonder..."

Robbie stopped, open-mouthed, but then decided he had no idea how to respond, so he went on as if Ian had said naught. "But I told you my truth, sir, in good faith and though it wasn't easy. Will you not tell me yours?"

*

Ian poured himself a cup of the strong tea before replying. Not that he didn't want to tell Robbie the truth of the matter, but there was only so much he could say.

"The laird's not my cousin," he said finally. "He's my uncle, although he's always been more of a second da to me. Not that I don't get on with my real da, but as Uncle Alastair says, there's no such thing as too much family, aye?"

He was quiet for a moment, letting himself get lost in thought, in memories of everything he'd given up for this task his uncle had given him. He'd been so lonely, as much of a lost soul as the white crests of the waves he so often went down to the beach to watch. He'd felt a kinship with the sea in a daft sort of way. It had been a constant in the months he'd been here, harsh, yet strangely welcoming.

"Ian?" Robbie prompted, a gentleness in his voice that made Ian look up and take heed. "You don't have to tell me your truth if you don't want to."

"Aye, I do." Ian wrapped his fingers around the welcoming heat of his mug, letting the soothing warmth seep into his hands. It felt right sitting in front of the fire with Robbie, like it was something meant to be, like this moment had waited for him, just out of reach. The feeling surprised him, pulled at him in the same way that harp of Robbie's did. Aye, it was a strange one, just like the lad himself.

Robbie believed in the tale he'd told. There was an earnestness about him, and Ian couldn't help admire that. He'd spent so long in pretending to be something he wasn't, in shoving his desires to one side. But this wasn't about desire; this was about two men talking, sharing what was in their hearts, even if what Robbie voiced was a wee far-fetched, like some faerie tale of old.

Ian shivered, despite himself. He'd always been more than a little scared of the old faerie stories. Magic was dangerous, and that was what Robbie claimed to be, wasn't it? Something of the old magic. Otherwise, how could he be speaking the truth? Normal men didn't live hundreds of years. The events he said he'd been a part of happened years ago. Long before Ian's time, before his da or even his granda were born.

For the time being, he'd go along with Robbie's story. Why upset the lad when there could be some truth to it? Yet Robbie believed it, and that harp... There was magic in the thing, that was for sure.

"How much do ye ken about the Jacobites? Are ye for or against the cause?"

"The cause?" Robbie looked puzzled, but more than a little curious. "I've heard the term, but a long time ago, and I'm afraid I don't know what you're talking about."

He was keeping to his story, and playing the role that went with it.

Ian sighed, not wanting to say too much until he knew which side Robbie was on. But surely the lad wasn't a spy for the redcoats? He didn't seem the type to work with that devil Campbell either.

"W—" He'd almost said *we* but stopped himself in time, wanting to see Robbie's reaction first.

"The Jacobites follow the king," Ian continued. "The true king of Scotland, not that usurper from England who wants the throne for himself." He spat into the coals, then wiped his mouth on his shirtsleeve. "Of course, the old king is getting on in years, so it's the young prince, Bonnie Prince Charlie, who's sworn to reclaim it, to put a Stuart back on the throne where he belongs. The Highlands are rallying. Rallying behind a cause that will go down in history."

"So you're a Jacobite, then?" Robbie eyed the sword Ian still kept close, but while he seemed nervous, he didn't appear to be scared.

"Aye, I am." Ian looked up and met Robbie's gaze directly. "If you're not, this would be a good time to tell me. I won't harm ye, I swear. I already made ye a promise I wouldn't, and I'm a man of my word."

"I know you won't harm me." Robbie's lips curved into a shy smile. He lowered the cup in his hands to his lap. His little finger on his right hand was deformed and scarred.

Ian wondered why he hadn't seen it before, but then he'd been more preoccupied with keeping them both alive.

"You haven't answered my question," he said, realising he'd been staring at Robbie's hand. He hoped the lad hadn't noticed.

"Last time I was awake, there was a rising." Robbie studied what was left of his tea. "That was the first time I'd heard about the Jacobites, but I didn't know that cause and the one you spoke of were one and the same. They'd just been defeated."

"Defeated?" Why did Robbie insist on sticking to his story? "But that was over twenty-five years ago." It was around the time of Ian's birth, and he had about five years on Robbie, if he was right in his guess about the lad's age.

"Aye, it would have been I suppose." Robbie grew quiet. "That's the thing. If I go back, I don't know when I'll awaken again. I'm spending more time asleep than awake."

Ian leaned over and put one arm around Robbie. There was such sadness in his voice Ian couldn't help but want to offer comfort in some way. "I've already told you, you're safe here with me."

"You were telling me about the Jacobites." Robbie leaned into Ian's embrace for just a moment before pulling away again.

He sounded bright, but Ian wasn't fool enough not to see it for what it was. A brave face and a deliberate change of subject.

"Aye, I was."

"I don't pretend to understand everything you're saying, Ian, but us Elliots fought on the side of Robert the Bruce. We might not be Highlanders now, but we were, and what you're saying makes sense. I'm not sure that makes me a Jacobite, but this cause doesn't sound like it's changed that much."

"You're not working with those English devils?" Ian wanted to be sure, to hear it from Robbie himself. He'd called himself a Borderer and many of those favoured the English crown.

"No, sir...Ian. I am not. I have good reason not to love any king of England."

Ian allowed himself a smile. "Good lad." He poured himself more tea and topped up Robbie's mug at the same time. "Drink up and warm your insides. There's a cold night coming our way. It's freezing out."

"The letter I saw. It tells a different story from what you told me." Robbie frowned. "I canna believe you're a man who deceives easily. You're honest. I can see it in your eyes. This doesn't sit well with you." He leaned in. "It said you were on a mission. That's not banishment."

"Aye, I try to be—honest, that is." Ian shrugged. "And you're a persistent one, I'll give ye that." But what exactly to tell the lad? He couldn't tell him about the treasure, not with the oath he'd taken to keep it safe. "I've told you Skye's not my home. I've always kept to myself a bit, but not always through choice. Sometimes it's easier, especially when some of the choices I've made haven't exactly worked out."

Ian still sometimes thought of Angus, although he knew he shouldn't. Angus had the life he'd said he wanted now. A wife, a family, and a position within the clan.

It wouldn't have been Ian's choice, but he hadn't been about to put his own needs above Angus. Nor above the wishes of his laird. Alastair was right. Ian and Angus hadn't a future together then, not one that would be welcomed by the rest of the clan. Angus had already been promised in marriage to someone else. What they'd had was in the past. Angus had a wife and family now. He had responsibilities.

So did Ian.

"Despite my mistakes, I've always tried to do what is right. Being here on Skye is a part of that. I canna tell ye what exactly the laird asked me to do, and why I'm here, just that it's important to the cause."

Robbie nodded slowly.

"It's a hard place, but the biggest hardship has been the lack of company. I miss my family, and listening to their conversation. Even if I didn't take part in a lot of it, knowing they were close, it's a comfort, ye ken?"

Robbie nodded again. "Being alone isn't a choice I made either. Does your family know about the letter?" He frowned, his brow creasing. "It said something about stealing?"

"I didn't steal anything." Ian brought his head up sharply at the accusation. He lowered it again in a flush of embarrassment. "People are supposed to think I did," he mumbled. "That way, they wouldn't come after me."

"They don't know, then?"

"My family? Nae." Ian had known it was a dangerous task he'd taken on, but in the first few months he'd been on Skye, he'd seen no one, apart from Fergus who had journeyed there with him, and so he'd begun to relax. Begun to have some hope he might survive this and one day be able to tell his family the truth. He'd go to his death if he had to, fighting to protect what had been entrusted to him. Yet Campbell's arrival five months ago, and Fergus's death, had made him wonder, for the first time, if his parents would ever know the real reason he'd fled.

"Your uncle knows," Robbie said. "And your family know you for what you are. They won't believe the lie."

"Aye, I suppose not." Ian hoped Robbie was right. "I miss them."

"Then perhaps you should tell me about them." Robbie smiled, that shy smile Ian had seen before.

Warmth filled Ian's heart, a fluttering of hope he hadn't known in months.

"I'm in sore need of some conversation, too," Robbie continued.

"We're neither of us alone," Ian said. Outside the wind howled, yet it was peaceful by the fire with Robbie. Ian didn't know how long the storm would last, or how long the safety of the cottage would last, but for now, he didn't care. "I'll tell ye a little of my life. Perhaps ye'd share some of yours in return?"

"Aye," Robbie said. He grinned. "Just a little?" He held his thumb and forefinger about an inch apart. "Like this little?" He widened the distance between them as far as they'd go. "Or this little?"

Ian chuckled. He held his fingers like Robbie's, then narrowed the gap to somewhere in between. "I'll start, and let's see where the story goes. A few minutes in and ye might fall asleep."

"I won't. Talk to me, Ian," he prompted when Ian grew silent. "Please."

"I don't know where to start."

"At the beginning? All stories start at the beginning."

"Aye, that they do." Ian poked at the fire, collecting his thoughts.

"My story begins in the village of Glenfinnan on the shores of Loch Shiel..."

*

Robbie woke in the cottage, the bed clothes gone cool and damp, and the sound of Ian's axe coming from outside in the wood pile. The wood was in a covered shed, protected and dry, so it wouldn't be long before warmth filled the old cottage. And wood fires had that sweet smell Robbie was coming to love—so different from the peat and dung fuels he remembered from his childhood. He loved the way the flames would 'speak,' too.

So very many things he loved about 'this time.' Not the least of which was Ian himself.

Thinking of the warmth he would feel when Ian came in—from the fire the man would start, but also from Ian's very presence, Robbie thought of staying put, right where he was in the bedclothes, simply waiting for good things to enter his day. What a luxury that would be! One he hadn't known since earliest childhood when his dear mother still lived. Before the king's sweep of the Borders. Before he'd been tricked into the domain of Lady Talwyn. The witch. With those thoughts came a shiver, climbing his spine, and suddenly, lying still wrapped in blankets was no longer a comfortable thought, no matter what he waited for.

He rose swiftly, smoothly, cinched up his breeks and grabbed his shirt off a peg as he went out the door. His bare feet didn't trouble him—he wasn't as tough soled as Ian or any Highlander, but he'd made it through a number of barefoot seasons in different places, and neither the prospect of a cool Skye summer morning, nor of the gravelly beach caused him to hesitate. He walked into the forest a few steps to answer the usual morning urges, then to the burn just beyond the rocks that guarded the cottage from view from the beach. It would be fresh water, as the tide was only beginning to return and the salt didn't pollute the burn until full high tide. He would just wash up in the pool there before returning to Ian and the cottage.

But as he came across the open stretch of beach on his way to the burn, he thought he saw a...sparkle, or a glimmer. Something that snagged at his eyes. But no, when he took a longer look nothing showed itself. Yet he knew something was there. Did he hear music?

Maybe.

No.

Still, out there near the sea, a source called to him. Insistent, like a beacon that found echo in his own pulsing veins. Robbie felt an undeniable need to move closer to the source of the call. Many strange things had happened since the witch laid her curse on Robbie, but this was new—unlike any previous time on the shore of life since the magic took him. Though mystified, he turned and began to walk towards the beach, as sure in his direction as a pigeon finding home.

By the time he'd gone ten strides, he knew what called him.

Yes. Of course.

And when he reached the shore it had begun to show itself.

The boat.

Chapter Eight

Ian finished splitting the final log, tucked the axe away in its hiding place—no need to leave a potential weapon in plain sight—and stretched his shoulder muscles. He'd always found hard work a good distraction from thoughts and feelings he didn't want to dwell on. He liked Robbie, more than liked. Ian hadn't felt attracted to another man in far too long. Hadn't allowed himself to be. But Robbie had got under Ian's skin. He smiled, remembering the warmth when their fingers had touched, and how he'd woken early that morning, his arm around Robbie. Ian had taken his time pulling away. It wouldn't do to wake the lad, and Robbie looked so peaceful sleeping. Ian could have kept watching him if it weren't for his body reminding him it was time to start his day.

Finally, he'd slipped from his—their—bed and taken care of his morning ablutions. Robbie hadn't woken, so Ian put some porridge on to cook and went outside to chop wood for the fire.

All this talk of magic didn't sit well with him. He wanted to believe Robbie's story, but he didn't know why Robbie did. Ian didn't doubt that Robbie thought the story he told was true. But... Ian shivered. His granda had told more than just stories about the old castle and had scared Ian shitless when he was a bairn. Although his granda hadn't claimed what he'd been told by *his* gran were true, he'd warned Ian to be careful. After listening to several of those tales in the dark around a fire, the promise to do so had come easily to Ian. He had no intention of getting anywhere near any ghosts or anything else that wasn't natural.

Yet, his fear of something befalling Robbie scared Ian more. Whatever the lad *thought* he'd been through already, he still needed someone to look out for him. The isle wasn't safe, not when Campbell or his men could return at any time.

His mind made up, Ian washed his face quickly in a bucket of cold water and pulled on his shirt. His body cooled now that he'd finished his chore, and with the memories of the song they'd shared at the castle, some of its earlier warmth returned. Robbie had a clear voice, musical while Ian's was not, and sweet and true.

Like the lad himself.

Was that the real reason for Ian's state of mind? Robbie didn't seem the type to tell tall stories, and Ian would swear he wasn't a liar either.

Ian's footstep faltered, and the thoughts he'd tried to shove to one side came unbidden into his mind.

What if Robbie told the truth? What if the magic he talked of was real?

"Don't be daft, man," Ian muttered, shoving open the door.

One look around the cottage and Ian felt the hairs on the back of his neck stand up. Robbie was gone. The porridge bubbled over the stove, not burnt but close to it, but there was no sign of Robbie.

Ian moved the pot of porridge off the heat, giving himself time to think. Robbie's shirt was gone, but...a quick search of the burlap by the side of the bed showed the harp was still where Robbie had left it the night before.

His shoes, the *brogan tionndaidh* Ian had cut down for him from a piece of deer hide, stood under the hook by the door. The lad had soft, Lowland feet—not the callused feet of a Highlander—and Ian thought he'd have taken them if he planned to go far.

But then he wouldn't need to, for someone else to find him. Although Campbell had gone, Ian didn't trust him not to have left someone behind. Robbie might put up a good fight if cornered, but that wouldn't be enough. Not against Campbell's men. No honour amongst the lot of them—not if they were anything like the brute they followed.

Fergus would have fought hard against the men who had killed him too. Ian blanched and gritted his teeth at the thought of finding Robbie with his throat slit or beaten to death because he'd been too stubborn to tell his captors the information they wanted. Ian had already seen the stubborn streak in the lad—his mam would have told him he'd recognised it as a reflection of his own.

Ian grabbed his sword and sheathed it. He stalked out of the cottage, pausing at the doorway to figure out what direction Robbie would have taken. He hadn't passed by Ian, so that limited his choice of route. Given where Ian had first found him, the nearby clearing was probably the most logical place, but Robbie could have gone somewhere different for that very reason. He'd talked of the sea, and looked like he came from it with those eyes of his. Perhaps he'd thought of going back to it?

Not that Ian believed any of it. But Robbie surely did…

Convinced he needed to go after Robbie, Ian started towards the beaten track he guessed the lad had followed, but he stopped short. Not knowing why, and cursing himself for it, he turned around, stepped back into the cottage, and picked up the damnable harp, slinging it over his shoulder by its frayed and sour-smelling leather strap.

It didn't take long for Ian to confirm his suspicions. A half-broken branch, and a footprint in the dirt path leading to the beach might as well have painted a signpost to point the way. Did Robbie want to be found? He'd left a trail anyone could follow, let alone an experienced tracker like Ian.

The scent of the ocean hit Ian before he reached the shore. It seemed stronger than usual, though he dismissed the thought as whimsy. Robbie's stories were prickling at Ian's mind, like an itch he didn't want to scratch, in case they were real. He would fight to keep Robbie safe, but what chance did he have against something unnatural? What if the sea wanted to claim Robbie as part of its own once more?

Ian picked up his pace, but before he'd gone twenty yards the sound of rough voices stopped him in his tracks. Between him and the beach lay a long, tangled cluster of stone spires, a bank of palisades worn by time into tall peaks joined at the base. On the other side of them was a narrow ledge of level ground before a brushy defile descended next to a waterfall in a precipitous drop to a well-like pool at sea level.

One voice called from below, breaking with fear or pain, or maybe cold, as the man must have fallen down into the frigid pond. "Niall," he shouted. "I think m' leg's broken. Ye canna leave me here to die!"

"Nay, I canna do that," Niall shouted back from just beyond the barrier of rocks. "You're the Campbell's cousin, and he'd flay me for it if I did." In a quieter tone, though no less angry, he said, "James, help me link the ropes to pull him up. We'll have to splint his leg somehow so we can get him home to cry to his mam. Donnell, take the others and go see if you can catch MacDonald at the cottage. Be wary—he'd like as not split your skulls if ye give him the chance."

"Niall, I dinna like this! There's something wrong here, maybe magic afoot. I can feel it! We need to collect Archie, fix his leg, and get back to the mainland."

Niall fairly roared his answer. "To hell wi' your superstitions, Donnell. Do as you're told. I've an idea I know where MacDonald's hidey-hole might lie, down along the beach. We'll get Archie to the boat and meet up wi' ye there."

Footsteps coming his way alerted Ian that if he didn't move, he'd be right in their path. He stepped back behind a second outcropping of stone on the other side of the path, and down into a ditch that lay just beyond, careful to keep his movements silent despite his size and weight. Crouching, he waited until the men passed, listening to their grumbling about "that arse Niall," who at least one of them thought was going to get them all "killed or worse."

It was always a good thing to know that your enemy had divided sentiments and questionable loyalties. Still, counting out the injured man, that left at least three men here, looking to capture him and steal the treasure. He might best them in a fight if their hearts weren't in it, but he'd prefer not to test that. From what Niall had said, he truly might have an idea where Ian had stashed the treasure. And Ian had an idea Robbie might be found down on that very same beach.

As soon as he deemed it safe, Ian moved, taking a second, less obvious path down to the beach. When he reached the rocky backshore, he detoured into an arch that formed the entrance to a shallow cave. He moved three rocks and reached behind another and pulled out the pouch of jewels that constituted half the fortune the MacDonalds had collected for Bonnie Prince Charlie. He stashed it into his sporran, then carefully put the rocks back exactly as they had been and left the cave, making sure to erase any mark of his passing.

From there, it was a short run to the gravel beach. He skidded to a halt as soon as he reached it and raised a hand to shield against the sun glinting off the water, scanning the beach for Robbie.

His gaze fixed on a lone figure standing close to shore, waves lapping around his ankles. The wind howled, as though taunting Ian, reminding him he had no hold on Robbie, that the lad wasn't *his* to claim.

Not yet.

He cupped his hands and yelled over the wind. "Robbie!"

Robbie didn't turn towards him, didn't give any sign he'd heard Ian.

"Robbie! Come back up the beach. The tide's coming in!"

But instead of turning around, Robbie seemed focused on something just out of reach. An old boat, battered, and looking like one could sink it like a stone just by looking at it. To his horror, Ian saw Robbie strip off his shirt and breeks, throw them further up the beach, and dive into the waves.

*

The boat. Oh, please don't let this mean...

When the harp had sounded as his eyes met Ian's, and then again when they'd sung together, and then the boat—the magical cobble that carried Robbie to sea and dissolved into the waves with him every time he left the world of living things—had not shown itself, Robbie hoped that maybe it wouldn't return. Maybe Ian was the one, and the boat would never come because it would never be needed again.

But…there it was, its faint outline visible just beyond the surf.

As Robbie watched the boat slowly materialise, bob on the waves, and drift inwards with the tide, he tried to remember word for word the witch's pronouncement about it.

This is not the same, he assured himself. *And anyway, Melisandre did not say it would always take me away. She said the boat would be my chance. "If ye've found the one ye seek, and that one wakes ye…"*

Just then, Robbie became aware of another presence away behind him, near the cottage. Ian, of course, looking for him. He *felt* Ian draw nearer, mentally followed his progress as he came down the rise, across the beach, and steadily towards him. But he didn't turn to greet him; his eyes remained fixed on the boat, which now seemed stuck in some doldrums, neither coming in nor drifting off, instead bobbing just out of reach from shore. Suddenly Robbie knew that the boat was necessary, that he couldn't disempower the magic—dissolve its cold hand on his heart—unless all the pieces of the witch's spell came into play.

The boat had to come ashore.

Without turning, and even though the big man moved nearly silently over the beach, Robbie knew Ian had come near. He took a deep breath and turned to face him.

"Robbie," Ian called over the sound of the waves and wind. "What are you doing down here, man. The tide's about to come in and cover ye waist-deep."

At Ian's words, Robbie became aware that, indeed, the tide had already brought the water lapping around his shins. But rather than stepping away, and rather than answering, Robbie stripped his shirt and breeks and threw them further up the beach. He took another deep, resigned breath, strode into the water, and dived into the waves. Surfacing once, twice, and hearing Ian call each time, he reached the boat and gave a solid tug. The boat came with him easily once he started swimming, as he'd hoped it would.

Apparently, though, Ian had feared Robbie would run into trouble, for as Robbie paused to breathe and switch to towing the boat with the other arm, he saw Ian striding into the incoming tide, waving his arms about. He was shouting too. Robbie couldn't make out all the words, but they included something about wasting time.

He's concerned for me! Or maybe not. Perhaps he's afraid I'll climb into the cobble and row away, attempting to escape my captivity. But what does he mean, we don't have time?

Robbie wanted to smile at these ideas. Of course Ian didn't expect him to row out to sea. *The man must know how I've begun to feel about him.* And the idea of a rushed Ian late for some pressing appointment seemed ludicrous.

Perhaps Ian felt the magnetic pull between them, too, but maybe he didn't—Robbie might be indulging in wishful thinking. It could be that Ian truly thought of Robbie only as a fairly agreeable, possibly useful captive.

The idea pained him, and he lost any urge to laugh. He resumed swimming, now towing the boat ashore, resigned to waiting and hoping Ian might truly see him, see *them*—what they might be together—before the sea's brine washed the chance away.

When Robbie came even with Ian, he found he was also close enough to shore to stand, the water coming just above his waist.

Ian stood alongside him, but then without warning, captured him in an embrace. "By all that's holy, Robbie. I swear you're driving me daft."

Robbie went wide-eyed, but melted into Ian's chest, glad for the unexpected opportunity.

"You're all right, then?" Ian asked, taking Robbie's shoulders and holding him away to look into his eyes.

Surprised and a little confused about what seemed too much urgency on Ian's part, Robbie only nodded.

"Good. But now we've a problem that can't wait. Come get your clothes and follow me."

Ian took Robbie by the elbow and tugged to get him started up the beach, but Robbie dug in his heels.

"Stop. I must bring in the cobble."

Ian's expression passed quickly through eye-flashing ire, to frustration, to confusion. He shook his head as if to clear it. "Are ye daft, then? It's just an old broken boat!"

"It's *my* boat, Ian. And it doesn't leak...per se."

Ian stared at Robbie. "Damn it all, man. This water is cold enough to shrivel me up in ways I don't want to talk about, and I'm short on both time and patience. Ye've got a minute, no more, to make sense. Ye say it's your boat. You mean to tell me *this* is what you went out to sea in?"

This type of question was a little hard to answer, but Robbie refused to lie to Ian about anything—he wouldn't set that precedent. "Well," he said. "Um...yes?"

At that, Ian's jaw dropped. Then, taking Robbie by surprise, he laughed out loud. "Oh! Well then, I guess that explains the shipwreck."

Robbie smiled at Ian's quip. He supposed the idea of him on a sea voyage in the cobble did seem funny. Not himself amused, Robbie enjoyed the way humour transformed Ian. But only seconds passed before Ian sobered.

"They're coming, and not far now."

Ian had spoken in a voice controlled but full of urgency, and Robbie thought he understood.

"They? You mean Campbell?"

"Not him, but his men, aye. Now let's—"

"Wait. Please, just hold," Robbie blurted, knowing he risked Ian's ire.

"Robbie," Ian growled. "I can see something is troubling you, but we must hie ourselves off this beach and climb. We'll hide—again—if we can, but if that doesn't work, we'll want a place we can defend. Campbell's man, Niall, is delayed pulling one of his laird's clumsier cousins out of a deep hole, but he'll finish that forthwith, and then he's coming down to this beach." He swung the harp off his shoulder and held it out to Robbie. "If you must bring this bloody harp, bring it, but forget about the boat, and let's go. Now."

Robbie took the harp but let it fall to lean against his feet. The surf pushed it about some, but Robbie knew it would stay with him. And other things were more important. He took hold of Ian's wrist. "Sir, put me in the boat."

"By God, move, or I'll pick ye up and carry ye up those rocks, make no mis—"

As bravely as he'd ever acted, Robbie interrupted, putting such urgency in his whisper that it felt like a shout. "Listen, please. I know you've got something Campbell wants—something aside from your life, that is. I could guess it from the letter, and now, well...that bulge in your sporran makes an unnatural sound as you walk, and I'm thinking it's the sound of gold or jewels—"

"What are ye talking—"

"Don't try to convince me otherwise, Ian. We've little time, and I know! After all, I was raised in a reiving clan, and leave it to a Reiver to know the sound of hidden jewels knocking together. So put me in the boat! Put me in the boat and line it with herbs, like a funeral boat, like I'm dead. I'll hold your treasure in my breeks, and ye can lay the harp over me!"

"If I'm going to hide anything in your trousers, it won't be Charlie's damn jewels!"

Ian mumbled, but Robbie heard, and as awful as the moment was, he smiled.

Speaking more normally, Ian went on. "I don't understand what you're raving about. You must know as well I do that they'll check—they're Scots, but even Scots aren't so superstitious they won't even check to see that an alleged corpse is really dead. When they find out you're alive—"

"They won't, I swear it. I...in the boat, with the harp, on the water, I'll...*I'll be as dead*, sir."

The colour drained from Ian's face. "*As* dead. What do you mean, 'as dead'?"

"I'll... Well, you'll see if you just put me in the boat. I won't breathe, my heart won't beat, my eyes won't change in the light. I'll be cold. No pulse of blood. I'll seem dead."

"But then...ye'll wake up?"

"Yes."

"Not truly dead?'

"No."

"By Mary, mother of God, you scare me, Robbie. I don't know how I could be so... Ach. This magic that's on you. It's an awful thing."

Robbie tried to keep the dread from his face. *Please,* he thought. *Please don't let him give in to the fear. It's what she wanted, the witch—that if, finally, I found the one who would love me, he'd run at me or away, just like all the ones that wouldn't matter. Oh, gods, please don't let Ian fear me, and so loathe me...*

But Ian drew a sharp breath and shook his head. "Ye ken we don't have much time, man. So, briefly, pray tell how do ye know ye'll be alive when this is over?"

"Sir," Robbie said, memory flooding in but crowding out emotion, sending his words rushing out in a rough stream. "I've been 'dead' in that boat many times. Yet here I am."

"Ach, aye, that's fine, then." Ian shook his head, his hair wet enough for water to fly from the loose red curls. "Well, I wish there was time for you to make me understand. I don't; make no mistake about that. But go on, then. Climb into the boat. There's a wee glade behind that outcrop of stone, there. An oak, I recall, with a small stand of holly. A witch's elder. Maybe some mint by the stream. Aye"—Ian nodded—"and some bluebells. That should do for funeral herbs, yes?"

Without waiting for answer, Ian turned to go up the shore, but Robbie didn't move. Undoubtedly the big man was aware, because he pivoted and stared, confusion and exasperation written plain in his drawn brow and flashing eyes. "Hurry, then; go now!"

"I can't!"

"What?" Ian's growl was about as full of frustration as it was possible for one syllable to be. He calmed only slightly when he said, "You've just told me you've done it many times."

"Yes, but…" Robbie's breath barely let him speak, but he was able to get it out. "I'm yet afraid. You must do it." Robbie thought he would surely break inside under the weight of Ian's ire and his own fears—fears he knew were irrational, but he couldn't help them. "Please. You see, before, always when I got into this boat, I did so because I wanted…needed to get away. And always I woke up many years later, many miles distant."

He waited for Ian's understanding, but the man just stared.

Urgent, he forced his voice into what surely must seem like anger, but it was no more than determination. "Sir, I do not want to wake up away in the future, I want to wake with you. I am so afraid to climb in that boat that I cannot make my limbs move." Robbie fell silent, gathering courage to continue—to declare his hand.

"Robbie?" Ian said, puzzled, moving closer.

"I canna bear it, for you are the one." A strangled laugh punctuated his words for he knew what that may have sounded like. Yet… "Ian, you are the one who can save me from this awful curse. And it doesn't matter that I reveal that to you because pitying me will not do it. But I…I have come to love you so deeply, man. And again, I know you are the one. I know in my mind—all the signs. And"—he chuckled—"believe me, I know it in my flesh, for never have I so craved even a touch. But most, I know here!" He grabbed Ian's brawny, swordsman's hand and held it flat to his chest, instantly feeling its warmth spread.

"Good sir, you are the one. I love you, and I know you can love me. I know it. And if you do, I am saved." He was again breathless at the finish, but that was nothing to the way his world tilted when Ian spoke, quiet and true, and without angst, as if nothing could be simpler, or more right.

"Aye. I can love you, and I do."

He leaned in and laid a kiss on Robbie's lips, brief and sweet but not precisely chaste. He left behind a flavour of saltwater, and tea, and sweet berries, and the rich, dark flavour of Ian himself.

"Aye," Ian said again. "But leaving much for later, because *they come.* One question for you. You said you will not die in the boat, but...how can we be sure you'll not go adrift into some other time? For I don't want that either, Robert Elliot."

"You're right, they come. They'll be here soon; I feel it in my bones, in the harp. She's uneasy. Understand: You must wake me before the moon rises this night, or I will be lost."

"And then I think we would be lost to each other, surely. For I cannot search through time." Ian swept Robbie into his arms and lifted him. Before he placed him in the cobble, he said, "You're shaking, man. Art so afraid?"

Robbie's voice came thin and wobbly, but he answered honestly. "Aye. I am."

"I canna stop to comfort you, or to comfort myself, with my enemies near." Ian laid him gently in the boat, but before slipping his arms out from under him, he said, "Look at me now."

When Robbie met his gaze, Ian's eyes burned with the passion of conviction.

"I will wake you before moonrise, Rob, or I will die trying. You...you have my heart."

Chapter Nine

Ian laid the harp gently on Robbie's chest, wishing he could lie there with him and keep him warm. He knew he couldn't, though, so he pasted a sad smile on his face and kept it there until Robbie closed his eyes. Robbie's chest rose and fell slowly a couple of times, then stopped. A chill ran down his spine. Although Robbie had warned him this would happen, seeing him lying in the boat still as death filled Ian with dread.

"Robbie?" Ian couldn't help himself. He reached for Robbie, stopping himself in time. It wouldn't do to wake the lad now.

What if he couldn't be woken? What if Ian had finally found someone he dared love, only to lose him to something he couldn't fight? How could he live, days following one after the other, cold lonely nights passing in between—nature's unbreakable rhythm? If he lost Robbie, only to face that...

Ian turned his back on the boat, the image of Robbie lying there burned into his mind. He didn't have time to grieve, and if he didn't move quickly, he risked losing Robbie forever. Although he'd told Robbie he'd die trying to wake him, a dead man couldn't keep his promise.

He ran to the clearing and collected what he needed for the funeral boat. His eyes pricked with tears as he picked the mint by the stream, but he blinked them back. Better to save them for later when they would be needed.

He'd only just finished decorating the boat when heavy footsteps approached. If they were attempting stealth, they'd failed miserably. Unfortunately, their incompetence didn't make them any less dangerous. But Ian had his sword and dirk. He'd go down fighting if it came to that.

Ian gently stroked Robbie's cheek with his fingers. "Ye better come back to me," he whispered. "My heart breaks seeing ye like this." He wanted nothing more than to lift Robbie from the boat and run, but he knew Robbie was right. This was the only way.

Tears came again, but this time, Ian didn't wipe them away. He felt someone right behind him, but he didn't move, for a moment as still as the man in the boat. He'd told the truth when he said he loved Robbie. Already, Ian couldn't bear the thought of losing him, however short the life he might live without him.

"What do we have here, then?" Niall sounded more amused than anything else.

"Go away," Ian muttered. "Can't ye see I'm grieving?"

"What do ye take me for?" Niall growled. "Face me like a man, not a woman crying at a graveside."

Two men grabbed Ian roughly, dragged him away from the boat, and forced him to his knees in front of Niall.

Niall took a step closer to Ian, his breath foul with a mix of ale and what smelled like fish. "Ye have the treasure. Where is it?"

Ian raised his head and faced Niall directly. "I don't have it," he said, keeping all emotion from his voice. He told the truth, but knew Niall wouldn't believe him.

Niall hit Ian hard in the stomach. Ian gasped in pain but said nothing. He continued to stare defiantly at Niall.

"Perhaps it's in the boat? Campbell said ye were too honest for your own good, and if that's the way of it, then you dinna lie," Niall suggested. "Donnell, search the boat! James, hold MacDonald tight."

The grip holding Ian loosened as one of the men let go of him. He could have freed himself easily enough from James, but he didn't move. Not yet.

"There's magic there," Donnell muttered. "Powerful magic. Can't ye feel it?" He shivered. "I dinna ken...It's unnatural, it is, and shouldn't be tampered with."

"You and your superstitions." Niall let out a long sigh. "I'll look myself, as you're too cowardly to do it."

Ian held his breath. It would only take him a moment to reach his sword. But if he reacted with force to Niall's words, the man might take it as proof the treasure was on the boat with Robbie. "Let the lad rest in peace," he growled instead.

"If he's dead, maybe I will. Or maybe I won't." Niall strode past Ian to the cobble, splashing through the water as he waded through the shallow waves to where it was moored.

James's grip on Ian loosened still further, and Ian pulled free as the action would be expected of him. He drew his sword. Niall was already at the boat. He'd not let Niall harm Robbie. What if Niall's interference meant the sleep that had taken Robbie couldn't be broken? Why had Ian agreed to this scheme?

"Let the lad be," Ian said, his voice rough. He didn't need to fake his anger or fear.

James backed away from him, his sword hand shaking. "Donnell's right. We shouldn't disturb the dead." He sounded scared but seemed more focused on the boat than Ian.

"I'm not afraid of the dead. But this…it's unnatural," Donnell repeated. His skin looked grey, and he was sweating. "Get away from the boat, Niall. For all our sakes. Can't spend treasure in hell. And hell's where we're going if we disturb this boat!" He crossed himself and backed further up the beach.

"You're both cowards!" Niall yelled at them, but there was a tremor in his voice that hadn't been there before. He touched the wooden edge of the boat, then removed his hand quickly. "Campbell will have our balls. I said I'd…"

"Get away from the boat!" Ian told him. "Or it won't be just Campbell ye need to worry yourself about." He stalked out to the boat until he and Niall were inches away from each other. Donnell and James wouldn't come closer; Ian was sure of it. "Not so full of yourself on your own, are ye?"

He towered over Niall, taking advantage of the six inches he had on the man.

"Come back, ye cowards!" Niall glared at Ian, as Niall's men ran further up the beach, their boots sliding against gravel in their haste to get away.

Ian stood his ground. Niall moved away from the boat, but not as far as Ian would have liked. Ian took another step towards Niall, and the man edged back towards the beach. Turning his back on the boat, Ian herded Niall until they were both close enough to shore so the waves were lapping around the tops of their boots.

"Ach, I dinna have any treasure," Ian said. "Ye can tell Campbell he's wasting his time." He raised his sword, matching the menace in his words with his expression.

Niall swallowed. His hand briefly hovered over the sheath of his sword, but he obviously thought twice about drawing it.

Ian nodded approvingly. "Good man." He'd figured once Niall was alone, his bravado would flee to join his men. Ian was lucky Campbell himself wasn't there. He wouldn't hold with the superstition that had made Donnell and James run. Once Campbell found out what had happened, he'd be angry and even more determined to hunt Ian and claim the treasure as his own.

Niall opened his mouth as though he was going to speak, then his gaze shifted behind Ian. He grinned, turned on his heel, and stalked off to follow his men.

"Wha—" It wasn't the reaction Ian had expected. He'd thought Niall would at least attempt a half-arsed fight before giving up and taking flight. Ian turned to see what had got Niall's attention. "Ach, nae!"

The boat was gone.

Ian forced himself to wait until Niall was well and truly gone from sight, then shaded his eyes as he scanned the sea. Nothing. He squinted, trying to see further into the distance. Reaching for his spyglass, he remembered he'd left it back at the cottage in his haste to find Robbie. If he went back for it now, he'd waste valuable time, and risk running into an angry Campbell.

"Where are ye, lad?" he muttered, glancing back and forth along the shoreline. But willing Robbie to appear wouldn't make it so.

Ian's stomach rumbled, reminding him of the porridge he'd made but not eaten. It would be cold by now, but that thought didn't stop Ian being hungry for it. Must be nearing midday, given the sun's position in the sky. He'd packed his fob watch away soon after his arrival on the isle, not wanting the reminder of the passing hours, yet finding himself reminded all the same.

"Ach, this isn't helping." Getting agitated wasn't going to solve anything. Ian needed a plan. Aye, one that would catch a ghost, as that was what Robbie would be if he couldn't be found. "I canna lose ye. I *won't* lose ye."

Ian took several deep breaths to steady himself and slow his racing heart.

Staring across the shore from here wasn't doing any good. He'd get a better look from further up the beach and climbing the rocks there. The boat definitely wasn't anywhere near, so it must have drifted.

If he still couldn't find it, he'd have to risk the cottage for his spyglass, waterskin, and a few mouthfuls of porridge. He'd need strength to swim out and pull the boat in, if it was a good way out to sea.

By the time he resigned himself to heading back to the cottage, he was frantic. Dusk was falling, and it would soon be night-time and with that came the moon.

Robbie's words echoed in his mind: *"You must wake me before the moon rises this night, or I will be lost."*

"Ye'll not be lost to me."

Luckily, Campbell wasn't at the cottage, but Ian moved quickly, only snatching what he needed, and shovelling some porridge into his mouth, swallowing as he headed back to the beach. He climbed up to the rocks again for a bird's-eye view. He'd been looking for the boat most of the day. If it had drifted too far, he'd never find it.

"Ach, I'm sorry," he murmured, although he knew Robbie couldn't hear him. Already, he felt a raw sense of loss, as though he was missing a part of himself he'd never known he had until that morning. Realising he could lose Robbie if their plan went terribly wrong had brought home how much he loved the lad.

Being with Robbie made Ian feel complete. But it wasn't just that. Ever since he found that bloody harp, he had a feeling he'd been reeled in by the thing like a fish, although he'd fought it at first. Not to the harp, he now knew, but to the man who owned it.

Robbie.

Was Ian really the man Robbie had waited for? Or was Robbie desperate for someone to save him from his never-ending torment? Ian shuddered. Being alone on this isle for months was bad enough. He didn't want to imagine what it was like for Robbie, only coming ashore for a short time, only to wake again to find everyone he'd known was gone.

Ian finished climbing the rocks. Robbie had enjoyed that brief kiss they'd shared as much as Ian had. *I want to be the one you're waiting for. I'll save ye or die trying.* But first, he needed to find the blasted boat. Ian checked the sky. No moon yet, but it wasn't far off. Robbie was running out of time.

Ian raised the spyglass, already resigned that he'd not find anything, yet determined not to give up until after it was too late. Maybe the moon wouldn't rise that night. Maybe this magic would work for them, not against them.

Give me more time. Please. I need more time.

Wait. What?

Ian swallowed and wiped the end of the spyglass with his sleeve before raising it to his eye once more. Aye, he'd seen something. A glimpse in the distance, by the sand spit. Hope welled in him. He grasped at it with everything he was and hung on tightly.

It was the boat. It had to be!

I'm coming, lad.

He shoved the spyglass through his belt and clambered down over the rocks, almost losing his footing in his haste. *Slow down, you're nae use to him if you're dead.*

But I'm running out of time.

Running out of time.

As soon as he was free of the rocks and back on level ground, Ian sprinted towards the beach, his breath coming in gasps as he ran. He didn't dare rest, wouldn't glance at the sky in case the moon took it as an invitation to show itself.

Finally, he reached the shore, his fingers fumbling for his spyglass. Aye! It was Robbie's boat, all right. A little way off, bobbing on the shallow waves.

Ian waded into the water, ignoring the chill as his wet kilt soaked him to the skin. He reached for the boat, but a wave pulled it just out of reach. Ian made an exasperated noise. "Come here!" Normally, he'd feel foolish talking to the thing, but it made him feel better hearing the noise. And perhaps…just perhaps…Robbie might hear him too, and know he was near.

"Got ye!" Ian grabbed the elusive boat and pulled it back to shore. He didn't dare risk glancing inside. He didn't need to. Robbie still rested there, sleeping as though dead. Ian knew it without looking. Fear rose in him.

You're too late. Too late…

The ocean fought him, wanting to keep what it considered its own, but Ian wasn't having it. Robbie was his, and to hell with giving him up. Not after coming this close to losing him.

Ian grunted as he yanked the boat onto the sand, wedging it between two boulders so it wouldn't drift away again. He walked around to the boat, his breath hitching as he saw Robbie there, the harp still resting on his chest. Ian put his arms around Robbie and lifted both him and the harp from the boat. He took care not to disturb the harp—if it fell and broke, he didn't know what that would do to Robbie, and he couldn't risk it.

He stumbled, losing his footing as a huge wave caught him unawares. Ian cradled Robbie close to him, the harp between them, protecting him as he fell towards the rocks. He winced as his shin caught a sharp point, cursing when he saw blood run from a cut on Robbie's arm from another.

"Ach, sorry," he murmured, struggling to right himself with the weight of Robbie still in his arms.

His back scraped against another rock as he used it as an anchor to stay upright. Ian glanced at Robbie, but he lay against Ian, unmoving.

Had this been for nothing? Was Ian already too late? He looked skywards once more, half expecting the moon to be shining down on them, taunting Ian, reminding him that he'd failed.

Around them, the incoming tide splashed against them, trying to draw Ian—and Robbie—into its embrace. Ian strengthened his grip on Robbie. If he didn't wake before the moon rose, Ian didn't know what he'd do—or what *to* do.

He slumped back against the rocks, watching his and Robbie's blood mingle together in the water, a thin trail of red, carrying their future away with it.

Another wave crashed against them over Ian's head, to splash the ledge above, and his grip on Robbie loosened.

The harp slipped as though trying to free itself.

As Ian grabbed at it, only just catching it in time, the harp sounded once more. But instead of the song he'd heard before, the sharp discord vibrated through him, a loud reminder that he'd lost. That the future he and Robbie might have had was gone.

*

Robbie had often dreamed, the times when he and the harp were one with the sea. Slow dreams, those were—distant and cold. Barely brushing anything that could be called awareness.

Not like this.

He *felt* this dream. He *knew* it.

Strong arms held him against warmth, against a beating heart.

This was a very good dream, and even though some memory of person and purpose hung on the horizon, like a mist Robbie knew he should pass through someday to see what was on the other side, he felt no desire to wake. It wasn't until seawater crashed over him, a mighty, noisy wave, that he realised he'd not been submerged, not been integrated into the sea, not this time like all the others. And then the wave touched the harp, which had lain quiescent and weightless on Robbie even as he'd been shuttled about by strong arms, and it sounded.

No song. No sweet chord, but a dissonant shout as if the harp had been torn harshly from its slumber. Robbie woke all at once, gasping for breath as the sea wave retreated with almost as much violence as it held coming in.

"Ian," he tried to say, but it came out a cough and a choke.

"Robbie! You're back! Thanks be to all the saints. But—ach!"

Ian's words were cut off when another wave came in and, with Ian struggling to keep his balance, Robbie slipped out of his arms to stand on his own feet. Still supported by one of Ian's strong arms, Robbie tried to keep a firm foothold on the rocks. It wasn't easy staying braced against the moving water while wracked with a persistent cough.

Ian said, "Tide's coming in again, Rob. We need to get to the beach."

Robbie resisted the gentle urging of Ian's arm around his shoulder. "The boat," he said.

At least he thought he'd said it. Ian didn't seem to hear. Still, Robbie closed his eyes and cast his awareness within until he felt the familiar connection, like an invisible rope, to the cobble that had been his ride from one future to another for more than two centuries. Within seconds, it surfaced—or perhaps came back into being—a long arm's reach from the rocks where Robbie and Ian stood.

Robbie repeated, "The boat," and this time, he made sure Ian heard. "My boat, Ian." He couldn't explain why, but thinking that the boat might drift back to sea without him set his already stressed heart galloping with panic.

Ian must have understood, for with another frustrated "ach" and perhaps some other choice words muttered under his breath, he reached out to grab hold of the cobble. After a couple of near misses, he grabbed it with one hand.

"Come on, ye wee bastard boat," he growled.

A torrent of confusion swirled in Robbie's mind. Maybe it was because he'd just woken from something deeper than sleep, but he couldn't make sense of Ian's struggle with the cobble. The tide was coming in; it should have been easy to pull the boat to shore. Instead, the harder Ian pulled, the more it seemed to resist. At the same time, Robbie could feel the connection between him and the craft stretching, strands of its fibre breaking, fraying.

Moonlight struck a sudden path across the bay and cast a thousand cruel stars agleam off the water pooling inside the boat. The same light glinted off Ian's wet skin. Then, when the big Highlander turned his head, although he frowned in frustration, the light of the moon shown in his eyes like lakes of deep blue peace.

Robbie understood. *I have no more chances. I either choose to fade into the sea with the boat and die, or I choose Ian and gamble that we can fulfil the spell and make a life.*

"Let it go, Ian!"

Ian held on to it, but stopped trying to pull it in. Exasperation exaggerating his brogue, he asked, "Eh? What's that, lad? Did ye nae ask me to fetch it in?"

Robbie couldn't help but smile, but he answered in earnest. "I don't want the boat. I want you. Let go."

The boat pulled back away from Ian and out of his grasp then, as if dragged by a powerful riptide that, less than a yard away, Robbie couldn't feel. He sighed as he watched it fade into the sea, gone from existence as surely as if the long years had laid it to rot. The connection between him and the small craft, thinned at last to but a single strand, snapped.

Robbie took a hard breath, feeling his weight and his tired muscles, truly earthbound as he hadn't been for more than a century. He sagged a bit and struggled to remain standing. Then Ian wrapped him up in two strong arms and flooded him with love, tentative but true. He clung to the harp, though, as Ian lifted him. Once more Ian began the careful trudge through the rock-strewn surf to safety on the beach, and joy and hope crashed over Robbie in waves more real, more tangible, more irrepressible than surf on shore.

By the time Ian reached the pebbled beach, the tide had covered it ankle deep with restless water. He stopped, labouring to catch his breath. After a moment, he asked, "Robbie, lad, can ye walk now? That harp may weigh nothing while ye hold it, but those jewels hidden in your breeks weigh a hell of a bloody lot! I swear to ye, I'll be glad when it's time to pass 'em on."

Robbie assured him he could manage on his own feet, and after Ian stood him upright, they made their way together up to a higher point on the beach. They stopped where soft sand had collected behind a tall boulder, and there they sat close with their backs against the stone. Robbie set the harp carefully next to him, thinking he almost heard its strings whispering as if the wind, blocked by the rock, still wandered among them. He sighed and gave the harp's mutterings no more thought. Respite from waves and weather felt like luxury.

"Robbie..." Ian said.

Robbie waited for Ian to continue. After a long moment of silence, he leaned forward to get a look at Ian's face in the scant moonlight. His eyes were closed. His breathing had slowed to a regular, restful rhythm.

"Ian," Robbie whispered. "Are ye sleeping?"

He was, apparently, as no answer came. Robbie smiled at the picture of the big, usually gruff man slumbering sweet as a baby. But then he sobered as cold crept in, and an achy fatigue took possession of every bone and fibre in his body. He felt the burden of his weight, unaccustomed, as if the chill earth he sat on was pulling him right down into it. He shivered, snuggled in close to Ian for the warmth his flesh offered. Then he rested his head on Ian's shoulder, closed his eyes, and breathed deeply once, twice, a third time and once more, weaving a dream from the smells of stone, and of life and the sea.

*

Ian woke with a start, confusion rushing through him like a tide trying to reclaim part of its own. The harp! He'd heard it play; he swore he had. Not the recent discord, but sweet music, tugging at his heart, a siren wanting him to follow it to the ends of the earth. He'd taken a step, then another, trying to resist, but it was akin to fighting a strong wind. Robbie's breath against his cheek had stopped him following, brought him back...

The harp lay still, leaning against the rock, silent as though sleeping. Ian frowned. He must have dreamed it, but it had felt so real. He eyed the thing suspiciously. The boat was gone, but the damned harp still needed to loosen its grip on his Robbie.

Robbie slumbered against Ian, undisturbed by the sudden movement.

Ian brushed two fingers against Robbie's cheek. The lad was freezing, cold as death. Ian shuddered, the memory of Robbie lying in the boat coming unbidden to his mind.

The boat is gone.

"The boat is gone." Repeating the words aloud made them seem more real. But it didn't change the fact that Robbie needed warmth. Ian had seen what happened to men too long in the water, the cold fingers of the sea refusing to let go even after reaching dry land. He had to get Robbie warm, and quickly, or everything they'd just been through would be for naught.

"You're still not having him," Ian muttered. "He's mine, and I take care of my own."

He didn't have anything out here that would warm Robbie. His own clothes were sodden and would take too long to dry in the cold. Ian shivered, the bite of the wind chilling him to his bones. He had blankets in his cottage, and could light a fire. Both might work, but a fire on its own wouldn't, and definitely not out here with nowhere to hide from the sea air. The moon was high in the sky now, and it would be hours before morning. Robbie might not last the night if they stayed where they were.

Did he dare risk being caught? Another glance at Robbie made the decision for him. If Robbie... Ian swallowed hard. Better to take the chance and be caught than remain here and let Robbie perish. The lad needed warmth.

Ian picked up the harp and placed it on Robbie. When he wrapped Robbie's arms around the harp to secure it in place, Robbie didn't stir.

"Ye'll be warm soon. I promise," Ian whispered lifting both the man and his precious harp into his arms. He adjusted Robbie's weight and started up the difficult path to the cottage. He nearly stumbled a couple of times but righted himself with a few curses without losing either Robbie or the harp.

Once in sight of the cottage, Ian took a few short moments to scan the area for any sign of Campbell or his men. Although he was taking a chance being there, there was no point in walking straight into an ambush. Being caught now wouldn't do either Ian or Robbie any good, and Ian was determined to give Robbie a fighting chance to survive this. If Ian didn't, a part of him would break, and he'd let Campbell do to him what he wanted.

But, whatever happened, the bastard wouldn't get the jewels. Whatever he did to Ian would be for naught.

Once he'd deemed the rest of the way to the cottage safe, Ian crept the final distance to the place he'd called home for so many months, spying as he went several likely places to stash the jewels.

First things, first though. He needed to take care of Robbie.

Ian was panting with exertion as he finished the last climb to the cot's door and stepped inside, shutting it behind him. He placed Robbie on the bed and covered him with blankets until he could do something about warming the place. The fire didn't take long to light, and Ian put water on to heat for tea.

"Aye, this will warm ye."

Seizing the moment, he stepped outside to see to hiding the jewels where they would less likely be found— outside in the confusion of trees and brush and vast, stony landscape. In the end, he settled on a place not too many steps from the cottage, in a small hollow under a ledge of stone hidden by a pile of brush waiting to be broken into kindling. Not ideal, but better than the cooking pot. Still, as he rushed to get back to Robbie, Ian searched his memory for safer places. He hadn't forgotten his oath to his uncle.

Back inside, he found Robbie still asleep, motionless and cold. The tea wouldn't do Robbie any good if he wasn't awake to drink it.

Ian didn't have any more blankets, and he doubted adding more would make much difference. There was only one thing for it. He double-checked the door was secured, stripped down to his shirt, pulled back the blankets, and wrapped himself around Robbie. If Robbie wouldn't respond to the warmth of the room, Ian would share some of his own body heat, lying together skin to skin.

His eyes itched. Ian blinked back tears. He was tired, that was it. The climb across the rocks and to the cottage wasn't an easy one even when he was well rested, and he'd carried Robbie and his harp too.

Ian closed his eyes, but he couldn't settle. Robbie wasn't warming, and he still felt too cold. He rubbed at Robbie's skin, hoping that would help, but it didn't make a damn bit of difference.

Not only that, but Robbie didn't wake. He slumbered on.

The sleep of the dead.

Ian shoved the words from his mind as soon as he'd thought them. "You're not dead," he whispered fiercely. "You're coming back to me. Ye hear me!"

But Robbie didn't stir. His chest rose and fell, but it might as well have not. Ian shuffled up into a half-sitting position. He laid a brief kiss on Robbie's forehead, and this time when the tears came, he didn't stop them.

"I can't lose ye. I only just found ye." Ian brushed Robbie's hair from his face and kissed him again. "Please, lad. I..." His shoulders shook as he wept. "Don't leave me. Not like this. I love ye." Ian's voice trembled. "I love ye."

*

Robbie came awake fully, brushing all the confusion of sleep away with a few blinks.

His sleep had been dreamless, though he remembered a sense of motion, of moving in and out of shadows in syncopation with the pattern of footsteps and a beating heart. He'd been down too far under the surface of life to respond for the most part, although once, just for a moment, he'd heard a voice making promises. The waking world had been too cold to touch then, so he'd let the rhythms lull him into the deep again. Now, though...

Ian is crying. Crying?

Ian lay close to Robbie, right up against him, so that Robbie had to crane his neck back to get a look at his face. Though Ian's eyes were closed, tears managed to escape one after the other. Robbie freed one hand from the blankets tucked around him and reached up to swipe gently at Ian's cheek with his thumb.

"Ian," he whispered.

Ian gasped, then snapped his eyes open and pulled back, fixing his gaze on Robbie's open eyes.

"Saints," he said, finally releasing his breath. He clamped his arms around Robbie, hugging tight, and laughed, choking out the words. "I thought ye'd died, lad. Ach, but I'm glad it wasn't true."

His laugh died suddenly, but he continued to hold Robbie close—too close, as Robbie had difficulty breathing. He pushed against Ian's chest, and Ian got the message, apologising with a kiss and a smoothing hand over Robbie's hair. The gesture felt right, but also odd somehow, and maybe that's why they both quieted— though Robbie felt Ian's heartbeat skip and thrill.

"It's fine ye are to me," Ian said.

Robbie marvelled, staring into the big man's blue eyes and wondering how he could say that now, with Robbie all salt-streaked and scraggly. He shook his head slightly and smiled, biting his lower lip, letting such mysteries slide as a far more certain, more immediate truth claimed his attention.

I'm so hard for this man. His breathing quickened, as did Ian's. Their cocks lay alongside each other, the blanket that had caught between them not enough to disguise Ian's erection. *And he's hard too—hard for me.*

Nothing else mattered much to Robbie right then, not the vague itch of salt-crusted skin, not hunger nor thirst, not even the witch and her bloody curse.

Ian!

The man's scent—salt, sweat, and sex—took him over, possessed him like a demon claiming his soul, and he thought of nothing but Ian, Ian, Ian. He saw Ian's look change from one of worry, care, and concern to one of hard, undeniable, desire.

"I want ye, now, Robbie," he said. "Is it yes?"

Robbie could scarcely speak for breathing hard, but he answered. "It is. The gods' truth, it's yes."

Under the blankets, hands roamed and flew, touching and searching everywhere, stopping to tug and pinch at nipples, to squeeze and tickle here and there experimentally and then linger where they found reaction.

Frustrated, Robbie flung the blankets off, getting them out of the way so he could watch as he moved his hand freely over Ian's prick—his stunningly hard, perfect erection. Ian opened his legs, and Robbie did the same. Robbie's gaze was drawn to his own cock as Ian's big hand stroked it, collected the crystal lubrication he'd charmed forth, and then slid his hand past Robbie's balls. Robbie kept his own hand busy on Ian, but let his eyes half close and his head fall back, overtaken by sensation as Ian slid his moistened hand over his hole, circling, and then dipped in.

The slight breach made Robbie arch back, wanting more, and he made some inarticulate sound even he knew wasn't a word, hoping nonetheless Ian would know what it meant.

Ian's breath rushed out as if he'd been holding it, and then he gasped. "Ye do want me, then? You're sure, aye?"

Robbie knew his answer was obvious in his every stressed breath, every squirming move, every quiver of touched flesh, but he schooled his tongue to answer anyway. "Yes...aye... Oh gods, please. I need you."

Ian seemed to force himself back from some edge to speak sensibly. "I've naught but spit and my own juices to ease my entry, though... I'm not small—"

Robbie surprised himself and Ian both with a chuckle, thinking he didn't need to be told that.

Ian chuckled once in response and kissed Robbie quick and hard on the lips as if to keep him quiet. "It'll hurt, I'm thinking."

"No. Maybe. I don't care. I need you to fuck me, man. Truly." Robbie nearly spat the last of those words, suddenly exasperated. His need rushed through him like a Norland wind roaring up a mountainside, and though some small part of him knew he'd wish later that everything had slowed down, right then, nothing existed except the race to the summit. He blew out a breath and pushed Ian down on his back—which might have worked only because of Ian's surprise—and got to his knees, bending over Ian's hardness. If spit was needed, he'd supply it.

He licked, sucked, laved, thoroughly wetting Ian base to tip, but only for a moment. Ian flipped them, pushing Robbie to his back, and again collected the slippery liquid off Robbie's engorged cock, applying it where it was needed. After an instant's prep, he sank one finger of his brawny hand deep, tapped Robbie's gland, and got paid for it with a buck and a shout.

"Ian!"

Ian took that as a call to action. He centred himself between Robbie's legs, and Robbie pulled his knees back, holding them apart, wanting nothing to get in the way of the fucking he so desperately needed. He felt Ian's prick poised to break in, then a sharp push past the head.

Ian grunted, stilled. "All right?"

Robbie wrapped his legs and arms around Ian and pulled, determined to sheath Ian's shaft to the base. He might not have succeeded if Ian hadn't joined the effort and pushed home.

It burned.

Quite a bit.

Robbie focused on Ian's face. Ian watched him, still as stopped time, apparently waiting for a sign that Robbie was okay. Then Ian bent to kiss Robbie's lips, and it was the sweetest, quietest moment since this quest for a solid fuck had begun. Robbie curled his hips, rotated them, and felt Ian against his gland. Pleasure washed through him, warm and pulsing, sweeping up the pain of entry until the two sensations were one and the same, augmented to fever pitch.

Ian sat back on his haunches, pulling Robbie's arse up onto his thighs, and in that position began fucking in a steady rhythm. He picked up speed and pounded harder and faster, not slowing, not teasing. Clearly he had no more inclination to wait for satisfaction than Robbie. "Ach, close, now!"

Robbie took his cock in his hand and started to stroke hard and fast, and in seconds all thought was impossible. Nothing in the world existed except the two of them and their sex. Ian called out some unknowable word when he came, and Robbie rode the crest, coming with Ian, too breathless to make any sound at all.

Before the orgasm was done, in the midst of the pulsing heat, Ian fell down over Robbie and, with his lips at Robbie's ear said, "Love."

Ian's word was but a whisper of wind, and if he hadn't been so close, Robbie might not have heard. For at that very moment, the harp—which Robbie had forgotten about for the first time in centuries—sang out, a sound as sweet and longed for as the first robin of spring.

They lay quiet, finally, catching their breath, and then Ian rolled off to the side, gathering Robbie close again, as if afraid he'd disappear.

"Did you hear it?" Robbie asked. "The harp?"

Ian's beard rasped against Robbie's cheek as he nodded. Then, into a silence that seemed oceans deep, Robbie said, "That was three."

Chapter Ten

Sleep had taken its time coming to Robbie, at first because he had joy jumping all around inside of him. Later he'd started to fret on what-ifs, and by the time he did fall asleep, he had a headache. He woke up with the same dull throbbing only a few hours later, cursing himself for an idiot.

Why is it you can never be happy, Robbie? Your whole life you've been chasing after love, and now it's come and you wrap it up in a skin bag and pick at it like a scavenger.

It was an ugly thought, but it went well with his mood, which he tried but failed to talk himself out of.

Sure, Rob. Why don't you just go around all glum and let Ian see your worst.

The scolding didn't help because he knew in his heart he had good reason to be pessimistic. At first, when the incredible sex he'd shared with Ian had been followed by the harp sounding that sweet, pure chord, he'd felt certain that meant his long trial had finally ended. But once his brain overrode the mindless joy coursing through his veins, he knew it wasn't—couldn't be—that simple.

When Melisandre had set her awful curse on him, she'd woven it of not two strands, but three: the boat, the harp, *and the key*. Not once during any of his sojourns ashore had Robbie caught sight of it—the harp's golden tuning key. It seemed likely, now he thought about it, that it had sunk to the bottom at the mouth of the Eden, and had since been washed to and fro. By now it had likely got buried in centuries of black mud. He didn't know how to find it.

He didn't know how to even *hope* to find it.

Disgusted, he picked up his and Ian's discarded shirts, his breeks, and Ian's kilt and plaid, piled them on the harp and carried the whole mess out to the fast-running burn not far from the blackhouse. The early morning sun on his shoulders taunted him as he stepped lightly along the bank in his bare feet, recalling to him the heat, the brilliant flash of pleasure he'd shared with Ian just hours earlier. He stopped himself just before wishing for clouds to cover it. One such as he couldn't afford to offer temptation to the unseen—whatever it might be— and after a few minutes in the cold burn, he'd be wanting the sun's warmth.

He found a large flattish rock at the edge of a deep pool, and a pile of smooth-worn, hand-sized stones just next to it, making it clear clothes had been washed there before. He set his burden down and jumped naked into the burn, not giving himself time to balk at it. He ducked under and came up blowing, combing his hair back with spread fingers. With sand from the brook's edge, he scrubbed his skin, then let the water soak away any remnants of soil and salt for as long as he could stand it. That wasn't long—he shivered by the time he climbed out, though once he'd wrung out his hair and slicked most of the water off his skin, he dried quickly and warmed in the sun.

He waded back in to wash their shirts, pounding them with smooth stones and wringing them repeatedly until the water that ran from them was clear. *It'll be nice,* he thought, *to wear a shirt that fits me for a change*, and he reflected that he really needed another. Maybe Ian had an old one he'd let him cut down. He liked wearing Ian's shirts because they were Ian's. On the other hand, he fairly swam in them, and the sleeves constantly got in his way. *To say nothing of the fact you must look a fool in them, Rob.*

Well, I am a fool, thinking of love and freedom from this curse, so why should I not look the part?

After he'd spread the shirts and his hempen breeks on the flat rock to dry, he took up Ian's kilt and beat the soil and dust from it until the colours of the MacDonald tartan shone like a beacon. He'd just started the same job with Ian's plaid when he heard a scatter of pebbles, which told him someone was coming down the trail. He immediately thought it was Ian, but then fear rose up. He was a good hundred yards or more from the cot, down a hill and in the trees. What if Campbell had come?

"Ach, there ye are, Rob! I dinna think you're using your head well this morning, love. We *are not safe* here. What were ye doing wandering off?"

Ian was bare to the waist, wearing only an old, frayed, faded kilt; the red thatch over his muscled chest looked fiery and beguiling in the sun. But his face bore a sour expression, and Robbie, already in a low mood, responded in kind.

"As you can see, sir, I bathed and washed our clothes. You might consider bathing yourself, as you don't smell the least bit pretty."

"And well, ye dinna seem to mind the stench of me in the night, did ye?"

Robbie laid out the clean plaid, and then—naked and wishing he'd had drawers under his breeks when the witch had cursed him—stepped up onto the flat stone, seated himself next to the clothes steaming in the day's rising heat, and picked up the harp. Cradling it, he stared at the water passing through the burn—clear but as unfathomable as any future, thanks to the hard reflections of the sun on its surface. He plucked at the strings as if he'd play the broken-down instrument, and he began to hum a tune. Soon, he laid a hand across the harp's strings to silence it, and he sang quietly, letting the ache in his heart dampen the soaring melody.

How blithe each morn was I to see
My lad come over the hill
He skipped the burn and ran to me
I met him with good will

Oh the broom, the bonnie, bonnie broom
The broom o' the Cowdenknowes
Fain would I be in my own country
Herding my father's ewes

"Ye'd like to be tendin' sheep, is it Robbie?"

Robbie chuckled, and though he didn't mean for it to be so, it sounded bitter even to his own ears. "No, then, I wouldn't."

He turned and looked into Ian's eyes, wondering at the change come over the man. Had he only been lusting after Robbie? Did his words...his *word*, "love," mean nothing after all? Robbie swallowed an urge to either cry or shout in frustration, and continued in a cool tone.

"But, now and again, I think perhaps I might have liked to have lived out my life in the usual way, in the place where I was born."

*

"Aye, I can understand that." Ian glanced away, deliberately forcing himself not to look at Robbie's naked body. "Cover yourself up, lad," he said roughly.

It wasn't as though he didn't enjoy seeing Robbie undressed, but he didn't want anyone else to pass by while he was. Ian also hadn't missed the tone of Robbie's laugh, and the coldness of his words. The rebuttal had hit Ian as though a tub of icy water had been poured over him, killing the interest his cock showed at seeing Robbie's state of undress almost instantly.

Surely for all his talk, Robbie wasn't planning to take his bloody harp and run?

He meant everything he'd told Robbie the night before, and he didn't use the word "love" lightly. Given Robbie's enthusiastic lovemaking, Ian had assumed his feelings were mutual.

Ian snatched his shirt from the rock where it lay drying and yanked it over his head, despite it still being damp to the touch. He stripped off his old kilt and dressed in the not quite dry plaid. "The harp sounded again, aye?"

Was that all Robbie wanted him for? To fool the harp into thinking he'd escaped having to return to his boat? Ach, it wasn't just the harp he'd fooled in that case.

"Aye." Robbie sounded cautious, as though he wasn't sure how Ian would react.

Ian sighed and used the motion of tying his hair back with a leather cord to work out how to approach the situation. He sat on the rock next to Robbie, taking care to put some distance between them. Robbie seemed worried, and Ian's heart melted at the look of him. Whatever doubts he'd had about Robbie's story disappeared when he'd seen Robbie lying in the boat. Death couldn't be faked like that, as far as he knew, at least not by natural means, so that only left magic, didn't it? He placed a reassuring hand on Robbie's shoulder, taking care to keep his touch chaste.

If Robbie didn't want him and didn't love him, Ian wouldn't force him to stay somewhere he didn't want to be, or to sleep with someone he didn't want.

"I told you to dress yourself." Ian handed Robbie his breeks. "At least put these on, will ye, and the brogans ye left on the other side of the rock?"

While Robbie dressed in silence, Ian chose his words carefully. "I'll nae hold it against ye if ye've changed your mind, Rob. I ken you're desperate to be free of the curse, and I'll do whatever ye need to be on your way."

Robbie turned to face Ian, his expression blank as though he'd carefully wiped it clean with a painter's rag. "You what—?" He swallowed and wrapped his arms around himself. "Aye, the harp has sounded three times, but that's not the end of it. I wish it were, but the witch...she's not made it that easy."

"Ach, the boat's gone," Ian reminded him, "but the harp's not given ye up." He eyed it suspiciously, not sure what Robbie would do if Ian snatched the thing away from him.

"Nae...not the harp. The curse. The witch, see, she made it so..."

"Aye, three times it's played." Ian shrugged. "You've told me that already." He was growing impatient, and very aware they weren't safe out here in the open. "I'll take ye somewhere safe, I promise. I'll nae leave ye until you're safe. This isn't your fight, and I'll nae have ye involved in it."

Robbie let out a loud sigh. "You're not listening. The harp's not complete."

"The harp's auld. It's bound to be missing bits." Ian glanced at it, surprised at the flash of emotion that sparked through him. Did the harp need something else to be complete? He remembered his dreams about it calling to him and shivered, then dismissed it as something out of the old stories. "Ye'll not find anything to complete it now." He wasn't surprised it wasn't in one piece, although he'd never tell by looking. He peered at it more closely. "I dinna ken much about music."

"It isn't what I mean." Robbie sounded exasperated.

"Well, then what is it ye *do* mean?" Ian frowned, trying to make sense of Robbie's mood.

"The damned witch…" Robbie stopped, almost choking as if the next words had literally stuck in his throat. He rose abruptly and started collecting the rest of Ian's clothing, draping the old tartan over one arm. "Ach, never mind."

He stood on the rocks, his gaze taken by the sea. Was he tempted to go back to it and try again?

"I have no more chances," he whispered so quietly Ian almost missed it. "I fear, sir, that this is the end of me."

"Ach, dinna talk like that." Ian doubted his words would reassure Robbie. His mouth felt dry, and he wanted to tell Robbie that even if Ian wasn't his true love, Ian knew Robbie was his. But when he opened his mouth to speak, he cleared his throat instead. He'd thought he'd found his true love before and been wrong. Yet, when he'd lain with Robbie, it had felt so right, like they were two pieces of a whole, and meant to be. How could he tell Robbie that? The boat might be gone, but Robbie didn't owe Ian a debt for his part in being rid of it.

Especially not if Robbie still wasn't free. Damn this witch and her godforsaken curse.

"You're still my captive," Ian said finally, although he had no intention of keeping Robbie any longer than the lad wanted to stay with him. "Best not betray me, aye?"

If he returned to the roles they'd taken when they met, he'd at least be able to keep Robbie safe. Once they returned to the cottage, he'd get some supplies and take Robbie a good distance away before deciding what to do next. Ian could fight to keep Robbie safe from Campbell and his men, but he had no clue how to fight a foe he couldn't see.

How did a man fight magic? Was it even possible?

But first they had a more pressing problem. Ian had slept well but woke up from a dream of Campbell descending on the cottage, and it felt like prescience. The more he gave it thought, the more certain he became that the jewels could not stay where they were.

"Ye'd better follow me back to the cot," Ian said.

Robbie did as he was told, but walked with eyes cast down. He said nothing, and that was just as well since Ian wasn't in the mood to continue their conversation. His mind went once more to the problem of the jewels, and though he didn't want to think it, he realised that, wherever he hid the jewels, his plans would have one potential weak spot—Robbie. If he knew where to find the jewels, he might tell.

"Ye'll not betray me, will ye?" Ian spoke the question softly, and the whisper of waves a long stone's throw away almost swallowed them. He wasn't sure Robbie had heard, but he couldn't make himself repeat the question.

"I'll not betray you." Robbie finally spoke minutes later, after they'd climbed through a patch of rough rocks.

"I believe you." Ian hadn't thought he would, not truly. Still, he might be made to tell—Campbell could be cruel.

As they walked the path on the crest of the headland, Ian's eye was caught by wings flying low over the sea. A sea eagle, its white tail and majestic size a clear giveaway. He shaded his eyes against the glint of a bright, mid-morning sun and gazed across the water. In the distance lay the Isle of Rum, a dark, secretive mound against the bright sky.

Perfect. And suddenly a plan lay before him.

"Take yourself back to the cot. I've an errand to run. Expect me gone several hours, but I'll be back before night falls. Keep your eyes and ears open. If my enemy comes, ye'll do best to take to your heels and run, and I'll hope to find ye again soon as may be. Mayhap the harp will aid us once more."

"Aye, sir," Robbie said, and although Ian could clearly see his admonition had troubled him, he slipped into silence again.

On impulse, he stepped back and enfolded Robbie in his arms. The words they'd said and not said that morning lay heavy over his heart, and he couldn't bring himself to speak his mind. Instead, he put as much feeling as he could into a brief, but deep and demanding kiss. Robbie stood stiff for only a fraction of a second, then melted and returned the kiss almost desperately. As they broke apart, Robbie schooled his face blank, but not before Ian saw moisture standing in his eyes.

"There, then. Dinna fash. Go now, and have a care on the path. Remember, look for me or my boat down the beach, here, if you must leave the cot before I return."

Robbie almost smiled. "I'll find you."

Ian's stomach rumbled, a reminder that he'd not broken his fast, and that Robbie wouldn't have either.

Robbie must have heard as his smile twitched a little wider and he quipped, "As your prisoner, it's your duty to keep me fed, sir."

"Aye, that is it. And ye don't…" Ian was tempted to remind Robbie he didn't need to call him 'sir,' as he preferred to think of them as equals, especially now he'd slept with the lad. But unfortunately, it didn't sit well with the pretence of captor and captive. "I said I'd protect ye, and I meant it."

The remains of Robbie's brief smile fell away, and he gave Ian a long hard look. "Ye'll protect me? I'd like to see how that goes for you when you're facing off with the damn Witch of the Badlands." He strode off in the direction of the cottage.

He made little sound while he walked away, and as Ian crept past the wee cairn he'd arranged earlier to mark his way, a chill swept over him, and the sun overhead didn't warm him. The temperature hadn't dropped, yet he couldn't shake the coldness he felt inside at the thought of losing Robbie. Dare he hope that little smile was a sign that not all was lost?

"As to that witch of yours," he muttered to Robbie's retreating back, "I never said I'd win, but that will nae stop me trying, should it come to that."

Once Robbie had left his sight, Ian turned along another little-used track and followed it around to the back of the cot to the woodpile, where he retrieved the jewels and turned back the way he'd come, heading for the boat.

Focus on the hiding the jewels. Ye'll be missing Rob soon enough.

He stopped at the edge of the shallow pool directly in his path. He squinted, peering across the pool, yet he didn't expect to see anything of his boat as it was well hidden. He'd figured the pool might fool someone into thinking the path stopped there. Would Robbie find him if need be? He hoped so, but a voice of self-doubt, one born of past heartbreak, wondered if Robbie would even want to. But the lad had said, *"I'll find you,"* and there was no point in worrying over it.

After a brief climb up a narrow path only wide enough for one, Ian headed down again towards the shore, got his bearings, and then waded through the water to the entrance of a small cave hidden by the rocks. The water was a wee bit deeper than the pool and reached the top of his thighs. He glanced behind him to make sure he wasn't watched, then reached inside, felt for the boat—as the opening in the rock was little more than the size of the cobble, leaving no room for a man to hide in there with it—and pulled it towards him.

The calm sea made for swift rowing across the water, though the climbing sun beat against the back of his neck by the time he made Rum. He angled slightly northwest as he went, judging direction from Rum's profile, and passed the island's northerly tip before heading back southwest close in to the coast. At a crescent beach on the west side, he pulled the boat out of the water. He judged it unlikely that Campbell's eyes—or anyone's—would spy the boat there and know it was his; nevertheless, he pulled it up the sand and behind a rough, barnacle-clad stone, and anchored its guy rope under a rock in case the tide should lift it.

Ian made a makeshift pack with his plaid and secured the jewels inside it along with the supplies he'd kept with the boat, then explored a few hundred yards inland to find an easily remembered landmark. The tall stone—with another atop it balanced by nature like a head on a long body—could be seen from the beach, and just to one side of it lay a another, larger stone with an indent like a small cave. Ian hid the supplies, with jewels inside the sack, in the little cave, and then piled some loose stones and brush in the opening. He was glad he'd taken the time to peruse the coast of Rum shortly after he'd arrived on Skye, else he might not have lucked on such a spot.

*

The sun rode low over the three peaks of Rum Island to the west when Robbie heard the already familiar rhythm of Ian's footsteps coming up the hill to the cottage.

He sounded tired, Robbie thought. It was a shame he couldn't rest. They needed to get away from here soon. He didn't know what made him so sure each moment at the cottage made them less safe. Perhaps it was the aggravated cries of the gulls, or the ominous dive of the sea eagle that had swooped through the yard moments before, or the way the harp silently demanded he pick it up—as if it wanted him to be ready to run.

Whatever the reason for the gut-churning certainty that something was about to happen, he stood where shadow would hide him just inside the cottage door, clutching the harp and peering out into the still-bright but failing afternoon. He'd been thinking it might be best to turn the cow and chickens loose to fend for themselves if need be, when he caught sight of Ian's red-gold hair glinting in the sun's low rays as he topped the hill. Robbie almost stepped out in relief, almost called a greeting, but that certainty of danger that had haunted him all afternoon swept over him in a new wave and stopped him.

Ian halted and turned his head quickly, as if something to his right caught his eye. Almost immediately, he turned and continued walking towards Robbie in a carefully casual manner, but his eyes were flashing a warning. He'd seen something, and Robbie would have known what it was even if he hadn't heard, just inside the trees, a muted commotion of heavy steps and drawn steel.

When Ian came within three strides of where Robbie stood in the shadows, he said in a low voice, "There's someone here. When I tell you to run, follow the trail down the beach and don't look back. Find somewhere to hide and stay there."

He reached down to adjust his shoe and on his way back up, drew his dirk from his sock. He handed Robbie the dirk with one hand, then quietly drew his sword from the scabbard at his hip, clearly trying not to alert his enemies they'd been spotted.

"I'll not leave you," Robbie whispered, determination turning the words into a fierce hiss. "You're not fighting alone."

They didn't have time to argue, but Ian tried anyway. He placed his free hand on Robbie's shoulder. "You're a stubborn lad, that ye are, but saints, I want ye *safe*. Run when I tell ye."

"Reivers run to get away with the stock, Ian, but not from a fight when our people need us."

"*Ye'll run*, and I'll be right behind ye," Ian said roughly, "I promise you that. They're not here for you, and they'll not have you just to torment me."

Robbie was no fool. He recognised the stubborn set of Ian's jaw, and he also knew it was Ian and the jewels Campbell's men were after. They'd let Robbie go if it meant taking Ian. *Ian won't run, though. Leastways not 'til he's sure I've got away.* If he'd had time to think about it, he might have wondered if that meant Ian loved him after all.

Ian interrupted him, beginning to sound exasperated. "They think you're dead, anyway, lad. Best they not see ye if we can help it."

"Ian—"

"Ach! I've let ye fash wi' me 'til it's too late." Ian stepped forward, an obvious move to shield Robbie with his own body, and raised his sword.

The red glint of a sword caught in late sunlight had announced a visitor, and now its owner came climbing over the rise to meet them.

Chapter Eleven

Ian couldn't see anyone else, but he knew Campbell wouldn't have come alone or left them the option of going back the way they'd come.

"Campbell," he said, giving the man a nod, although he didn't lower his sword.

"MacDonald." Campbell's eyes widened when he saw Robbie who had moved forward to stand at Ian's side. "Your friend is looking well for a dead man."

"I don't have what you want, Campbell. But if ye let the lad go, I'm prepared to talk to ye." Ian phrased his reply carefully.

"Ian—" Robbie protested, but Ian shushed him with a glare.

"*You're* prepared to talk to *me*?" Campbell chuckled. "Still as arrogant as ever, I see." He gestured a forward motion with one hand and his men came out of hiding, surrounding Ian and Robbie. "We both know I'd lay hands on ye, eventually, aye? I'll thank ye for making it easy, coming back to your wee homestead."

Donnell crossed himself when he saw Robbie. "The lad was dead, I tell ye. I dinna want to fight a demon."

"Pull yourself together, man." Campbell shook his head in disgust. "I'll not hear any more of your superstitious nonsense." He turned his attention back to Ian. "Give yourself up, MacDonald, and I'll consider going easy on the lad."

"Ye expect me to believe ye?" Ian tightened his grip on his sword. Anyone trying to take Robbie would have to go through him.

Campbell raised his sword. He took a step forward at the same time as Ian. The two men circled each other warily. Campbell parried too late. Ian struck the first blow.

Ian smiled grimly. Blood welled from the wound in Campbell's arm.

Niall attacked Robbie from the other side, a sword against a dirk. Robbie put his foot out as Niall lunged, then quickly stepped out of reach. Niall hit a protruding rock with a thud.

Distracted, Ian brought his sword up to block Campbell's blow just in time. Ian stumbled back from the force of it, barely righting himself.

"Donnell! James!" Campbell roared. "Do what I pay ye for, or I'll kill ye meself."

Both men approached Ian, three against one. If he could take down Campbell, the others might run scared. Ian jerked his sword from left to right. He took a step forward, thrusting in a stabbing motion. Campbell dodged, missing the blade. James moved behind Ian, Donnell to his left, enclosing Ian in a circle.

"Ach," he muttered. He couldn't escape this, but he might hold their attention long enough for Robbie to get away. Ian moved his sword from side to side again in an unspoken invitation. They wouldn't kill him. At least not yet.

Ian lunged again. Campbell parried. Ian glared at Campbell over their joined swords. Too late, he felt someone move behind him. He jabbed his elbow back to land a blow, but his assailant dodged it easily and grabbed

Ian, holding him tight. Ian felt the nip of cold steel against his throat.

"Stop fighting, lad, if ye want him to live," Campbell called to Robbie. He gave James a nod. Ian felt a sharp pain as James increased his pressure on the blade. Blood dribbled down his shirt from the wound.

"Ye'll not kill me." Ian kept his voice calm. "I can't tell ye what ye want to know if I'm dead."

Robbie's dirk clattered as it dropped to the rocks.

"Ian," Robbie said. "A Reiver knows when to take the loss so he can live to win another day. I'll not take the chance with your life."

Campbell smiled. "Reiver, aye? And that's unlikely. Nevertheless, you're a good lad." He ruffled Robbie's hair.

Niall shoved Robbie over to join Ian. Blood beaded along a line on Robbie's calf. Niall, the bastard must have scratched it during the scuffle.

Ian growled low in his throat. "Keep your hands off him." He'd seen that look in Campbell's eye before. His temper flared, his need to keep Robbie safe overriding his intention to not give Campbell any advantage., his intention to not give Campbell any advantage abandoned in his need to keep Robbie safe. "Touch him like that again, and I'll kill ye."

"Idle threats from a man in no position to make them." Campbell's smile widened into a self-satisfied grin. "Bind them once we're off these rocks, and make sure they're kept apart while ye search the cottage and its surroundings. I'll nae waste my time trying to force ye to talk, MacDonald, as much as I'd enjoy it. You're too stubborn, and my—he wants you alive." Campbell looked thoughtful for a moment. "Dinna fash; I'm sure he has a good reason."

Ian climbed down the rocks carefully, his mind racing. He had a good idea who Campbell was working for, and the direction he marched them in would confirm it. He spoke the truth about wanting Ian alive, or why give him the freedom to get down to the beach unhindered? The rocks were slippery, and there was good chance of falling without his hands free to steady himself. He glanced at Robbie, but whatever the lad was thinking, he gave no outwards sign of it. He'd had the chance to run, but had chosen to stay and fight, and then given himself up to save Ian.

Had Ian been wrong in thinking Robbie planned to leave? If... Once they were restrained, Ian would lose his chance to remind Robbie of how he felt about him. He couldn't go to his fate with Robbie thinking Ian viewed him as a captive and nothing else.

He stood as James bound his wrists in front of him. Robbie kept his head down as he was bound by Niall in a similar manner.

Once they were restrained, Niall pushed Robbie in front of him. "I'll be watching you at all times," he warned Robbie, "as will Donnell. Ye have nowhere to run, so don't try. And remember your friend is also well guarded."

Robbie nodded.

"Good, lad." Campbell inspected the ropes, then leaned in close to Ian, his breath foul, spittle covering his lips as he spoke. "Alive doesn't mean uninjured." He lowered his voice to a whisper so only Ian could hear. "Your friend is a good-looking lad. Would be a shame if that were to change, aye?"

Ian glared at him but said nothing.

Campbell laughed. "We understand each other. Good." He waved his hand. "Move out. We've a good distance to travel, and I want to reach Sconser by nightfall."

So they were heading to Sconser. Ian doubted it was their final destination, but if Ian was right about whom Campbell had aligned himself with, all might not to be lost. Given the distance they were travelling, he'd wait until they reached Sconser before taking any action.

Campbell led the march, and Donnell positioned himself at the back. The man was still nervous around Robbie and kept giving him sideways glances. His superstition was something Ian could use against him later to aid their escape. James held Ian back, waiting until Robbie and Niall were well in front, then pushed him towards the trail.

Ian couldn't help but grin. Although their situation looked dour, that arse Campbell had no idea the route he'd planned for tomorrow headed in the opposite direction from the very treasure he sought.

Rocky ground dipped and rose, difficult terrain for a group of men carrying arms and herding a couple of unhappy captives. When the skies blackened with clouds, they lost the benefit of moonlight. Campbell grumbled loud enough for everyone to hear, but they trudged on until thunder let the rains loose on them, turning the trail to mud too slippery to trust in the dark.

Two of the men Ian could hear but not see began bemoaning the ill luck of having evil in their midst. Ian's mouth grew tight as he grimly tried to figure his chances of breaking free to make a rescue if Campbell's soldiers decided it would be worth their leader's wrath to rid the band of the cause of their misfortune—Robbie, as they saw it.

But Campbell had heard them, too, and he was having none of it. "Shut it, or by the de'il hi'self, I'll boot ye both into the gulley and leave ye there."

He called a halt, though, when they found a sheltering overhang. "We'll wait 'til we ha' moonlight or morn. Nae sense losing our lives to this treacherous isle. Be ready to move when we can, and we'll hope the lads bringing the horses to Sconser ha' the brains to wait. It's a long walk to the castle."

Robbie and Ian were tethered and guarded, but close enough to each other for Ian to watch. No one approached Robbie in the hours they stayed in their rough camp except Donnell, who stood over him for too long. Ian picked up a stone and planned to heave it if Donnell took one step closer. The gruff soldier spit to the side and walked away.

Ian kept his eyes open until the sun rose bright in the east, and Campbell started the day's march with a shouted obscenity.

*

The sun beat down, the day hotter than Ian expected. Robbie kept up, but Ian could tell by the way his shoulders had become more hunched that he was struggling. Perhaps that wound to his leg was worse than he'd thought?

"Can we stop for a wee bit?" he asked Campbell. "If ye march us all day without any more food or water, we'll nae be able to answer your laird's questions when we get to the castle."

Campbell seemed to consider, yet didn't deny Ian's assumption that he answered to a laird. He'd slowed his pace, too, his limp becoming more pronounced, although no one else seemed to have noticed, or was brave enough to comment. Ian certainly wasn't going to remind him of it, considering he'd inflicted the wound on the man in the first place.

"James!" Campbell called ahead. "We'll rest for half an hour before continuing." He glanced at Robbie. "Give the lad some of your bread and water."

"Thank you," Robbie murmured.

James took a swig of water, then held the water skin to Robbie's lips. Robbie took great gulps of the liquid until James snatched the skin away again. He gestured for Robbie to sit on the ground at his feet, and then pressed some torn off pieces of bread into his hands.

Campbell watched Robbie with interest, shoved Ian towards Donnell, and walked over to talk to Niall in a low voice.

He didn't offer Ian any food or water, but Ian hadn't expected him to. He'd asked for Robbie, and ensured the lad was taken care of.

"Robbie," Ian called now he was close enough that Robbie would hear.

Donnell elbowed Ian in his side. "No one told ye to speak."

"Robbie!" Ian spoke louder, this time determined to get Robbie's attention. They'd been kept apart since their capture, and he wanted to be sure Robbie heard him.

Robbie turned this time. The slight smile he wore left his face as soon as he noticed the other men watching him. Ian gave him a nod. He'd seen it all right, and that was all that mattered.

"I meant what I said when I took ye off the boat."

Robbie's eyes widened, relief chasing surprise across his face. He opened his mouth to speak, but Ian shook his head, knowing he'd get into trouble for doing so.

"Dinna forget, lad." Whatever happened now, at least Robbie would know Ian loved him.

"I told ye to be quiet!" Donnell shoved his elbow into Ian's stomach this time.

Ian held his head up and matched Donnell's glare with one of quiet defiance.

"Fucking arse," Donnell muttered. He hit Ian in the stomach. Hard.

Ian grunted in pain, stumbled, but righted himself.

Robbie stood. "Ian!"

James grabbed him and held him back.

Donnell glared again, this time in Robbie's direction. A slow smirk tugged at the corners of his lips. He punched Ian again, this time across his face, and grabbed his hair, holding him in place so he couldn't move. "At least this proves you're human," he snarled, "though I'm nae sure your friend would bleed."

Ian kicked Donnell as hard as he could. Donnell let go of Ian and staggered back. Ian scrambled onto his feet and put his bound hands over his would-be tormentor, capturing his head between his arms. He pulled up sharply. Donnell gasped.

"Touch the lad, and I'll kill ye," Ian ground out in Donnell's ear. "Say ye won't, or I'll snap your neck." He yanked his hands up when Donnell didn't reply. "Promise me."

"Ian, don't—" Robbie started to speak, but James cut him off, his hand over Robbie's mouth.

"Stand down!" Niall bellowed. "Both of ye."

"He lets go of the lad first," Ian warned. "Leave him be, or I'll give ye a reason to hang me."

Campbell strode between Ian and James. "Both of you let go."

"But sir," James protested. "He'll kill Donnell." He tightened his grip on Robbie.

Ian growled low in his throat.

Campbell held up his hand. "Let the idiot go, MacDonald—Ian—and they'll leave ye and your friend be. Ye have my word on it. For now."

"And how much is that worth?" Ian had believed Campbell's intentions were honourable once before, and it had put his cousin—someone Ian cared about—in danger. He'd not make the mistake again.

"I promise ye, I swear." Campbell shook his head. "I'll not harm either of ye if ye dinna make a fuss. I'll nae pay ye if ye harm the lad, James. Let him go. It's the only way this pig-headed man will let go of Donnell!"

"Fair enough," Ian said. Although Campbell had proven himself to be anything but a man of honour, he'd left Ian with little choice. Even if he'd killed Donnell, Ian wouldn't have got far, and Campbell knew it. But with several hours left as Campbell's captives, at least his men might think twice before harming Robbie.

James let go of Robbie, although it was obvious he did so reluctantly. Ian, being a man of his word, released Donnell a minute later. Donnell edged away quickly, rubbing at his neck, which was already showing signs of bruising.

The other men eyed Ian with trepidation, and turned away from him, but not before he saw fear in their eyes. Campbell handed him a water skin and some bread.

"You'd better have this. I'll nae want to have to lug ye the rest of the way."

"Thank ye," Ian said, surprised.

"If it were up to me, ye'd be dead already." Campbell turned his attention back to his men. "The wind is coming up. We're moving out in five minutes. Be ready."

He strode over to Niall, and the two of them bowed their heads deep in a conversation Ian couldn't hear. Niall glanced in Ian's direction and shook his head.

Ian made short work of his bread and drained what little water was in the skin Campbell had given him. His belly was far from full, but at least he'd had something.

He spent the rest of the march in silence, and so did Robbie. They exchanged a few glances when they were able, making sure they weren't noticed doing so.

By the time they reached Sconser, night had fallen. Niall ordered James to set up camp and added a comment that he and Campbell would return shortly. He bound Ian and Robbie's legs so they couldn't run, and shoved them down hard in the dirt, a distance away from the fire.

James and Donnell spoke in whispers after Campbell left. Donnell seemed nervous, and Ian caught the name Archie in their conversation. Campbell hadn't taken kindly to his man being so clumsy as to break a leg and had left him to fend for himself without any food and water.

Ian leaned towards Robbie, taking advantage of their captors' distraction. "Ye all right there, lad?" he whispered.

"Aye. That was a brave thing you did back there, Ian. I was scared for your life." Robbie wriggled over closer, risking a brief touch of his hand over Ian's. The harp was still on his back as neither Campbell nor his men would touch it.

"I told ye I'd protect ye, and I meant it."

The sound of horses' hooves in the distance confirmed Ian's suspicions of their final destination. Campbell might manage half the distance on foot, but he'd never last the rest, not with his leg. He must have arranged for someone to meet him there in Sconser with horses for the final part of their journey.

"I have a good idea where they're taking us, Rob." Ian had considered other options, but this was the one that made sense, especially if Campbell was working for a laird. "Dunvegan is MacLeod's seat, and Campbell knows he'll want the jewels for himself and betray our Charlie."

MacLeod was also a two-faced liar. Just because he'd told Campbell he wanted Ian alive, he'd not hesitate in killing him—or Robbie—once he realised he'd not get the jewels or any information he sought about the rebellion.

Robbie paled. "We'll die there, Ian, once this laird figures out we're no use to him."

"We have time before that happens," Ian reassured him. "Don't worry, lad, we'll find a way out."

*

The sun had long since faded when they reached MacLeod's Dunvegan lands and made camp. By then, Robbie seemed to have retreated into himself completely.

Ian woke at dawn to find Campbell watching Robbie. The other men were asleep, having taken turns to keep watch. Ian had slept lightly, snatching enough sleep between the change of shifts. Each time he opened his eyes, he'd seen Robbie wide awake. Ian hoped Robbie hadn't sat up all night, but he hadn't wanted to anger Campbell any further so hadn't dared to ask the lad.

When they were heaved onto the horses, Campbell ordered that Robbie ride with him. Ian wasn't happy about it, but he couldn't do anything, so he settled for a warning glare. If Campbell noticed Ian's reaction, he didn't acknowledge it.

Robbie slipped from the horse at one point, but Campbell righted him quickly. They arrived at the castle without much incident, and Ian was surprised when they weren't brought in front of MacLeod but instead shoved into a guard room downstairs. Given the look of the room, it had once been the kitchen.

Campbell, too, seemed unusually quiet, and left Niall and his men to tend the horses while he went to speak to MacLeod.

Robbie heaved a sigh of relief once he and Ian were alone. "I'm sorry," he murmured. "I'm tired. Will you keep watch while I sleep?" He limped over to the far wall, rubbed at his leg, and lifted the hem of his breeks to reveal a much deeper gash than Ian expected. It had spread with use, revealing layers of tissue beneath. The entire outside of the calf from knee to ankle had begun to bruise.

"Did Niall do that to ye?" Ian asked angrily, guilty he hadn't seen it happen.

"Aye, he got a swipe in with his sword when I was fighting him. My leg's stiff and sore, but I'll be fine. I think the cut is healing—it pulls a bit. Mostly, though, I'm tired. That's all." He gave Ian a shaky smile. "And this is not my first time in a dungeon. I'm not fond of them, but I can't deny I feel less desperate knowing we're together." Robbie ducked his head, clearly rethinking his words. "Not that I'm happy you're in a dungeon, mind, but—"

"'Tis all right. I know what ye meant." Ian sat, gently bringing Robbie down to the thin straw pallet on the floor. "Ye get some rest. The floor's nae comfortable, and this layer of auld straw won't help much, but ye can rest your head on my shoulder if ye want."

"I do want that." Robbie smiled at that, one that lightened his face, although it didn't quite hide the weariness about him. "I hope they feed us soon. I'm hungry, and my stomach's wanting food."

"I'll wake ye when someone comes," Ian promised. No wonder Robbie seemed weakened. Not much food, very little sleep, and carrying the ache from his bruised leg.

"Thank you." Robbie rested his head on Ian's shoulder, but before he closed his eyes, he turned his head to look up at Ian. "I never forgot what you told me. I never wanted to leave you, for I love ye too."

Ian brushed his lips across Robbie's forehead, but the lad was already asleep. "I never wanted ye to leave. I still don't," he whispered. If the chance arose to thank Niall properly for the injury he'd given Robbie, Ian would take it, and ensure the man got at least as good as he'd given.

The sound of footsteps alerted Ian to the approach of the guard before he reached their cell. Ian lowered Robbie gently onto the rough straw bed and stood.

"Stay where you are," the man ordered as he opened the door. He held a lantern which he used to peer into the darkened cell. "My laird has ordered ye be fed tonight. He'll see ye in the morning. When he does, remember ye owe him a debt for not having ye thrown into the pit." He shoved in a tray, slammed the door shut, and relocked their cell with one of the keys hanging from his belt. They jangled as he walked away.

Ian waited until his footsteps faded before grabbing the tray. He carried it over to the corner where Robbie still slumbered. "Wake up. Ye need to get food into ye and get your strength up."

Robbie stirred and then went back to sleep. Ian shook him gently a couple of times before Robbie finally opened his eyes and sat up.

"Ian?" He rubbed sleep from his eyes and glanced around the cell. "Ach. I thought it was a dream."

"Nae, sorry." Ian handed Robbie a cup of water and set about splitting the bannock in two, making sure to give Robbie the bigger piece. To his surprise, it didn't rip apart easily. He frowned and moved over to the other corner of the cell where the tiny window offered more light to examine the bannock more closely.

Robbie stopped drinking. "What is it?" He started to stand and grabbed at the wall for support.

"Stay where ye are," Ian said. "Ye need to get some food into ye first."

Someone had cut a slit into the bannock and shoved something inside. Ian found the end of it and pulled gently so not to destroy it. His eyes widened when he saw the note, and he read it quickly before coming back to sit beside Robbie.

"It's a message from someone I know—used to know."

"Will he or she help us escape?"

Ian scanned the note again, then folded it and put it in his sporran for safekeeping. Angus hadn't signed it as that would be foolish, but Ian recognised his penmanship immediately.

"He," he started absently, then figured he owed Robbie an explanation. "We were lovers...once, but...I kept his identity a secret, and this is repayment for that debt of honour. My uncle—the laird—knew, but I beseeched him to keep it to himself."

"So your lover left you to take the brunt of the punishment?" Robbie made a noise of disgust. "He wouldn't have lain with you if he didn't want to."

"I thought he did." Ian winced, the note having brought with it memories he didn't want to dwell on. "Last I heard he'd married and had a bairn. I didn't take him for a traitor and working for the likes of the MacLeod!"

"I'm sorry." Robbie took the share of the bannock Ian gave him and munched quietly for a while. "Sometimes men find themselves in situations not of their choosing. Perhaps that's why he's here at Dunvegan." He frowned. "You didn't answer my question. Will he help us escape?"

"Aye. He'll be on watch after midnight." Ian doubted he'd see the man, and for that he was glad. "He'll make sure our cell is unlocked and will leave us a rope which we can use to escape over the wall. He'll only risk leaving it for a one pass along the wall. If we can't reach it by then, he'll take it down and consider his debt paid." Angus had only ever risked himself up to a point. Even with Ian's life at stake, that hadn't changed.

"Then we'll have to make sure we reach it." Robbie yawned. "Sorry, I'm still tired." He looked less pale than he had but still not well as Ian would have liked.

"Ye've eaten all you can?" Ian wouldn't eat anything that remained until he was certain Robbie had finished.

"Yes, and anyway, you need to eat too. I've been hungrier than this in my day. Ye worry too much for me. But I'll allow I'm more tired than I should be, and my leg hurts a bit."

Ian leaned over to take a look at Robbie's leg. No sign of infection, but the healing seemed slow. He sighed, then spoke gently. "We have a few hours before we can make our escape. Rest, and I'll keep watch."

Chapter Twelve

Ian jerked awake with a start. Despite his intention to keep watch, he'd drifted off to sleep. The moon's rays illuminated the cell, bathing his surroundings in a harsh light. Ian got to his feet immediately. Something had woken him. He glanced over at Robbie still asleep, his chest rising and falling steadily, the harp cradled in his arms like a baby. Before Ian had opened his eyes, he could have sworn someone was watching him, but it must have been a dream.

He eyed the harp suspiciously for a moment. The thing wasn't alive. It couldn't have been what was watching him.

A memory tugged at him. Angus used to watch Ian as he slept. "It's so I'll remember," he'd told Ian as they lay together.

"Ach, why speak like that?" Ian said, running his fingers through Angus's long hair. "We have our lives ahead of us. There's no need to worry about making memories just yet."

Angus shook his head sadly and then distracted Ian with other things.

In hindsight, Ian realised what Angus had meant. Even then, he'd known their being together wouldn't last. Or he never intended it would. Why risk a life that could lead to execution when he could be free to love someone and not hide it?

"Damn you, Angus," Ian muttered. The man owed him a debt all right. No wonder he'd thought too easily that Robbie wouldn't stay. He shivered, shaking himself out of his musings.

Something had woken him from his dreams—dreams of Robbie, not Angus. Dreams of making love, of a future together with Robbie. One that would never happen if they didn't escape from this place.

Ian strode over to the cell door. Taking care to be quiet, he pushed the door, and it opened silently. Angus had kept that promise at least.

"Robbie, lad, we need to go." Ian shook Robbie awake. He wasn't sure how long it had been since Angus had left the rope, or when the guard would pass by next.

Robbie stood quickly although he looked bleary-eyed. "Go Ian. I'll follow your lead."

Ian smiled at Robbie's words, hoping the lad's trust in him wasn't misplaced. "No talking after we leave the cell unless ye have to, and then keep your voice down, aye?"

Robbie nodded and picked up the harp, slinging it onto his back by the leather strap. When he and Robbie had been led to their cell, Ian had noted the route carefully, knowing they'd need to retrace their steps.

According to Angus's instructions, from this part of the castle, there were only two ways out—one leading to MacLeod, and the other to freedom.

Ian and Robbie crept down the hallway silently, Robbie keeping a couple of steps behind Ian. Before he'd slept, Ian memorised the details Angus had left, and carefully pictured their escape route in his mind. They'd need to get out of the castle, then use the rope to get over the wall.

He ducked down, pulling Robbie with him, as two of MacLeod's men walked past them heading towards the cell. Once they'd gone, Ian and Robbie made their way to the door leading out into the night. Ian shoved at the door, but the stupid thing refused to budge. He swore under his breath. Angus had promised he'd leave it unbolted. Voices sounded from the distance, men coming closer. Ian butted the door with his shoulder. Still nothing, although he could have sworn it had groaned slightly. Angus's directions had seemed clear enough. This should be the right door though he'd warned the old thing had always been stiff. Robbie glanced behind them nervously.

"We're close to being undone!" he hissed.

Ian slammed his body against it. The door groaned, then creaked, before finally opening. He ran through it, dragging Robbie with him, shut it behind them. He put his weight against the door, the rough wood digging into his shoulder, but he couldn't risk someone coming after them.

He heard voices. The handle turned. Robbie joined Ian in securing the door. The handle turned once more, then no more. The voices grew distant. He hoped the men were convinced the exit was still secure rather than going to find reinforcements.

Ian supposed the men on watch were focused on any possible intruders from outside the castle, not prisoners making their escape—a bit of luck for him and Robbie.

Ian glanced around to get his bearings. He'd half expected the door to come out in a tunnel leading to the sea gate, but that exit would be well guarded. The safest way out would be to climb the wall well away from the thing.

"Ach, where did ye leave it?" he murmured. "Straight ahead fifty paces, turn sharp left, and follow the undergrowth. Follow the undergrowth to what? At least ye didn't leave it in plain sight, but ye dinna say enough about how to reach the damn thing either."

They'd just have to run for it, and hope they reached the safety of the shadows before they were seen.

"Don't stop lad," he whispered. "Run, and whatever happens, keep going."

Robbie nodded, his expression grim. "Yes, I will," he promised.

"Go first," Ian said. That way, if Robbie's wounded leg caused him to stumble, Ian could pick him up and carry him the rest of the way. After getting this far, Ian wouldn't be leaving him behind.

By the time they reached the wall, Ian was breathing heavily. Robbie stood with his hands on his knees, struggling to catch his breath. He straightened and brushed his hand against the wall. When his hand came away, he was holding the end of a bottom strand of rope. He looked up at the wall, then at the rope, and finally at Ian.

"I'm not sure I can make the climb, Ian. I don't want to fall and alert anyone that we're here. Perhaps you should leave without me. At least that way you'd be safe."

"I'm nae leaving ye," Ian told him firmly in a tone that brooked no argument. He tested the rope, making sure it was secure. "I'll climb up first. Once I'm up, secure the rope around yourself, and I'll help pull ye up."

"If someone comes—" Robbie's argument died on his lips when Ian started to climb.

As soon as Ian reached the top, he pulled the rope up, knotted it in sections, and sent it back down. Robbie tied the rope around himself and used the knots as handholds to help him climb so Ian wasn't left to support his full weight.

Finally, Robbie reached the top of the wall. He gave Ian a shaky smile as Ian pulled up the rope and threw it over the other side. Going down was much easier. Once they reached the bottom, Ian gave the rope a sharp yank, and it slithered to the ground. He tucked it beneath some gorse so it couldn't be easily seen.

The way down to the shore was steep, but they could use the rocks as handhelds. Luckily, the moon was full and gave them enough light to see by. Ian tried not to think about whatever was in the darkness further ahead. They'd just started down when Robbie almost slipped, steadied himself, then put one finger to his lips.

A moment later, movement flashed in the distance. Ian held his breath, letting it out again when a lone bird flew overheard before heading out over the water.

Robbie grinned and shrugged, his expression reflecting Ian's relief. He reached over to brush his fingers against Robbie's. Robbie's skin felt chilled to the touch. They needed to get off the rocks and into the cave where Angus had promised to leave them some supplies.

The climb down felt like it took much longer than it should. Ian kept a close eye on Robbie, grabbing him when he slipped a second time. "You're still tired."

"I'm sorry. My leg isn't doing what I tell it. We're almost there. I'll rest once we find the cave."

"I can help—"

Robbie shook his head. "We'll go faster if you don't. I don't want to slow you down. And besides, as I said, we're almost there."

"You're stubborn." Ian caressed Robbie's cheek with his fingers, feeling the stubble of several days' growth of beard under them. He figured he looked a sight, too, unkempt and dirty.

"So are you." Robbie smiled, a softness in his eyes when he met Ian's gaze.

Ian pulled him close and slipped an arm around Robbie's waist before he could protest, taking most of his weight as they finished the climb down. When they reached the bottom, Robbie leaned into Ian's embrace and let himself be carried over the rocks to shore.

"Ach, he could have said where the cave was," Ian muttered. If there was one nearby it wasn't very big, and difficult to spot.

"And then anyone else finding the note would have known too," Robbie pointed out. He scanned the area, then pointed to an outcrop of rocks a short distance away. "I think I see it."

Ian looked closely to where Robbie pointed, squinting in the darkness. Moonlight reflected off the water, highlighting a wee gap in the rocks, the tips of the waves glistening white. "Aye, that does look as though it might be it. Good spotting."

The sea breeze felt cool against his skin, and his hair blew into his face. He tucked the loose bits of it back into his braid and allowed himself a moment to watch Robbie's arse, and how his long golden hair caught in the wind. A wee smile tugged at Ian's lips, despite their situation. Aye, his Robbie was a good-looking lad, that he was. Determined too. And stubborn as a mule.

Ian caught up quickly, but this time when he tried to offer Robbie help, Robbie shook his head.

"We're almost there. I can manage. Save your own strength."

The closer they got to the cave, the more obvious it became that Robbie had been right. The cave was small, its entrance almost hidden by the cliff above it. Ian grunted as he squeezed through into the cave, thankful it was bigger than he'd expected from the look of it—or else he'd gotten thinner on short rations and lots of running. Robbie slipped through more easily.

"There's a sack over here." Robbie picked it up, then sat down to pull out its contents. "There's some bread, cheese, and a full waterskin. Your friend has kept his promise."

"Aye, that he has." Ian noticed a large branch near the entrance. He arranged it over the way in, leaving enough of a gap so they could look through and have enough light to see by. With the cave not easily found, hopefully disguising the entrance would keep them safe—at least for now.

"Do you think we're safe here?" Robbie tore off a piece of bread and handed it to Ian.

"For a while, but not too long." Ian munched the bread, then washed it down with some of the water, taking care to leave plenty for Robbie. "MacLeod knows all these caves, and once he realises we've gone, he'll send someone to drag us back. He'll nae give up so easily. Nor will he risk Charlie getting the treasure. MacLeod's in bed with the English, traitor that he is, and will be wanting to stay in favour with them."

Robbie struck a match and the cave filled with a warm glow of a candle. He laughed at the surprised look on Ian's face. "Your friend left us light as well." He glanced suddenly towards the entrance. "Should I blow it out? It won't give us away, will it?"

"Nae, leave it burning."

They were well back in the cave, and Ian doubted anyone could see the wee flicker of a candle through the sliver of a gap he'd left at the cave entrance. Nevertheless, he moved so he was between the light and the opening. Robbie secured the candle in an upright position using a pile of small rocks as a makeshift holder, then shuffled closer to Ian.

"Lean on me if ye want. Ye'll be more comfortable that way, and ye should get some rest." Ian let out a contented sigh when Robbie rested his head on his shoulder. He kissed the top of Robbie's head, breathing in his scent. "Ye still smell of the sea," he murmured.

"So does this cave." Robbie placed the rest of the food on Ian's lap. "I've eaten all I want. The rest is yours."

"Ye have hardly touched it," Ian protested. "Don't go hungry for me."

"I've had enough." Robbie grew quiet, although he didn't close his eyes to sleep. "I know you didn't eat all you could when Campbell had us."

Ian swallowed the last piece of cheese quickly so he could put the lad's mind at rest. "I had enough." Ach, he'd thought the lad hadn't noticed. "And I've plenty now, so don't ye go worrying about it."

"I've come to care, so I'll worry even if you tell me no." Robbie linked his fingers through Ian's. "But I'm worried about more than whether you eat. There's a reason you are the only one I've found to make the harp sound. I'm meant to be with you, but with MacLeod hunting us down, I'm...afraid."

"Aye, I ken what you mean—and about the two of us." Ian couldn't help but shiver. The thought of Robbie lost to the sea forever still filled him with dread. "But surely, it's not the magic that worries ye. The sea can't claim ye now...can it?"

"I...I don't know. Perhaps not, but I still feel it." Robbie's gaze darted here and there as if he was restless. "All this business with Campbell—I know the threat is real and present, and we must deal with it. But I fear I've not quenched the witch's spell." He reached behind him and yanked at the harp, wanting it off, but it had become tangled in his hair.

"Here, let me." Ian worked the knots of hair loose, pulled the harp from Robbie's shoulder, and laid it on the floor of the cave. He peered at the thing, almost expecting it to speak. "I dinna understand all this about the magic, but I trust ye. As long as ye believe there's that to fear, I'm scared for ye. I'm nae sure how to fight something unnatural, and this magic harp seems a wild thing—like it possesses a mind of its own."

"The harp will not harm *you*, and the witch's spell isn't *your* punishment. It's mine." Robbie bit his lip.

Ian pulled Robbie onto his lap and drew him into an embrace. Robbie's breathing sped up, and his heart thumped in his chest. "I might nae ken how to fight it, but that dinna mean I won't. I won't let go of ye. I promise. I want a life with ye; I want to be able to hold ye like this until we're both old and grey."

"You can't know how right that sounds to me. You and me and a long life together." Robbie leaned back against Ian, his head resting on Ian's chest. "But I've been so long on the sea—or in it. I hear it in my dreams. I wonder if I'll ever be free of it. Even in this cave, I can hear it taunting me."

Robbie fell silent and then whispered, "If I listen hard enough, I can almost hear the waves singing. I can't hear any words, but the waves call to me and remind me how easy it would be to stay with them."

"They're nae siren, and neither is that damned harp of yours," Ian said more roughly than intended. "And if they're taking ye, they have to take us both, and I'll nae have it."

"You almost sound like you hear the song, too."

Ian drew in a hard breath at the thought, but then blew it out and shook his head. "Ach, that's just the sound of the water dripping down the walls." Ian caressed Robbie's hand with his thumb. "But I dinna mean to dismiss your fears in saying that, mind. I know what it's like to be haunted by something ye have no control over. But we control what we can and adapt to the rest, aye?"

Robbie grew silent again and didn't speak for several minutes. "Do you know of An Uaimh Bhinn?" He used the old Celtic name for it. "I've never been there, but I heard of it once when I was on land. People say the noises it makes can be mistaken for song."

"The cave of melody? Aye, my granda took me to see it once. It's a wondrous thing, verra tall, and deep with great pillars for walls. Do ye know of the legend?"

Robbie shook his head, so Ian continued, warming to the tale. It was a favourite of his grandfather's. Speaking of those stories always reminded Ian of happy memories of when he was a bairn and the time he'd spent with his grandfather while he was growing up.

"It's said there is a similar cave in Ireland, and that the two are end pieces of what was once a bridge built by Fionn mac Cumhaill, the Irish warrior, to reach Scotland so he could fight the god Benandonner." Ian shrugged. "There's nae sign of the bridge itself now, just each end of it. I never believed it, but when I saw the cave, I figured it was certainly big enough for giants. Not that that makes the story true..."

"Sometimes stories exist because some part of them used to be true."

"Aye, I expect you're right." Ian wouldn't have believed it before he'd met Robbie, but after hearing the harp, and seeing him in the boat, Ian wondered how many of the old tales might have some truth to them after all. He watched the candle for a few moments, its light bending this way and that as it caught the whisper of wind bringing air into the cave. In a few hours, it would be morning, and he didn't dare risk staying that long.

"What are you thinking, Ian?"

"We need to leave this place before MacLeod sends his men after us. If they find us in this cave, we'll have nowhere to run, and I dinna want to be caught like rats in a trap."

Ian threaded his fingers through Robbie's long locks, finding the feel of his hair soothing against his skin. His thoughts drifted, his mind looking for answers that weren't particularly forthcoming, and he found himself glancing at the harp once more. "Perhaps that's the answer..."

"What is?" Robbie turned his head so he could look up at Ian.

"The cave of melody is on the wee Isle of Staffa, which is owned by MacQuarrie. He's nae taken a side for or against Charlie, so if we're lucky, MacLeod wouldn't think to look for us there. And MacQuarrie has been a friend of the MacDonalds at other times—so mayhap we can look there for succour if need be." Ian felt hope rise in him. "Are ye rested enough to leave, Rob? It won't be an easy way ahead as we've a distance to travel both by land and by sea. I'll help ye when I can but—"

"We can't stay here." Robbie brushed his lips against Ian's leaving a taste of salt and sea. "I meant what I said before. I'll follow where you lead."

Ian cupped Robbie's head before he could pull away. He kissed him, deepening it, the action a promise of the future he wanted for them.

"Aye, and I'll protect ye so ye can. I swear."

Chapter Thirteen

After making their plans to leave Skye and make for Staffa and An Uaimh Bhinn, they'd rested another hour. Or at least Robbie had rested. He was pretty sure Ian had kept vigil and never even blinked the entire time. Robbie had needed the sleep, but that delay left them squarely in the black hours after midnight with no moon overhead. As they got close to the cave's entrance, it seemed the light they carried might give them away against the backdrop of deep night.

"Ian," Robbie whispered. "Put the flame out. I'm afraid it will be like a beacon."

"I dinna disagree, lad, but the way is rough. I'm a Highlander, and my feet can likely find the path under dim starlight, but I'm worried you'll stumble and make your injuries worse."

Robbie shook his head. "You forget yet again. I'm a Reiver; I've been sneaking in the dark since a babe. I'll walk in your footsteps if it seems better to you. But no matter, we can't risk the light."

"Ach, aye, and you're right. But sling that harp onto your back again so's you'll have your hands free. I don't know why you're trying to carry it like a bairn."

Robbie chuckled and thought of some likely answers, but kept quiet and did as Ian asked.

Robbie expected Ian to start walking then. Instead he took Robbie by the shoulders, turned him around, and leaned down to plant a rough kiss on his mouth. Robbie returned the kiss with fervour, thinking it might be some time before they got a chance to steal another one. Ian sighed as they ended the kiss. He put the light out, then took Robbie's hand and hooked the fingers in the waist of his kilt.

"Hang on to me, then, so I'll ken you're with me. We'll be going east for now, through the wood, and then put some hills 'twixt us and MacLeod's eyes."

The way was rough and rocky, and the trees thick and crowded. Robbie became convinced the hills must be enchanted to block the way. Still, Ian only had to carry him on his back over one particularly rocky stream bed, where Robbie's injured leg made it impossible for him to negotiate the crossing. By the time they reached the flatter, open lands on the other side of the hills, the sun was a handsbreadth above the horizon, and Robbie felt bruised and ragged and hungry. Ian looked about the same, but neither of them suggested a rest longer than necessary to catch a clear breath and slake their thirst from a rivulet flowing among the broken stones that covered most of the field.

They turned north, which surprised Robbie as the cottage, Ian's boat, the Isle of Staffa, and the jewels—as far as he knew—all lay to the south. After giving it some thought, he said, "North, then, Ian? You're hoping to lead them astray?"

"Aye, we'll head on up to Duntulm. It's a MacDonald holding, but half took down to ruin, as the laird there took the stones with him when he abandoned the place. Yet I know there'll be boats sheltered there in the cove, and as MacLeod expects us to head south, it may be some time before he thinks of Duntulm."

"But…your treasure?"

Ian smiled, but Robbie could only think of the expression and the spark in Ian's blue eyes as mischievous. It reminded him of the look on the faces of his older brothers when they thought they'd pulled off the perfect prank.

Smiling back—because how could he not—Robbie said, "You look like the mouse that caught the cat."

Ian laughed quietly at that but motioned for Robbie to follow as he started on the faint track he'd chosen. "Well, I think there's nae danger of that dunderhead Campbell finding the jewels, anyway. We'll swing o'er and gather them on our way down to Staffa."

They walked on throughout the heat of the summer day, trying to stay hidden in the shadows of rises and tors, cottage walls and solitary trees. Miles from the sea, Robbie felt as though something was missing—some small hitch in his heartbeat that should be filled with the rhythm of waves lapping the shore. To move his thoughts from what was missing to what he needed, he stayed close to Ian, usually a step behind him as the best track was often narrow. He looked on Ian's red-gold hair shining under the sun, his back and shoulders braw and bonnie, his fine form from head to toe. He breathed deep to catch Ian's scent, salty sweat maybe a bit sour—days since a wash—but necessary for Robbie just the same.

Ian's closeness may have kept Robbie going longer than he otherwise could have, but after several times assuring Ian he didn't need to rest, that his leg was fine, he finally got to the point where the injury throbbed. This time, Ian didn't ask.

"We'll stop here by the burn, ye sweet, daft lad, and ye can rest that leg and tend it while I break out some trail fare to tide us 'til we can sup properly."

Robbie didn't have any argument in him. His leg needed the rest, yet after he soaked in the cold water and tended the wound, the throbbing receded to a dull, steady ache. After slaking his thirst and eating some of the biscuits and hard cheese Ian had set out, he lay back against Ian's broad chest and closed his eyes against the summer sun just starting its westerly descent. The breeze coaxed faint harmonics from the harp's strings, small sounds like echoes of Robbie's distant, yet recent, past life in the Border Marches. Surrounded by Ian's warmth, he fell asleep and dreamed.

The king's condemnation.

The hanging.

The witch. The boat, the harp, and the ironwood box.

He woke with a start, the image sharp in his mind of the harp's key lying against midnight velvet in its small coffin. Ian's arms tightened around him, and Ian's breath warmed his neck, calming him.

"You're all right now, lad. Whatever fear ye found in your dreams, it'll nae have ye whilst I hold ye."

"Aye, Ian, that's true enough," Robbie said, and he squeezed Ian's hand before moving to stand. *Yet, your strength is nothing against the magic and the sea.* He understood then why he felt melancholy and 'in-between.' Nothing had truly been resolved. The harp had sounded, yet Ian was not his, and he was not Ian's. The sea still claimed him, still drew him in and under. The harp's key had a siren's song of its own, and the sea still called him.

No point trying to explain that to Ian, not now while he had things to do that were for him more urgent. It would only worry him, and he would be powerless to help the situation in any way. Robbie's only hope, then, was the sea itself. Once they were again upon the water, perhaps the magic would guide him.

They laboured over stony fields, through thickets, and over tree-clad hills, and then struck a path close to the coast. But as dusk turned from lavender to lightless cobalt, Ian stopped, turned, and pulled Robbie briefly into his arms. He leaned his head down so it almost rested on the smaller man's shoulder and spoke quietly into his ear.

"Ach, Robbie. I'm about asleep as I stand, and your limping has grown so harsh it's paining me just to watch ye. We've got two hours' walk yet, and it lies across open land. I'd rather have my wits about me before we begin that trek. A wee burn runs behind that willow bank, I'd wager. Let's cosy up for a rest."

They found the burn running too swiftly over rocks for moss to form, and they drank their fill of the water, finding it refreshing. Off his feet for a few moments, thirst slaked, and sitting still in cool night air, Robbie contemplated trying to coax Ian to continue on to Duntulm. But once his belly was heavy with the trail food Ian's one-time lover had supplied, sleep came over him irresistibly, and he barely kept his eyes open long enough for Ian to lay him down under the tartan plaid. Ian cozied up and slept beside him, his nearness doing more to keep Robbie warm than the plaid could ever do, and his bulk like a seawall to hold him safe.

If Robbie dreamed, he didn't remember. The last he knew before sleeping was the sound of peepers and a distant owl, and the first he knew upon waking was a bright moon hanging in the east, casting threads of satin light into the black predawn hush.

Ian had stirred beside him as if they'd come to some agreement during sleep, and now Ian mumbled an "ach, sweet lad" and rose, pulling Robbie to his feet and brushing twiglets from his hair.

Robbie wet his throat with fresh water and spoke quietly, just loud enough to fray the edge of the night's silence. "The dark is good cover for us to cross the open land, aye, Ian?"

"'Tis that, Rob," Ian answered.

With no more words they stepped out of the cover of the willows and onto the path. There'd been no sign to worry them as they met the trail, and no one disturbed their solitude as they travelled through the dwindling trees. Ian took a long moment to survey the wide fields that lined the coast as they approached the abandoned castle. It stood, lonely and broken, atop an upthrust headland that made Robbie think of a mighty beast ready to devour anything approaching from the sea.

Once Ian deemed them unseen and unlikely to be challenged, they set off across the swath of green, holding a decent pace—now that Robbie's leg had improved with rest—and staying to the low swales when they could. They met with no alarm or trouble despite their fears, and came at last to Duntulm's ruins just as grey dawn shot flame across the east to burn the last trace of the sinking moon to cinders.

*

The rest in the willows by the burn had not been enough, not by any measure. As Robbie let Ian half pull, half support him up the inland trail to the top of the headland and then to the Castle Duntulm ruins, he felt barely alive, much less awake. His eyes burned. His throat rasped, raw with laboured breath. His leg throbbed.

Ian had him sit with his back against the stones of a partial wall, looking out to the sea. He left him there while he gathered moss and the plentiful cleavers growing up through the floor, cleared debris from a place where a roof and two and a half walls still made shelter, and once again laid down his plaid to cover them in their makeshift bed.

As Robbie watched the sea wave and wander through an incoming tide, his strength began to return. His breathing eased, and the ache in his leg dulled—as if just being near the sea was a cure for his ills. He wanted to walk down there, bathe in the salty water, and that desire troubled him, for he feared that senseless call. He was freer now, he knew, with his cobble gone for good and the harp naming Ian as the fulfilment of the spell. But that damned song still played through his veins. *The key*, he thought. But then, to put it from his mind, he asked Ian about the place they'd come to, Duntulm.

"This is a strange place, Ian. The stones look almost newly hewn, yet it stands as little more than a ruin. Is there a story to be told here?"

"Aye, there is." Ian stepped over to lend a hand and pull Robbie to his feet. "I'll tell ye of it as soon as we're wrapped in the plaid. I've got some tea made to restore ye as well before ye sleep."

Robbie followed Ian to the dim, protected corner, laughing a little. "It's a bedtime story, then?"

Ian laughed too, and after they were both comfortable with tea and the plaid and each other's closeness to warm them, he began the tale. "Not much romance to it, Robbie. It's a MacDonald laird that holds this castle, but he didn't find it comfortable—old and draughty, I suppose, though most of the place is less than a hundred years since its making. Anyway, he made a new hall and moved his people there. It's not far, and rather than get new stone he took down some of these walls. That's why the place looks a ruin after a few years empty."

They sipped their tea, and Robbie lay down next to Ian, glad to close his eyes against the bright day. Even with his eyes closed, he could feel Ian's eyes on him. They felt nice. If he wasn't so very tired and sore, the touch of that gaze skimming over him would have roused him for other things. As it was, he opened his eyes and looked into Ian's sea-blue gaze, and peace blossomed.

"Ian, I'm sorry. I confess I thought ill of you yesterday. Before...all this with Campbell and MacLeod..." Robbie drifted off, catching himself just before letting sleep take him. "I thought you'd only said words in my ear you didn't mean. It's not so, is it? You meant...what you said?"

"Ach, Robbie. And there was me thinking it was you who hadn't meant to say ye loved me. Tell me, then, you're nae just wanting me for stopping the magic? It's me ye might love?"

Ian hadn't actually answered his question, but the distress in his voice woke Robbie to Ian's true feelings. "Yes," he said, forcing his eyes to stay open and hold Ian's deep gaze. "It's true I love ye. And I think ye don't understand the fine craft of the witch who laid the curse. The harp would know if we were trying to pretend. It would be no use at all."

"Aye, then, that's at least one good thing." Ian fell silent, running a hand over Robbie's back as he held him.

Another time, the rhythmic motion might have brought heat to Robbie's groin; this time, it only tipped him into sleep. He barely heard Ian speak once more before he fell deep into dreams of dark islands and sparkling seas.

"I do love ye, Robbie. Know that, and take it with ye into your dreams."

*

Robbie woke to the smell of seafood and a wood fire and thought perhaps he'd arisen in an afterlife. If so, he guessed it would be the one prayed about in the kitchens and groves of his youth, rather than the sterile one the priests promised in the churches. He hadn't opened his eyes as he contemplated this, but when he realised he needed to empty his bladder, he looked around.

It was neither angel nor fair folk at the fire, but Ian, tending flame and food under the partial roof of the ruined castle they'd fallen asleep in. Robbie blinked out the last of the sleep, then rose to stumble away and tend to the morning's business. Though the clouds were high now, revealing the sun not far past its noon, it had rained at some time in the morning. The long grasses were wet with droplets, cooling his sore feet. Robbie crouched to wash his hands, wiped them once on his breeks, and left them to dry in the summer air. The calluses he once sported on his fingers from hours and hours of harping had all but disappeared. He wondered suddenly if the harp would vanish as well, like the boat had, and the thought of losing his closest companion through sea-washed time sent him scurrying back to the broken castle to make sure it was still there.

It was, and he touched it to reassure himself, shaking his head at his anxiety, which surely was misplaced in light of more immediate troubles. Still, at the fire with Ian, he found the tantalising aromas a reason to smile. "Smells good," he said, "and I believe I'm hungry."

Ian's smile was his answer, and it was enough—brightening their little shelter as though sunlight had peeked in.

"But where'd you find wood for the fire?" Trees were notably absent from the headland and the valley that stretched up from the beach all around.

"Apparently, someone thought a great wardrobe—taller than me, the width of a room, and made of oak—was too much trouble to move. I broke it up a little worse than it was, I'm afraid."

It was hard to feel serious about things with the midday sun shining past the broken stones, the promise of a good meal, and Ian's wit to smile about. After a few minutes, though, the soughing of gentle waves lapping the shore on three sides of the headland wormed its way into Robbie's conscious thought, and his belly tightened with resistance to its call. He felt the weight of Melisandre's curse fall over him, and he let it pull the corners of his mouth down, banishing the short-lived smile.

Ian's back had been to him as he fussed with the oysters roasting on half shells near the edge of the coals, but he seemed to hear—or sense somehow—the change in Robbie's mood. "What is it, then? What's got hold of your mind of a sudden?"

Robbie couldn't answer immediately, but without meaning to he let his gaze settle on the harp, its wood shining golden under the sun.

Ian stood straight and rolled his shoulders as if to shrug off a clinging rat. "Ach, Robbie. Tell me you're nae thinking of that damnable curse again? It's done! Leave it be."

Robbie did not want to tell Ian how wrong he was. He wanted to play along and hope somehow the solution to the magic's last mystery would arise of its own accord. *But Ian should know what's true.* "It's *not* done," he said. And then, feeling somehow that it truly was his fault, he added, "I'm sorry."

For a moment, Ian's expression looked like a storm was rolling in fast, but he breathed deep, and his features settled into a half smile as he shook his head. "Aye, then. Let me serve ye some breakfast, and ye can tell me more of your tale as we eat."

The oysters had a delicious flavour, roasted to steamy perfection and seasoned with hunger and the salt off the seaweed they'd been covered with. For a few minutes, Robbie had no attention to spare for conversation. When he stopped for a breather, he looked long at the harp, remembering all it had been to him in a capsulised second. Then he met Ian's gaze and told him about the harp's key and the box made of ironwood that would neither float on the sea's surface, nor fully sink.

Ian's first response surprised Robbie.

"How in all the possible hells of man or god did that bloody witch ken about wood from trees on the Isle of Man that wouldn't act as ye'd expect wood to behave?"

Robbie stared open-mouthed and then, unable to stop himself, he laughed. "A very good question," he said after a moment. "I don't know, of course. But I suppose those who do magic know of such magical things because someone else told them."

"Like a grandmother's tale, is it?" Ian had smiled too, but now he set down the flat rock he'd used for a platter and moved closer to Robbie. Placing a protective arm around him, he said, "I see then why 'tis ye continue to fash over it. The sea troubles ye still. And now it troubles me too, for if ye've no idea how to find this box wi' the tiny key inside, I'm sure I don't either."

*

Robbie leaned into Ian's embrace, and Ian kissed the top of his head. He wished he knew how to find the damned key and end the curse once and forever. That witch had gone out of her way to ensure it wouldn't be broken easily, that was for sure. His stomach rumbled, reminding him that he hadn't eaten. He'd been too busy watching Robbie eat—no, making sure he had. The lad had a bit more colour in him now, but Ian still didn't like the way he favoured the leg he claimed was fine.

"You need to eat, Ian." Robbie nodded towards the pile of oysters Ian had put aside before they'd got distracted by talk of the key.

"Aye, I will." He reluctantly removed his arm from around Robbie, shuffled over to retrieve his meal, and wolfed it down. Once finished, he wiped his hand across his mouth, licking the juices left on his lips. When he looked up, Robbie was watching him. Ian took a swig of water, and then handed the waterskin to Robbie.

"Drink up, lad. You're looking a wee bit flushed." He suspected the reason for Robbie's colour wasn't thirst but couldn't resist teasing him, especially as he felt himself grow warm. "I think it's a good look on you, I do," he added quickly, not wanting to embarrass Robbie too much.

"It's a good look on you too." Robbie finished drinking and wiped his hand across his mouth the same way Ian had done. Droplets of water still clung to his lips, and Ian leaned across without thinking and brushed them away with his tongue.

Before he could move away, Robbie threaded his fingers through Ian's hair, using the motion to pull him closer, and brought their lips together in a soul-searing kiss. Ian groaned into it, ignoring the part of his brain that told them they needed to discuss...

"Something," he murmured. It could wait.

"Something?" Robbie broke the kiss and grinned. "Is that what we're calling this? I enjoyed that kiss far more than just 'something.'"

"Aye, I enjoyed it too." Ian didn't bother to hide the hunger in his voice or eyes. "We should stay here 'til nightfall," he said roughly. "It's not safe to—"

"So we have all day." Robbie nodded. He caressed Ian's cheek, slowing his touch as he reached the stubble of Ian's several days' growth of beard. "I like the feel of you like this. Unshaved and rough under my fingers."

Ian captured Robbie's fingers and kissed each one in turn. "You want to make love? Now?"

"Yes, I do. Very much so, and definitely *now*." Robbie let out a sound that reminded Ian of a cat purring, but made his cock stir and harden. "I want to, while we still—"

Ian shushed him with a kiss. "I'll nae have talk of that. Not now. We're both here, and that's what I want to think about. And how good we'll make each other feel." He scooped up Robbie in his arms before Robbie had a chance to protest. "We'll be more comfortable on my plaid. The ground here is damp and rough." He laid Robbie gently on the plaid he'd spread over the cleavers and moss for a rough bed for them the night before. "Much better."

He kissed Robbie once more, then sat up on his haunches, taking the time to fill his soul with the sight before him. *Enjoy being with him while ye can.* Ian's eyes misted over as the words came unbidden into his mind. *How long do I have him for?*

Damn that witch and her curse. Even if they survived Campbell and his men, what kind of a future did they have with that harp still wanting to claim Robbie as its own? No, not the harp, but its key. Still the same. In all the ways that counted, still the same. Ian had almost given up hope of finding someone he could imagine spending his forever with, but he'd found Robbie only to be faced with the knowledge he would almost certainly lose him.

"We'll survive this," Robbie whispered fiercely as though he knew what Ian was thinking. "Or…"

Ian didn't want to put his thoughts into words. "No talk about that now."

He let his gaze travel over the smooth skin of Robbie's chest and then laid kisses along the curves and hollows near his heart. "We're staying here today. Today is here, and now, and us. I can't promise ye anything about tomorrow, though I can promise ye I'll do what I can to keep ye safe. But, for now…I want good memories, Rob. Memories of you to keep for when I'm old and grey." *In case I don't have you by my side when I am, or I don't survive that long. I'm not sure I want to survive that long without ye.*

Fortunately, Robbie didn't answer him in words, as Ian wasn't sure he could have listened to any reply that might have confirmed what he wanted to ignore. Or forget, just for this day.

Robbie reached for the ties on Ian's shirt, undoing enough of them to ease it off his shoulders. "You're a fine-looking man, Ian." He licked one finger and traced the damp digit down Ian's chest. "But I don't want to just look at you. I want to touch. I want to feel."

"I'd like that too." Ian heard the unspoken question in Robbie's words. "I want to be touched and to touch you."

"Oh yes." Robbie's voice shook with emotion.

Ian kissed him on the lips, putting all his love for Robbie into it. Not just his love, but his hope for a future with the lad, however unlikely that might be. Long and tender. Both of them lingered, neither wanting to stop although Ian forced himself to break it first. "I love ye," he murmured, "but ye need to breathe. So do I."

Robbie chuckled, a light sound that brought with it a twinkle to his eyes. He tugged at the bottom of Ian's shirt. "I've decided to be greedy. I want to look *and* touch."

"Nothing wrong with wanting both, but fair is fair. Ye need to sit up so I can take your shirt off too." Ian held out his hand. "I'll help ye."

"Very gallant." Robbie took Ian's hand, sat up long enough to pull his shirt over his head, and then lay back down again. "Aren't you forgetting something?" The question began politely enough, but the way Robbie licked his lips made it clear he wouldn't take no for an answer.

"Am I?" Ian teased for only for a moment as disappointment filled Robbie's eyes. He yanked off his shirt and threw it over Robbie's. "Aye, but you're a fine-looking man too. You must think me daft repeating your words. But seeing ye like this takes *my* words away." He blew a breath over each of Robbie's nipples in turn, watching as they hardened before swiping them with his tongue.

Robbie reached under Ian's kilt, his fingers brushing against Ian's hard cock. He stroked the shaft a couple of times, slowly at first, and then more firmly.

Ian let out a long breath and knelt over Robbie, holding him in place on either side. He rose up enough on his knees to edge up Robbie, the bottom of his kilt swishing against Robbie's bare chest. He groaned once, then louder as Robbie kept stroking him. "Wait," he managed to grind out. "I have an idea."

It only took a moment to undo Robbie's breeks and yank the material down. Robbie's cock stood to attention, as hard as Ian's. Ian bent and kissed the tip of it. His own cock was weeping glossy liquid, but this time he didn't want to fuck Robbie. He positioned himself above Robbie's cock, straddling him. Balancing himself, he ran his tongue down Robbie's chest. "I want ye in me. As ye touch...me like that. I want to give ye pleasure too. I want it to be verra good for ye too."

Robbie's eyes widened and then he smiled. Ian felt as though heaven opened at that moment, and he allowed himself a slither of hope that perhaps they might both get the future they wanted. "You *are* giving me pleasure. Watching you and knowing you're hard because of me makes me happy."

"Please." Ian wobbled slightly, yet kept his balance before Robbie could put a hand out to steady him. He'd not ask again. Perhaps it was something Robbie didn't want to do.

"Yes." Robbie swiped at Ian's cock, collecting the slick natural lubrication in his palm, then spat in it. "But let me prepare you first." He wet his fingers with the mix then slid them into Ian's hole.

Ian tensed at first. "Aye, but it's been a long time since I've had a man." He sucked in his breath as Robbie's fingers moved inside him, stretching him.

"Been had by one, you mean." Robbie stilled his fingers but didn't remove them. He reached up and threaded his fingers through Ian's hair, bringing his head down until they rested their forehead together. "You felt so good inside me, Ian."

"Aye, it felt good for me too." Robbie's breath was hot against Ian's face. "And aye, that's what I meant."

Robbie slipped one slender finger further in.

Ian cried out, in spite of himself at the wave of pleasure that cascaded through him. "I..."

Whatever he was going to say was lost as Robbie moved his fingers again. Ian gripped Robbie's shoulders, hard, then kissed him, his tongue stroking Robbie's. Robbie removed his fingers, and Ian cried out again, this time in frustration.

"Robbie, please."

Robbie took a deep breath, kissed Ian again and pulled him down, his cock seeking Ian's entrance. Ian hissed, then groaned as he felt himself being filled. His fingers free, Robbie began stroking Ian's cock, lifting his hips, one rhythm matching the other, then one following the other, playing Ian like some sensual instrument.

Ian rode him, following Robbie's lead, the two of them dancing to a tune as old as eternity. He was flying, floating on a haze of pleasure, heat filling his body. He groaned louder, his mouth on Robbie's, wet tongues stroking frantically. Ian sped up, wanting more friction, more...more. Robbie matched him with his fingers on Ian's cock, note for note.

"Rob. Rob..."

Robbie moaned loudly, his eyes glazing over.

Ian tightened around him. His vision went white. He felt Robbie let go, fill him with warmth, his cock spurting over both of them. Ian shook, both physically and emotionally.

"Robbie." He collapsed onto Robbie, then rolled them so they were facing, the two of them joined in body and soul. Ian stroked Robbie's hair and buried his head on Robbie's shoulder. "I love ye, Rob. With every part of me, I love ye."

"I love you, too, Ian."

They clung to each other. It felt as though the moment stretched to eternity, yet Ian knew it would never be. Reluctantly, he eased himself off Robbie. Robbie sighed as Ian was free of him. Loss flowed over and through Ian, a sense of sorrow, a song of despair. He blinked back tears.

"I don't want to lose you, lose us." Robbie whispered the words. Ian looked up to see Robbie's eyes were full of tears too. "Being with you feels right. More right than anything I've ever felt before."

Ian held Robbie to himself tightly, daring for a short breath to believe he could keep Robbie safe from what was to come. Their cocks brushed against each other, yet this time, it wasn't lust Ian felt but an emotion far deeper. He breathed in Robbie's scent, clinging to it in his mind, needing to remember it for when Robbie wasn't there.

"Aye, for me too." Ian kissed Robbie's eyes, trying to kiss away the tears but scared that whatever comfort he might offer, it would never be enough. How could he fight against magic? "I'm scared, Rob. Not about being found, but about this key of yours. I don't know how to fight something I canna find nor see."

Robbie slipped free from Ian's embrace, quietly cleaned himself up, and dressed. Not wanting to break the silence, Ian used some of the moss he'd used for their bedding and some of the water he'd collected earlier that morning to do the same. He didn't blame Robbie for not replying and preferred the silence to promises that might easily be broken.

"I'll not go far," he murmured, knowing Robbie would follow when he was ready.

The view outside the ruins didn't take his breath away as it usually did. He kept close to the outer wall of the castle, not daring to walk to the edge of the cliff in case he might be seen. Water stretched for miles, clear and blue apart from the shoreline in the distance. He found the dark trees hiding the two boats in the cove. He'd been down to check, so he knew they were there—one seaworthy, one best kept in the shallows—even though he couldn't see any sign of them.

He couldn't see any approaching danger either, but that didn't mean he and Robbie were safe. The last of the exhilaration from their lovemaking leaked away like the tide left behind on the shoreline the longer he thought about what was ahead. They couldn't stay where they were. It might be safe now, but come nightfall, they'd need to make their way south. Travelling by water at night would be dangerous, but a better option than taking the risk of being found by MacLeod or Campbell, and their men.

Ian crossed his arms over his chest and leaned back against the wall of the ruins. He scanned the water again, yet it was more of an automatic response rather than anything. He could fight a human foe, but he knew naught about magic. How long would it be before the sea and that damned key claimed Robbie as their own?

His gran had always told him there was no point in worrying about the future, as it would do what it wanted to anyway. Live in the present and do as best as he could with it. Ian pushed away from the wall and growled, annoyed at himself for slipping into such melancholy. It wouldn't help Robbie, nor keep him safe. He needed to be doing something practical, to keep himself busy so his mind would get the hint and stop its incessant nagging.

Ian shivered in the chilly wind, remembering his plaid was still in the castle ruins. He should go back and build up the fire, and make preparations for their evening meal. They'd need to eat well for the night ahead and get some sleep before their journey if they could. He'd take first watch and gut the fish he'd caught earlier that morning. Yet, with the few steps he took, he found himself closer to the edge of the cliff and looking out to sea again, rather than back to Robbie and the reminder of how little time they might have left.

He felt rather than heard Robbie walk up behind him. He straightened as Robbie slipped his arms around him from behind.

"If I had an answer, I'd tell you." Robbie spoke the words quietly. "I'm scared too. If we could find the key, we might stand a fighting chance, and I swear I'll do what I can to stay with you. I feel the sea calling, and I can hear Melisandre taunting me."

"I'm not one for backing down from a fight, and neither are you." Ian leaned back into Robbie's embrace, taking comfort from his lover's arms around him. "The sea can call all it likes, but it doesn't mean it will have ye. As for that witch—I want to hope that together we'll find a way to break the curse but…" He turned in Robbie's arms and kissed him. "You're mine, and she can taunt all she wants. If she were here, I'd—"

Robbie placed a finger over Ian's lips. "She's not," he said so firmly Ian wondered if he worried she might appear and add to her curse somehow. After Ian kissed Robbie's fingers, Robbie removed them from his mouth, caressing Ian's cheek instead.

"Nae, she's not." Ian threaded his fingers through Robbie's free hand. "We have a few hours before nightfall.

I'm nae sure I can sleep, but I have a few ideas of how to fill in those hours." He looked Robbie up and down and licked his lips. "More than a few, I'm thinking."

Robbie grinned, although it seemed forced. "I've a few ideas of my own," he said, "although I liked your last idea. A lot." He turned to walk back to their makeshift bed. His next words were almost a whisper, and nearly carried away with the wind, but Ian heard them clear enough. "I'll have you for as long as I can."

"Aye, Rob. Me too."

Even if their forever ended up being just a few short hours, it was still better than naught.

Chapter Fourteen

Duntulm Castle bumped and rattled stone against stone, and the sea chanted Robbie's name. Despite thinking he wouldn't, he slept. Yet, somewhere in his mind, he remained aware of these things even though they didn't pull him down into dreams. When he and Ian had first gone back to their pallet for another session of lovemaking, the castle's sounds gave their coupling a second rhythm, like the heartbeat of the place. As to the whispers of the ocean, the waters seemed another lover, watching, spurned but not yet hopeless. And when Robbie let his thoughts furl into slumber again, Ian's heartbeat was shield and comfort, and for once his sleep was dreamless and sound.

As on all summer nights in the high latitudes, dark came late, yet no more than a glow remained of sunset when Ian woke Robbie to eat before they began their journey west across the water.

When he stumbled back from the burn—where he'd splashed around enough to wash away sweat, sex, and sleep—he found Ian picking shellfish and roots out of the coals of a small fire.

"More oysters, I'm afraid, for now," Ian said. "Didn't want to waste them. But I spied a croft just a mile or so northeast from here, and I paid a little coin for some small stock of hard bannock, smoked fish, and dried mushrooms, so we'll have those for the journey. They had little to share, but they offered what they could. And they're MacDonald's people, so I feel they won't cause us grief."

"Oysters are fine. I've hunger as sauce, so ye won't hear me complaining."

Ian sat next to him on the wall, close enough to balance the stone holding their simple meal across their knees. A light breeze out of the east ruffled Ian's hair, but otherwise the twilit land seemed perfectly still. Suddenly restless, Robbie impulsively pulled free the meat from an oyster and reached over to pop it in Ian's mouth.

Unfortunately, Ian didn't open his mouth at the right moment, and it all went wrong. The titbit fell down the front of Ian's shirt, so Robbie went fishing for it, both of them laughing so hard they nearly spilled their entire meal in the weeds growing against the wall.

After they shared a quick kiss, the laughter calmed to chuckles. As night cloaked the land, a sombre mood swooped in to take possession of them both. Silence prevailed until they'd finished their meal.

They stood, and Robbie took the stone to scrape the remains into the fire.

"It's time we start o'er the water," Ian said. "I've checked the boat over, and it's good, it'll hold. I've packed up everything too. We've but to carry it down to the boat."

Robbie grunted in reply and started kicking dirt and pebbles over the flames, though he didn't suppose it mattered much. He stood with hands on hips and looked quizzically at Ian. "So why didn't ye wake me earlier? I could've been some help."

"Ah, Robbie. Ye looked so peaceful, and it seemed no dark dreams disturbed ye. I thought your rest a good investment. Besides, there wasn't so much to do."

Ian ducked his head sheepishly, making Robbie smile. *Here*, he thought, *is a much sweeter man than anyone would guess to look at him.*

"Well," Robbie said. "Thank ye, then, Ian." He picked up the harp, which chimed softly as the breeze struck it, slung it over his shoulder, and followed Ian to the water's edge.

*

The Inner Sea flowed around their small boat as though parting to make way for their passage. The water glittered, but beneath the shining tips of the wavelets swirled the darkest sea Robbie ever remembered. Not even when the witch's spell first took him late in the night on the Firth of Forth had he seen waters so black and fathomless.

In that moment hope left him.

How would he *ever* find the small ironwood box that held the key in that depth of black ocean? But Ian was singing low, a tune to row by, and he was so very alive and real, Robbie didn't know whether to smile and sing with him or cry and roll overboard and let all his dreams go.

"I'm grateful for the dark, then, Robbie," Ian whispered so low the sound was almost lost among the soft sweep of the oars.

Robbie gasped, as Ian's words called him back to reality—the present threat of Campbell and MacLeod. Suddenly Robbie's thinking righted itself, and he realised the dark wasn't the product of any curse, nor a cause for despair. The dark sea simply reflected a cloud-covered, moonless night sky. And as Ian said, it favoured them.

"And ye'll ken, I've crossed these waters before, but always I've had to battle the wind. Seems the sea favours us as well."

As soon as Ian said it, Robbie knew it was true—knew it in the part of him where the magic made its home. *Perhaps the witch's curse isn't pure evil.* The thought wasn't new. More than once, he'd sensed that the magic opened a door to him or helped him to safety. The enchantment seemed now to link him to the waters of the Inner Sea and ease his passage. He didn't say that to Ian, thinking it best to let him wonder.

When they reached the southeast coast of Harris, they put ashore in a deep inlet, dragging the boat up betwixt rocks on a narrow shore with a wide green bank above it.

"This part of the Long Island is home to a cousin. He stands with the Jacobite cause, to be sure, but if he knows of me at all, he'll think me a traitor. At the least, I can't be sure of a kind reception. We'll stay down here by the water and be on our way as soon as we've had a stretch."

But Robbie climbed up to the top of the rocky hill that blocked their view inland, and he could see a house fit for a laird and an old church, each with a candle burning in a single window. When he came back down, he told Ian what he'd seen.

"Aye." Ian was rummaging through their meagre stores, looking for something, and he sounded preoccupied. "Likely they're burning a candle for the prince, if he should happen to come in the night." He stopped and peered at Robbie as if suddenly wondering why he'd brought it up. "Surely you know it's not for us, lad."

"Of course," Robbie answered, and he did understand, but the simple existence of a welcoming light burning against the loneliness of night out here in the islands made him homesick—though for what home he didn't know. Wanting to shake off the desolate mood, he changed the subject. "What is it you're looking for, Ian?"

"Uh...well, I... Ach! Here it is!"

He held up a package wrapped in slick oil skin and layers of sackcloth, and his face wore a look of such proud triumph, Robbie couldn't help but chuckle. "What is it?"

"I asked could they spare any butter..." He cleared his throat. "But they couldn't spare any. They have a son who goes a-whalin', though, and they said sometimes they grease their bread with the blubber."

By now, Robbie had gotten the idea, and he smiled as he teased, "What if we have no bread?"

"Well, now, bread isn't the only thing what can get buttered, is it?"

Robbie laughed and stepped down from the green bank onto a rock that lent him just enough height to be eye to eye with Ian, who gathered him into a strong hug, cupping his arse and squeezing for more effect.

Gruff, Ian said, "Ach, and we've nae time for such now, but come opportunity, I promise ye I'll come knocking with me whale well greased."

Laughter felt good, and the talk of sex set Robbie's imagination afire, but Ian was right. They needed to keep moving until they were south of Dunvegan. Earlier, Ian had strained a muscle in his shoulder, and Robbie had watched his involuntary wince from time to time as he rowed. When it was time to go again, Robbie stepped into the boat and sat at the oars.

"What are ye doing, lad?"

"I can row well enough. Ye need to rest that shoulder a while longer."

Ian pushed the boat out into the water and climbed in more gracefully than Robbie might have expected for such a big man. He settled at the tiller, and turned his head to look towards the east.

"No sign of the sun, yet. We've made good time. You can row a short while, but then I'll put my back into it. We'll be needing to make the best time we can, get to Rum and collect the jewels, and get out of the waters McLeod will be prowling."

Robbie smiled. He felt the sea beneath him, not singing to him and calling as it did at times, but singing *with* him. A song rose in his mind, and he was just ready to sing when Ian broke into a brawny version of a Gaelic song. Robbie didn't speak the language and was surprised that Ian did, but the rhythm and repetition in the song was so perfect for the oars, he figured it must have been a rowing song. Soon he was tapping a foot, and the harp sounded a sympathetic chord. By the time Ian had sung the chorus thrice, Robbie could sing along, and away they went out into the Inner Sea. They turned and hardly noticed the wind at their backs as they sang—not too loudly, as they didn't want any to hear them—and smiled at each other, passing swiftly by the coast of North Uist.

'S iomairibh eutrom ho ro
'S iomairibh eutrom ho ro

They stopped singing at last when a wind pushed them hard to south by southeast—directly towards Rum Island.

"Stop rowing lad," Ian said. "We've a sail!"

Robbie did stop rowing, and he smiled. He of course knew they had a sail—it lay furled around a mast in the bottom of the boat, and there was a tongue-and-groove stub near the tillerman's seat. True, he'd been enjoying the feel of the sea enough, he'd not even thought of the sail, but they could make better time across the water if they raised it.

Working together, they quickly had the mast and sail fitted and lashed, and it filled with wind and carried them forward in a great leap. Before thinking it through, they both raised a cheer that boomed out and echoed between the islands.

They worried about whether they'd given themselves away to pursuers for a time after that, but soon their spirits grew quiet.

"Being raised Catholic, Robbie, I'd almost think God were on our side. I'm not so sure, but this wind is following the sea, and they're both going exactly where we want to be. How is it so, do ye think?"

Robbie said, "Aye. It's luck, then, Ian," and he kept his knowledge of the magic at work to himself, for while it gave him hope, it would worry Ian, and he had no need to know.

The wind held, and the two men struggled to stay alert while nothing about the waters or the skies brought a threat to them. As they neared Rum, the wind still didn't turn away, but it died to little more than a whisper, and they took down the sail. With Ian at the oars again, they ran as best they could for the western shore of the island, then followed along it to the deep inlet that would bring them in to where Ian had hidden Prince Charles's treasure.

For all the quickness of their sail through the night, by the time they shoaled the boat into the crescent beach, dawn had come, washing a rose tint over sand, water, and stone.

"Ach, and it'll be full light by the time we get back out on the water," Ian said, his voice low as though the tors and free-standing stones might harbour hidden enemies.

"Aye," Robbie agreed. He stepped out into water a foot deep and helped pull the boat higher on the sand. That done, he stretched his cramped muscles and enjoyed the sight of Ian doing the same. Somehow, after the long trip with sail and oars, he felt more like himself, like he'd slipped fully into his body and his mind for the first time since the witch had floated him down the Eden to the belly of that fabled god, Manannán mac Lir. It seemed odd, though, that it should be like that—that salty waters should drive him into his true self—because before the curse, he knew little of the sea.

Yet it was so, and Robbie slid a tiny bit further into his own stubborn, pragmatic, Reiver-born personality, not unlike the tongue-and-groove fit of the boat's spar. After a deep breath, he opened the conversation he and Ian needed to have right then, and it wasn't about sex, magic, or love.

"So what do ye think, Ian? Should we stay here, then, hide ourselves until dark, and then go west and south again? Or do ye think we should grab up your treasure and run?"

Ian stood gazing at the morning light peeking over Rum's twin peaks, scratching thoughtfully at his bare, slightly sunburned chest. "That's the question of the hour, lad," he finally said. "And thank ye for bringing my mind back to it. One thing's sure, I don't feel well enough hidden where we stand. Let's pull the boat around to the back of those rocks there—there's a growth behind it that should hide it well. And ye see that tall stone with a head on its shoulders?"

Robbie peered in the direction Ian had indicated and smiled, for that was indeed what it looked like. "Aye, I do. That's where ye hid the treasure?"

"It is. I'll go and fetch them back while you make your way to that beachhead to the south and keep an eye out for traffic in the sea lanes."

"I can do that. But I don't know how to signal if I see something."

Ian nodded in agreement, then squeezed Robbie's shoulder. "Nae, ye'll not be able to do that. Take note of what ye see and meet up with me, and we'll decide from there. Just keep out of sight as best ye can."

Robbie stretched up to give Ian an innocent peck on the cheek and started to walk away, but Ian pulled him back into his arms.

"Nae, then. We won't be leaving it at that." He kissed Robbie long and hard before letting him go, then smacked his arse playfully as Robbie stepped away towards the ridge.

Robbie laughed, but after he was a safe distance away, decided a little payback was in order. "Ian, turn around." When Ian faced him looking a little worried, Robbie languidly rubbed at his own half-hard cock through his breeks and ran his tongue languidly over his lips.

"Ach, don't do that now! I need to keep my mind on other things!"

Robbie laughed again and winked, then turned and saucily strode away.

But it was true, their attention needed to be on plans and dangers, so Robbie quickly sobered. He kept low as he climbed—sparing half a thought to the fact that his wounded thigh no longer ached, even with use. *Maybe more of the sea's favour*, he mused. *Maybe the water has healed me.*

At the top of the ridge, he lay on his belly to peer out to sea. He had a vista to three sides with the peaks behind him, and for the first ten minutes, the view was clear, the long dawn of summer gradually lifting the shadows. It was a pleasant view, and the breeze played lightly over his skin, ruffling his abundant but too-fine hair. It had been hours since he'd slept, and he started to drowse, but a square-rigged boat, high at both stern and prow, heaved into view from the north and brought him fully awake.

A birlinn.

He identified its type from its profile and rigging, though he knew of the midsized sail-and-oars craft only from songs and a single sighting during a raid of lands on Solway Firth when he was a lad of sixteen. The design, which Robbie thought might be called ancient by this date, gave the sighting a ghostly feel, and when a thick grey fog came rolling across the water to surround it like a shroud, that feeling was underscored. Robbie shivered, but the imagined apparition didn't distract him so badly that he lost track of reality. Chances were good that boat belonged to MacLeod of Dunvegan, and it was almost equally likely the sailors were looking for Ian. In a moment when the fog thinned, he made out a device on the sail, more or less circular, with two flags and something in the middle, though he couldn't tell just what.

The ship slipped from view heading south and somewhat west, and Robbie had just determined he needed to go give Ian word of the sighting when two more ships cut through the fog. These were a bit smaller and also more distant, but it seemed likely the three were sailing together. He waited, but no more boats came over the water, and Robbie went down off the ridge, carrying information he hoped wouldn't spell their doom.

Just about where they'd parted ways, Ian came towards him carrying two packs, one large slung over his back, and one quite small tucked against his chest. Robbie didn't have a chance to say anything before Ian read his expression.

"Ye've seen something, then, Rob?"

By the time he'd reported what he'd seen they came to the rocks where the boat was hidden. Looking west across the Inner Sea, they could see the fog lying in cloudy patches over the water. To the north, it seemed thicker, and Ian said he thought it best they try cutting back to the north, into the fog, to cross to the west.

"It's morning still, aye?" he said, not expecting an answer. "The fog won't be so thick we can't find the sun in the east and take our direction from it."

Robbie thought before speaking. A personal history of reiving, even as little of it as he himself had done, should help him figure the best way to evade an enemy, but this was water, not land. It wasn't the same. Still, he voiced his thoughts. "We can't tell how far that fog extends westward. We can't tell if boats are already hidden in it. We can't know if the wind will rise and blow the fog away, leaving us in plain view of our enemy."

"All that's true, lad. Shall we go, then?"

"Aye, then." Robbie smiled encouragement. "We'll take our best chance, and perhaps the sea will favour us again."

As Ian shoved the craft out from the beach, Robbie took the oars, shooting a look to Ian begging him not to argue about who should row. Perhaps Ian understood, for he looked as though he'd object, then sat once again in the tillerman's seat. Robbie pulled hard against the water once, twice, three times, and then the harp, still propped in the bow, sounded a single soft chord. Immediately the craft settled into a current driving it north, swift though Robbie barely dipped the oars and no wind came.

They sped north along a high bank offering a shadowed passage. Ian touched the tiller to send them northwest, but it seemed almost to be after the fact, as if the waves themselves chose that heading before any human could have given the direction. Robbie held his breath and peered left and right as the boat glided almost silent through an unsheltered space. The morning light was yet dim and grey, but visibility along a north-south axis was clear and far. Robbie saw no boat, and no cry went up across the water. They slid under the frayed, curling edge of the thickest fog bank, and then they were inside the cloud.

Robbie kept pulling, but the thick fog and shrouded silence imparted an eerie feeling that they stood still while the water and the world moved away around them. Ian began to hum a melody, so faintly sounded Robbie wasn't sure he heard it at all until the harp whispered back a low harmonic. Perhaps Ian had been elsewhere in his mind, for he fell silent at the sound, and then gasped, wide-eyed, as though the harp called him back and reminded him that silence might mean life. It seemed they'd passed undetected, until from somewhere on the water—it was impossible to say where or how far—came the clunk of an oar or a bootheel against wood.

Robbie's heart slammed into his throat at the sound, and seconds later, he felt the craft heel towards the southwest and right itself on a slightly altered course.

They left the fog and entered a bright morning, like passing through a curtain into a window-lit room. Robbie had never in his life felt so exposed—not even running hard from an interrupted raid, not even that day in King James's solar. Certain discovery seemed a matter of when, rather than if, so Ian's quiet, calm statement surprised him.

"We're heading directly into Canna Isle, there, see?" He gestured, made sure Robbie looked, and then continued. "Let's go ahead, try to get onto the beach without being seen, and rethink our plan. Aye?"

Robbie wasn't sure why Ian's practicality calmed him, but he breathed easier as he began to row towards the shore behind him. "Aye," he said in answer, then fell silent again as they entered the shallow, glass-still water of a small crescent cove. "It's beautiful here, Ian," he whispered, and though he had much to hope for now, he realised something in him longed for the rocking sleep of non-being in the sea.

Ian spoke as if he'd read that thought. "Ach, it's true, but listen to me, now. Don't go yearning for the quiet dark of the sea. I need ye here. With me. It's where ye belong. It's what's meant to be." He leaned forward and laid a hand on Robbie's knee, their gazes locked.

Ian's words, and especially his touch, his gaze, came as a shock to Robbie, and it came clear to him that though the magic may not be evil in itself, and it may favour him at times, he couldn't trust it. It protected and aided him some, but it also lulled him, called him back to the beckoning sea. He'd stopped rowing, but the boat drifted swiftly shorewards. When they were all but run aground, he played the oars one against the other to turn the boat into a narrow beach between a cliff and a sea stack topped by what looked like a horrible prison tower. He shuddered, looking up at it after they'd beached the boat.

"Pay that nae mind, Robbie. It's a prison built cruelly by a man to house a wife he thought too beautiful to trust. Empty now, and ne'er a threat to us. This is a Clan Ranald Isle, though Argyll himself once claimed it. The Jacobite cause has been strong here, and Ranald is the cousin of MacDonald. Again, if they know of me, they'll think me a low traitor, so it's best we keep away from folks. But I've got the plaid, and mayhap that will buy us safety here."

With the boat dragged into some gorse and hidden as well as they could hope to do, they grabbed the packs and the harp and crossed as quickly as possible into a long grove of trees set against an inwards curve of the cliffside. Once in the trees, they smelled the friendly smoke of the hearth and roasting meat, and spotted some way back the rectangular shape of a blackhouse. Robbie breathed deep the smell of home and comfort and then leaned against Ian for a moment before, as one, they turned away to the other end of the wood. They found a cleft rising up the cliff. They could climb it, and though Robbie's limbs ached already, he suggested they go up.

"Aye," Ian agreed with a slight nod and wry face. "But I think we'll nae go to the top—it's likely to be open to the sky with little shelter. Let's find a perch in the gulley, take a cold meal, and work out where to go from here."

The climb wasn't as difficult as Robbie had expected, and the sun was still well east when they found an indent into the rock. Soil had collected there, and grasses had taken up residence along with a few clumps of low heather.

Ian set his packs down and sat next to them on soft but dampish ground. He spread a corner of his kilt to one side and beckoned Robbie. "Come, sit."

Robbie leaned against Ian's side, grateful for the warmth, as he shared out some of the dried fruit and hard bread from Ian's pack. They ate and passed the water skin between them, and when Robbie was full, he found himself nodding towards sleep.

"We canna stay here," Ian said, rubbing the muscles of Robbie's back and shoulders. "I get a sense of things building up, and the need to move—if for no more reason than I'm nae longer able to rest whilst I carry these jewels."

Robbie sat up straighter, rubbing his eyes in an effort to ban the sleep from them. "Aye, and I feel the harp is restless too. And the magic—don't fear this, please, but it stirs in me still. Out on the seaway, it drives me onward. There's a destination, and thus far it seems to agree with your plan to make for Staffa, the cave there, and the MacQuarrie. Do we head back out, then? Do ye think MacLeod's boats have given up the chase?"

Ian's brows had drawn inwards, and his mouth was set grim. He turned to meet Robbie's gaze. "The magic, is it? I'd wish I ne'er heard such a word, if it weren't for the single fact it brought ye to my shores." He took a deep breath and let it go, his troubled expression relaxing as he turned his attention to the practicalities of their present circumstances. "As to heading back onto the water, nae. I think not. That fog isn't enough to keep us from being seen, and I think 'tis nae safe to say MacLeod has left off chasing us. We'll need to go overland."

Surprise brought Robbie fully awake. "And leave the boat?"

Ian's wry smile told Robbie what he was going to say before he said it. "Nae. We'll portage."

Robbie stood, stretched, reached for a crust of bread and the waterskin. After he'd chewed and swallowed and slaked his thirst, he turned to Ian, but he didn't get a chance to speak.

"Now don't look so worried. 'Tis nae far. Only five miles or so. True, we canna take the coast route—too visible, but there's a passage between the high ridges that should serve. Your wound's well healed. Two hours, maybe three with rest. Aye?"

Somehow, Robbie knew it wouldn't be so easy as Ian made it sound. He sent Ian a smile that meant surrender and said, "Aye, I suppose so."

Chapter Fifteen

The portage across Canna was everything Robbie had hoped it wouldn't be. The boat was only about twelve feet long, but it was clinker-built, and with mast and sail lashed on, it weighed, Robbie guessed, at least thirteen stone. Ian could lift that weight with ease, and Robbie could lift it with planning and a little more trouble, but carrying its odd shape over rough ground for five miles was not easy even for both of them together.

They managed it nonetheless, first dragging the boat back to the shallows until they reached an easier passage between bluffs. There, they lashed the oars so they could rest on Ian's shoulders as he carried the boat upturned, and then Ian lifted the back of the boat to rest on a tall rock, so he could get under it. Robbie shouldered the packs and took some of the weight of the prow, carrying it in front of him and trying to see around Ian and the bulk of the boat to know what was coming.

The route took them from shore to shore via a fairly level passage between scattered uplands and tall stones, but level didn't mean smooth. They had to rest frequently, and by the time they made it to the far end of the island, the sun was on its way down in the west. Ian had what looked like permanent imprints of the oars on his shoulders, and Robbie limped. Not only had he stubbed toes and banged shins numerous times, but the wound in his thigh—which had been healed to a red, slightly puckered stripe—had reopened, and a dark stain spread once more across the rough cloth of his breeks.

Ian clearly worried about Robbie's condition, but the truth was he was in no shape to do much about it. He pulled Robbie down to sit in the sand against a thick chunk of bleached driftwood. "Sit here wi' me, lad. We've got to stop. Rest. Eat."

"We're there, though, right, Ian?" Robbie tried to force his eyes open wide enough, long enough to take in the landscape, but he was certain that bright path the sun made was the glimmer on water.

"We are, but as much as I'd love to toss our boat onto the water and row south, I'm afraid I can go no further. We'll stay as secret as we can behind the hillock and hope nobody gets too curious." He handed Robbie some of the dried fish and fruit from his pack. "All the food one could want lying on the beach in need of naught but shelling and a fire, but I'm too beat down to do it, and so are you. Let's eat, then I'll look at that wound and see if there's aught to do about it before we sleep."

Robbie only grunted, chewing a tough dried apple. By the time he'd finished eating his handful of food, Ian had laid his aside and fallen asleep. Nature called Robbie, though, so he rose from the ground—which wasn't easy. Not sure why, he picked up the harp and held it to his side as he made his way from camp. Once he'd had a good piss, he picked up the silent harp again, thinking he'd just wander to the shore and cool his aching feet, feeling quite safe in the orange glow of the day's farewell.

He watched the tide recede for a time and then stood gazing into a large tide pool. Brilliant purple-red anemones tucked in corners betwixt stones on the outer edges, and small crabs scampered here and there, but in the centre all he could see was soft sand, lifting slightly with the faint movement of the water. He didn't think about stepping in, or sitting, or curling up in that aqueous bed; he just did it. He placed the harp outside the pool, leaning it against a large black stone. The tide pulling away took his cares and his conscious mind and left him with only sleep.

The stones and sand of the tide pool transmitted the rhythm of the shore's small waves to him, and he dreamed first of Ian's arms, Ian's heartbeat. But as the sun sank lower and the breeze flattened to nothing, the smell of salt and steady beat of the water's pulse pulled him into a deeper peace. In his dream, bodiless once more in the ocean's depths, he drifted, only aware enough to appreciate contentment.

Something shifted in his mind, though, and Ian's face appeared before him. Robbie opened his mouth to speak, ready to share his quiet joy with the man he loved, but darkness clouded Ian's image. The sea towed Robbie under and away from the image of Ian, and he realised the empty sea was not what he wanted. *Not peace*, he thought. *Oblivion*. Above all things, now, he did not want to let the waters take him away from Ian. He struggled into his flesh-and-bone body, felt the pulse of his blood coursing through his veins, searched with all his being to catch hold of something, anything that would keep him near life and Ian.

He started to drown.

All at once, Ian's strong arms cradled him against his warm chest, lifted him from the sea and the dream. Robbie's dream and waking worlds collided and mixed and didn't sort themselves until Ian's rough voice broke in.

"Robbie! What are ye doing here lying in the pool? The tide was about to cover ye over and take ye from me for good! Can ye grab up your harp? Though truth, I'd be just as happy to let the sea have it!"

"No!" Robbie choked the word out and reached out blindly, but his hand nevertheless made contact with the harp. He picked it up and held it weightless as Ian carried him away from the hungry tide.

Ian set him on his feet and gave him a perplexed look, his eyes narrowed and brow wrinkled as if Robbie posed a great puzzle. "What were ye thinking?"

"I...I don't remember. I only meant to sleep, perhaps?"

"Aye, well ye slept all right, and nearly stayed asleep for all time to come!"

Robbie drew away, unable to face both his own fear and what he thought was Ian's anger, but Ian grabbed hold of his hand, stopping him.

"Wait, now. I'm not angry wi' ye. It frightened me, is all. Come, you're all covered wi' salt, and I'm still sour wi' sweat. I found a fresh burn just o'er that rise there."

Robbie breathed easier, flashed a ghost of a smile, and entwined his fingers with Ian's. They stepped away, Robbie still carrying the harp, holding it to his side with his free arm.

The small burn was open to the rising moonlight and glimmered silver and blue as it bubbled past a clutter of fist-sized stones. Ian began to strip, and Robbie followed suit. Naked, he washed himself down and then dragged his clothes through the clean water several times, pounded them with a stone, and wrung as much wet as he could from them. He did the same with Ian's.

"We'll likely have to put them on wet," he said. "But do ye think a fire will be all right? It's not awfully cold, but..."

"Aye...a fire."

Robbie turned at the growling sound of his whisper and saw Ian's lean, muscled body gleaming damp and clean in the silvered light, saw his rising sex, the deep rise and fall of his chest, his half-closed eyelids. "Ah," Robbie breathed, his own body responding in excitement. "That wasn't exactly the flame I was thinking of, Ian, but yes."

He bent to gather up their clothing, but Ian took it from him.

"Get your harp, man. We'll be making that fire ye asked for. More ways than one."

Robbie heard the humour in Ian's voice, and it made him glad, recognising something he loved about Ian— nearly always he could find a smile. Robbie smiled too as he tripped along, doing his best to keep up with Ian's determined, long-legged stride. Robbie leaned the harp against the overturned boat, which was propped on a waist-high stone, and took possession of the bundle of clothes. While Ian gathered stones, tinder, and sticks of driftwood, and drilled and blew a fire into existence, Robbie spread the clothes over the boat's hull, facing the flames. Both of them worked fast, anxious to move on to a more pleasant activity, and Robbie kept glancing over to catch glimpses of Ian's body.

"For such a small fire, it's throwing a lot of heat," Robbie said, surprised at the throaty quality of his voice.

Ian turned towards him, his smile all but wicked now, "It is at that," he said.

He opened his arms wide, either beckoning Robbie into them or putting his fine body on display in the moonlight. Robbie took advantage, first drinking in Ian's beauty, letting his hand stray to his own cock, which had filled so hard it threatened to weigh him down. After seconds, he stepped in close to Ian, planting his body bare skin to skin and stretching up to meet his waiting lips. As the kiss deepened, Ian's arms wrapped Robbie tight and never loosened even as his hands travelled Robbie's back and arse.

"Moment," Ian said, breaking away. "Wait."

He nearly ran to the rocks where they'd propped the overturned boat, pulled out from under it the larger of the packs, and ran back to Robbie seconds later, holding the small packet of whale fat, a self-satisfied smile flashing in his eyes. He laughed aloud, wrapped Robbie in an exultant hug, and spun him around. After setting him back on his feet, he gently pushed Robbie back to arm's length.

"I should be too tired for this, Rob, but you fill me up with a need that will nae let me rest. I want ye now, and I mean to take ye, if ye'll be having me."

Robbie's breath rushed out, and instead of answering, he dropped to his knees and pushed his nose deep into the red-gold hair surrounding Ian's engorged shaft, drinking in the sweet musk of his arousal. Turning his head to the side, he licked along Ian's shaft to the smooth, slicked crown, the smell and taste of the liquid he harvested making him want to stroke himself to orgasm as fast as possible. He did stroke himself a few times as he continued to enjoy sucking and licking Ian's perfect cock, but resisted the urge to rush things. He concentrated a while on the lovely ridge around the head of Ian's prick and then, with just the tip in his mouth, sucked as his tongue played against the ultrasensitive triangle of soft flesh just under the opening.

Gods how he wanted the taste of Ian's seed! When Ian gasped and made as if to pull him away, he pulled back.

"Please, Ian."

Ian groaned and gave in, cradling Robbie's head and letting him have his way. Robbie laved and sucked with abandon, and then took Ian in as deeply as he could, sucking while closing the muscles of his throat around Ian's erection.

"Ach! No," Ian said, but instantly changed his mind. "Yes! Yes, Rob!" A long loud groan accompanied his bucking, spurting orgasm as Robbie curled the front of his tongue under the shaft and let the creamy liquid coat the back of it, savouring the sensation, the heat, and the salty, bittersweet flavour.

Ian recovered for only a moment before dragging Robbie up to suck his own taste off his tongue. "So good," he said, "but that won't be all." He pushed Robbie gently until he leaned against the boat. "I'll be having my turn too. When I'm hard again, I'll be taking your fine arse."

He kissed Robbie's mouth hard, then moved his lips over his neck, breathed into his ears the word "sweet," stealing Robbie's breath completely. He moved to lay his tongue over Robbie's chest, biting at the nipples and then licking them as if in healing. Trailing kisses, he travelled down the centre of Robbie's belly, stopped to dip into his navel, then moved on. When he got to Robbie's straight, slender erection, he gave his man the same treatment he'd received.

But Robbie wasn't shy, and when he got too close to the brink of orgasm, he said, "Stop! I want you to fuck me 'til I come!"

"Ach, and that's done it, then! Feel this, man. Ready."

Ian took Robbie's hand and closed it around his hard shaft, and Robbie let out a delighted breath.

"Will ye turn around then? I've a mind to fuck ye hard o'er this boat."

"Yes," Robbie said. He flipped over without hesitation, leaving only enough room to insert a hand to cradle and stroke his own cock. He couldn't remember ever having anticipated anything with such impatient joy, but he didn't have to wait long.

Ian's greased fingers plied his arse, and then his hard, slicked cock pushed in, neither too hard nor too slow. Robbie delighted in the feel—half burn, half sweet stretch—of his arse being opened.

"All of it," he said when he felt Ian hesitate.

He got a chuckle and a "patience, man" from Ian in return, but soon after, Ian began to move, setting up a sweet rhythm that somehow timed itself perfectly with Robbie's need. The steady, repeated prod against his gland brought him first to quiet bliss, then to a place of roaring need.

"Oh," he said. "Almost."

"Let it come, then. Let me feel it." Ian leaned down and pushed his arms under Robbie's chest, wrapping his hands up around his shoulders. Using that leverage to fuck hard and steady, he breathed close to Robbie's ear. "Now, man! With me!"

In time with the fucking, Robbie pulled at his own cock once, twice, only three more times before bliss exploded into euphoria. He shuddered through his orgasm, his arse clenching Ian's cock in a hard rhythm, his cum filling his hand, even as Ian's rhythm broke and hot sperm shot against the inner walls of Robbie's arse.

Ian collapsed for a moment against Robbie, and though he was heavy, Robbie relished his weight lying over him like a shield against every single thing. With kisses and care, Ian broke away, and Robbie waited, weak, dazed, and happy, while Ian spread the sail over the sand beneath the boat.

Then Ian was beside him, leaning over him with a deep kiss. "Ach," he said. "I love ye, Rob." He picked Robbie up in his strong arms and laid him down on that makeshift bed under the boat and crawled in beside him.

Feeling Ian's warmth surround him, his breath play against his hair, his heartbeat tap a rhythm against his back as they spooned towards slumber, Robbie whispered, "I love you, too, Ian." He wasn't sure if he heard the harp whisper in agreement, or if it was only the beginning of a sweet dream.

*

Ian grabbed for Robbie's hand, too late. He watched in horror as Robbie sank into the water, the sea reclaiming what it thought rightfully its. "He's mine, not yours!"

The boat lurched to one side as Ian leaned into the water, the upper part of his body partially submerged as he hunted frantically for Robbie. But he was already nowhere to be seen. Someone or something tugged at Ian's kilt, trying to get purchase to pull him from the water. Ian fought, but to no avail. Wind tugged at his hair, yanking at his braid so tightly he yelled out in pain. Seawater flowed into his mouth. He coughed, spluttering to disgorge it.

The boat tipped, throwing him into the sea, then upended on top of him. He pushed up with his hands, frantically trying to dislodge it, but the boat stubbornly sank lower, taking him with it.

"Ian..."

He heard Robbie's voice as though from a distance.

"Ian." Strong arms wrapped around him, reclaiming him.

Ian coughed, his breath coming in gasps. The water had disappeared, yet the wind still tugged at him, taunting him, although now it was an empty threat. He leaned into Robbie's embrace. The wind howled around them, enraged that its intentions had been thwarted. Ian forced his eyes open to meet Robbie's concerned gaze. He struggled to sit, realisation crashing into him.

For a dream, it had felt so real, the malice of the elements not easily shaken.

"Aye, I'm here." Ian wrapped his arms around Robbie, holding him close. "Sorry if I woke ye."

"You were crying out in your sleep. I was worried for you." Robbie leaned his forehead against Ian's. "I am yours," he whispered. "I'm staying for as long as you'll have me."

Ian smiled at the fierceness of Robbie's words and his tone. "I have ye now, and that's not going to change."

Above them, rain pounded against the boat. Ian peered around their shelter, yet instead of the dawn he expected, it was still dark. He shivered, despite the warmth of the wind, trying to shake the remnants of the ghosts from his dream. "We're in for a storm. Best shift the boat crosswise before the wind tries to rip it in two. We'll nae get far with a broken boat." He shrugged on his clothes and handed Robbie's to him.

Robbie nodded, and as soon as they'd dressed, they turned the boat together, using nearby rocks to secure it in place. By the time they'd finished, they were both wet to the skin, but thankfully, their clothing had protected them from being too badly scraped against the rocks and the rough wood of the underside of the boat. Ian crawled into the wee hiding place they'd made between the boat and the rocks, and motioned for Robbie to join him.

"The storm will take a while longer to blow out, but at least it won't harm us here." Robbie stared into the distance, his eyes glazed as though he was looking at something not quite there.

"Too much wind to light a fire." Ian kissed Robbie's brow, needing to feel skin against his lips, and proof that he was real and they were together. "At least it's not freezing cold."

He reached under the bow of the boat, hunting until his fingers connected with his pack. He removed the parcel of food and placed it on the ground between them. Robbie helped himself to a piece of the dried fish and chewed thoughtfully, growing quiet. He'd left Ian the bigger piece. Ian broke the piece in two and took part of it. Their supplies were dwindling. They'd have to replenish them before taking to the water once more, as they wouldn't be able to afford to linger in one place for too long.

Robbie finished his fish and offered Ian the final apple. Ian cut it in half with his dirk and shared it between them. Robbie shuffled forward and leaned his head against Ian's shoulder, a tiny sliver of juice trailing down the side of his mouth. Ian kissed him, then licked the juice. He began to smile, but it changed to a frown before it half-formed.

"Ye didn't wince when we moved the boat, Rob," he said slowly, thinking through the words before speaking.

"And I'm not seeing any fresh blood on your breeks. Surely your wound is still troubling ye." He doubted the nasty cut on Robbie's thigh would have closed up again that quickly, not with the way it looked last time he'd seen it.

Robbie paused mid-bite. He straightened and flexed his leg without any effort. "You're right. It does feel better. I didn't notice—was busy helping you move the boat. And last night..." He grinned. "I was a little too distracted by you to be thinking about it."

"When was the last time it pained you?" Ian painted a picture of Robbie's naked body in his mind, but his memory skimmed over the very detail he wanted. Truth be told, he'd been focused on another part of Robbie's body at the time.

"It still ached after we stopped here and had our first meal." Robbie frowned. He glanced in the direction of the sea, although the boat blocked his view. "I only meant to rest in that tide pool. I remember laying the harp by the side to keep it safe, and then... It was so easy to sleep. The sea wanted me."

He fixed his gaze on Ian, determination dancing in his eyes like a fire so ferocious Ian was in parts taken aback, and wanting to embrace it.

"I thought of you, Ian. Of how I wanted you, even though it would be so easy to give in to the sea again."

"When I found ye I thought ye were drowning." Ian took Robbie's hand in his and squeezed it tightly. He didn't attempt to hide the echo of fear he'd felt, didn't worry Robbie might see it. "I thought I'd lost ye to that damn pool. That it had found a way to rip ye from me."

"I was drowning. I think..." Robbie paused. When he continued, he sounded more certain. "You saved me."

Ian crinkled his brow. "That doesn't explain your wound." He rolled up one leg of Robbie's breeks. Instead of the ugly gash he expected to see, Robbie's skin was already partly healed, the different shade of new pink overwriting what had been there before. "It's healing, Rob. And a lot faster than it should."

Fascinated, he leaned in for a closer look and touched it gingerly, ready to withdraw if Robbie showed any sign of discomfort. "I dinna understand," he said finally. "Ye say the sea wanted you, so why would it heal you and then spit you out?"

The words sounded crazy said out loud, yet it was the only explanation he could think of. Robbie's long sleep was magic of sorts, and his wound healing could only be more of the same. A short time ago, Ian would have recoiled at the idea, but now...

"It didn't spit me out," Robbie said quietly. "I didn't want to stay. And...as I think back on it... I know you won't like hearing this, but the witch, she told me I had a bit of my own magic. Maybe that helped me break free. Or at least it helped me call you. You pulled me out."

"Aye, and I would again too." Ian let out a long breath, before saying hesitantly, "Unless you didn't want me to."

"I want you to. Always." Robbie kissed Ian with some of that same fierceness he'd show before. "I don't want to go back to endless sleep and dreams that might never come true. I'm grateful for the healing, but I wouldn't be if losing hope—losing you—was the cost."

"You've already paid whatever it thinks you owe." Ian cleared his throat. "Listen to me, will ye. I'm talking about the curse like it's alive." He shivered. "I dinna ken if it's some kind of ghostie, this curse of yours, but it needs to know its place, and keep the hell away from you. You've made your choice, and it's done."

He wanted to raise his voice, to shout above the wind to tell the damn thing Robbie was his, and this magic could go to hell, but stopped himself in time. While he doubted Campbell and his men were out in the storm, it would be foolish to reveal his and Robbie's position. "I've been thinking about our route to Staffa. As soon as this storm blows out, we should get started."

Robbie nodded, yet seemed distracted.

Nevertheless, Ian pressed on. If Robbie had anything to add, Ian expected he'd do so in due course. "If we head east to Rum, then south, hugging the coastline, we'll be as safe as we can be, and more likely to find food, and somewhere to shelter along the way."

He drew a rough map in the dirt using the tip of his dirk. "Galmisdale on Eigg, then Muck, down the coast to Ormsaigmore."

Ian dragged his dirk from each circle to the next, stopping at each place as he mentioned place names, then marking spots on the larger shape he'd drawn to represent the Highlands. He paused for a moment, thinking of Glenfinnan and wondering if he'd ever see it again, before continuing, "Then Mull, and across to Staffa."

Robbie frowned. "Do you trust me, Ian?"

"Aye, I do." Despite his words, Ian felt unease bubbling up inside him. "Why?"

"I have a strong feeling we should launch the boat now, and set out."

"If we wait, the storm—"

"We'll be safe, despite the storm. I know it." The words tumbled from Robbie. "Since we left Duntulm, I've had this feeling that I'm—we're—being guided. It's the reason we've been lucky so far. We've been safe here, haven't we?"

"Aye." Ian couldn't help but nod, yet… "I trust ye, Rob, but…you're thinking the magic is the reason we found this shelter, and that it will keep ye safe?"

"Keep *us* safe. The witch, she bound me with magic to the sea, and I can sense it."

"It's not having you back," Ian grumbled. "How do we know it's not using this to try and get ye to return to it?"

"This feels different." Robbie used his own knife to draw in the dirt. "When we're on the sea, I feel the magic more strongly, like it's a part of me. We need to find the key if we're to end my curse, but we need to stay safe while doing this. Not only that but we need to stay together. It's the only way."

"Ending your curse won't be without risk." Ian wanted to believe what Robbie thought to be true, yet he couldn't ignore the fear that he'd be left watching Robbie claimed once more by the sea, and helpless to do anything about it.

"Yes, I know that." Robbie shrugged and glanced at the lines he'd made in the dirt.

Ian's eyes widened as he realised what Robbie had drawn—a direct route across the sea to Staffa.

"We go south to Staffa," Robbie continued. "I don't think it's a coincidence that this Northeast wind is blowing the very direction we need to go."

"If we don't end up at the bottom of the sea first." Ian shook his head. "The boat isn't that big. We won't last long out there."

Robbie smiled. "You're forgetting something—the storm will favour us. Mayhap we'll travel in the calm at its eye, or else the wind and waves just won't hinder us. Either way, it gives us an advantage over Campbell and MacLeod. They won't dare launch their boats in this weather. They'll be waiting for it to pass."

"Aye, that's true. They wouldn't think us idiot enough to go out in it either." Ian cringed at the hurt expression on Robbie's face, but it was too late to take his words back.

"Is that what you think I am, Ian?" Robbie asked softly. "An idiot? For believing in magic I know to be true, and risking our lives in a storm on a sea I know will keep us safe."

Ian caught Robbie's arm, and met his gaze intently, holding it for a few moments. "You're no idiot, Robbie Elliot. I might not trust this magic of yours, but as I told you before, I trust you."

He bit his lip, his mind racing, a sudden exhilaration warming his body. "If we wait here until the storm is over, we'll be easy pickings for Campbell. I think you're right. We need to do something they'd never do, something they'd never expect us to do. I'm going to take a leap of faith, and follow you on this. It's a huge risk, but there's some chance in it. I've been looking at this the way I've always known, but I've seen enough to believe in your magic, to know something unnatural is at work."

He leaned in and kissed Robbie hard. "But this sea of yours...if it tries to take you back, I'll fight it, I swear, with everything I am."

Chapter Sixteen

Ian clung to the boat, his muscles aching as he tried to pull it towards him, to ease it onto the beach on the eastern shore of Staffa Isle. The wind howled as the water beat down on him, the sky working in tandem with the sea to whip the boat from his grasp. A wave crashed into him, and he spat saltwater from his mouth.

"Leave it," Robbie yelled above the wind. He grabbed his precious harp. "We can't win this fight, Ian. We're close enough to where we need to be. We don't need the boat now, so just grab what ye most need, and let's get out of the waves before we're dragged back to sea with it."

Instead of wasting energy in a reply, Ian gritted his teeth. If they lost the boat, they'd be stuck on Staffa waiting for Campbell to find them. Another powerful gust yanked the boat from his grasp, claiming it for the sea.

"Aye, you're working together, I swear." He muttered the words and strode out into the waves, but the tide was already taking the boat out of reach with its precious cargo. He caught up with it, barely, and managed to grab the jewels and a sack full of supplies before another gust ripped away any hope of retrieving anything else.

At least they wouldn't starve, and he hadn't lost the jewels. Yet why did he feel as though he'd failed?

The wind tugged at his plaidie. Ian tried to grab it, but his hands were already full. "Ach, no!" He could only watch as it blew towards the sea, a victory flag for the enemy pursuing them.

The water lashed against his thighs as he stomped back to shore, the landwards journey a little easier as he was walking with the wind instead of against it.

Robbie waited for him at the shoreline, cradling his harp close to his chest. "We're here. Out of the water and safe."

"Aye, but we can't stay on this isle forever." The warmth of Robbie's lips against his cheek reminded Ian that while they were together, they still had hope. "It's a good hiding place, but I thought the same of Skye."

"The sea wouldn't have brought us if we weren't meant to be here. And ye said there'll be MacQuarrie people on this isle—allies, or close to it." Robbie craned his head and pointed to a narrow path leading around the side of the cliff face. "That is the way we're meant to go if we want to go into An Uaimh Bhinn." He studied the terrain in front of them. "The island seems to be made of columns that fit together. I've never seen anything like it before."

"I remember the first time I was here. I thought it wasn't like any isle I'd been to before either."

Most of the rocks on what Ian wasn't sure he'd call a beach were a decent enough size to stand on—flat, and joined together to form an uneven but solid mass. The path itself would be manageable although it wasn't wide enough for them to walk side by side.

"The cave is easy enough to find, if my memory of it is right, but once we're across the rocks, we'll need to climb upwards, off the beach, as we head towards the southern tip of the isle. Then we come back down to a path over those columns at the shore. They lead right into the cave. Though I'm nae sure that's where we should go. There's other hiding places on this island. Lots of them, as I remember."

Robbie swung the harp onto his back, looping the decaying leather strap over his shoulder. "I *am* sure. We're meant to go into An Uaimh Bhinn."

"Aye?" Ian searched Robbie's face for a sign of doubt but found none. "Your magic is telling ye so, then, I'd guess?"

Robbie nodded and gave a small shrug as if to say he was helpless against the demands of the curse. But then he explained. "I do think it's the magic leading me, but I think it means we could find the way to beat it once and for all inside that cave."

Ian set his shoulders, resigned. The rain was beginning to ease, although the wind still tugged at their clothing and hair. A chill hit his buttocks as the bottom of his kilt pulled up and slapped across the small of his back.

"Do you want to lead, Ian? As you know the way?" Despite the innocent-sounding question, Robbie's lips quirked into a smile. "And I can carry one of the sacks, if you'd want a hand free."

Ian glanced behind them, wanting to satisfy himself as much as he could that they were alone, but he couldn't see anyone, only a movement in the distance, at the top of one of the cliffs. He squinted for a moment, then relaxed as a couple of birds flew over them before returning to what was probably their nest. There'd been puffins on his last visit, but that had been later in the year, so he hadn't been sure he'd encounter them again. Strange-looking creatures they were, unlike anything he'd seen elsewhere.

"Aye, I'll lead." That way, he could scout ahead for any danger. Ian hesitated then handed Robbie the sack holding their supplies. He put the other down for a moment and hooked the bottom of his kilt into the material at his waist so it wouldn't blow up any further.

Robbie made a frustrated noise, and Ian couldn't help but grin. "We need our wits about us. I don't need ye distracted by my arse."

"Lead on, then. You can make up for my disappointment later." Robbie glanced behind them. "I'll keep an eye out this way, as you're doing the same ahead."

Despite Ian having his back to Robbie, he could feel him following, although as they got further from the sea, Robbie's steps started to slow. "Are ye all right?" Ian turned at Robbie's heavy and laboured breathing.

"I will be." Robbie waved Ian forward.

Ian retraced his steps and reached for the sack Robbie carried.

Robbie tried to hold on to the satchel. "I can manage—"

"You're already weighed down by that harp of yours." Ian pretended he'd forgotten the thing didn't seem to weigh anything when Robbie carried it. He took the pack forcefully from Robbie's hands. "I can carry both, and we've still got a fair climb ahead of us."

He peered upwards. From the distance, it hadn't seemed as though the journey would be that long, but now the narrow path seemed to go on forever, although, logically, he knew it couldn't. The last time he'd been here with his granda, he was a small lad, and he and the old man had made the climb together, then walked along the narrow path. Ian had run ahead in his excitement, so had to wait for his granda to catch up.

Rocky cliffs tufted with tough grass towered over them to the left, the sea crashing over rocks to their right.

He'd feel safer once they were out of sight and couldn't be seen by an approaching boat, although anyone who knew the area would try to land on the eastern side of the isle as they'd done, or risk being dashed against the rocks. The existence of An Uaimh Bhinn was only known to a few, yet he couldn't shake the feeling that—magical call or no—they were walking towards danger rather than away from it.

Finally, Ian could see the entrance of the cave just ahead. It rose high to meet with the cliffs and reminded him of a castle entrance hall. Or a house for giants as if the giant himself held it upright on his shoulders. It wasn't the first time he'd seen the cave, yet the sight of it—and what he knew lay inside—still filled him with the awe. He wanted to watch Robbie's expression once he discovered the inside of it for himself.

"It seems to have a magic of its own." Robbie took a step back and tilted his head to one side. "I can feel the music in this place," he continued softly. "Like calling to like. We'll find what we seek here, Ian, I'm sure of it."

"I'm more concerned about keeping safe...and that's beginning to look like a problem."

Ian pointed down to the foot of the cave mouth. The cave floor was covered as always by a deep channel, but it seemed the tide at present was high—higher than usual if he didn't miss his guess. All but the tallest of the rock columns that usually formed a path into the cave were covered with roiling brine.

Robbie looked down where Ian pointed, gasped, and nearly pitched forward.

Ian caught him and found his skin clammy to the touch; he looked so pale Ian wondered how he was still upright. Guilt rolled over him like a wave. Why hadn't he taken more notice of how unwell Robbie had seemed earlier?

"Ye don't look well." Ian held up his hand to shush Robbie when it looked as though he was going to protest.

Ian adjusted his grip on the sack he carried and slipped his free arm around Robbie, taking as much of his weight as he could. Together, they walked through the cave entrance, Ian carefully helping Robbie to climb up to the rock-strewn path.

Water flowed between them and the opposite wall of the cave. Ian took an instinctive step back when a large wave lapped at his feet.

"We need to get further in and higher up. There's a cave entrance we can climb into up top. It isn't An Uaimh Bhinn, but if we follow the passage, we end up in another fair-sized cave right next to it. I guess there's no reason to choose An Uaimh Bhinn over that one, aye? The passage going in is narrow and steep though. Do you think ye can manage if I go first and help you?"

Robbie nodded. He leaned against the wall, his breath coming in shallow rattles. "The wound hurts, but it isn't too bad. The sea's been kind enough to help it heal, I think. Wears me out a bit dealing with it, that's all." He took a breath as if he wanted to say something else, but after he stayed quiet for a minute or so, Ian spoke again.

"It's been a long while since I was here, and I was but a child, but I remember the caves—they fascinated me. We're almost to the entrance from the hill, and we'll follow it through. The lower cave opens on the beach next to An Uaimh Bhinn. Ye can stay out of sight of the entrance and rest there while I go for help. There'll be a MacQuarrie outpost somewhere on Staffa. I just need to find it."

When Robbie still said nothing, Ian turned to look at him. Robbie's brows were scrunched together as if something worried him, or perhaps he puzzled at something. "What is it? Something's troubling you, that much is clear."

"I can feel something, here... Maybe something about the magic? I'm not..."

"Ach, and that's some awful news! Of course there's still something left undone about that curse... Could it be your key? Maybe it's...I don't know, calling to ye, or such?"

They'd come to the opening in the hillside that led into the cave, and Ian stooped to the ground to enter. "Sorry, this is a bit tight for the first few feet. I'll go slow so ye can stay close, and I'll help ye out when we come out below. Ye'll be all right?"

"I don't like it a lot, but, yes, I'll be fine."

A few scrapes and grunts later, Ian dropped to the cave floor, turned to catch Robbie up, and placed him down gently to keep him from jarring his injured leg. It was damp in the cave—water ran through the centre of it— and dark. The seaside entrance was lower and smaller than that of An Uaimh Bhinn and a few hundred feet away, so the afternoon glow was faint. Once Ian's eyes adjusted to the dim light, he glanced back at Robbie just in time to see him wince and pull his hand away from his leg coated in blood.

"Your wound is bleeding again," Ian said. "It's seeped through your breeks."

Robbie shrugged. "I thought I'd been healed, but it must have been temporary." Fear danced across his eyes. "Ian, if we can't find the key..."

"We'll find it." Ian had to believe they couldn't have come this far only to lose each other. Otherwise, why had

Robbie's magic led them here? He'd heard stories about how ghosts liked to play tricks on unsuspecting folk, but this wasn't like the magic in the old stories. This was real. He seen enough to know that, and he knew Robbie wouldn't lie to him.

"Go, Ian. Ye need to find MacQuarrie's people. It's what we came here for. Take the jewels with you. Maybe ye'll need to give them to MacQuarrie, if he's got instructions from your uncle the laird. You did say he's a friend of the MacDonald." Robbie sounded weary, his voice flat. "By the time ye come back, I'll be rested. And if I still need help then, maybe you'll have your hands free."

Ian hesitated, torn between moving on with the plan, and not wanting to leave Robbie alone. In the finish, practicality won out. Robbie was right. "Do you want me to take your harp?"

"I'll keep it. It's no weight to me, and...I'll just keep it." Robbie slid the harp around to his front. He cradled it, holding it tightly to him like a bairn.

Ian still made no move. Finally, he threw up his hands, exasperated, and exclaimed, "Ach, I hate to leave ye like this!" Moving quickly now, he retrieved the sack holding the jewels. "I'm going to find the outpost; then I'll be back for ye."

"What happens if you can't find MacQuarrie?" Robbie's eyes were bright, a little too much so. Ian brushed his fingers across Robbie's forehead, but the lad didn't seem overly hot. Too cold, if anything. Unfortunately, they didn't have any blankets, and Ian had lost his plaidie, so he couldn't leave that with Robbie either.

Ian took the now empty waterskin from Robbie. "I'll head west over the water and find help that way." He sighed. "We do need help. The supplies will only last so long, and—"

"We have no boat," Robbie pointed out, agreeing. "The sea is still too rough to swim, and it's too far." He shivered. "Promise you'll come back to me, Ian. If ye go wandering we may not meet again."

"Aye. I promise. We'll have to hope I find the outpost—or the boat." Ian reluctantly stood. The sooner he started his climb to the top of the isle, the sooner he'd be back. He turned at the entrance of the cave, his expression softening when he met Robbie's gaze. The lad was tough. He'd wait for Ian; Ian was sure of it. "I promise."

"I'll be as quick as I can."

Ian slid the cloth bag holding the jewels into his sporran and set off. After going to the beach entrance of the cave and discovering the tide still quite high, he struggled back out through the narrow, steep passage to the hilltop. The clouds had apparently dropped a rain shower on Staffa as they passed towards the mainland, and some of the rocks were slippery. In a hurry, Ian almost lost his balance.

"Slowly does it," he murmured. After a few false steps he found a rhythm and soon reached the summit of Staffa Island.

Ian took several deep breaths and rested his hands on his knees. The climb had been harder than he expected, especially with the wind battering him from all sides. His hands were bruised and red, but he'd made it. The way down would be easier. He hoped.

He lay down on the grass, his thoughts racing as he took a few moments to rest. He needed to work out a way to find MacQuarrie or one of his men. MacQuarrie might be cautious, but he was loyal enough to his friends. Ian still had the jewels, and he could use that to ensure MacQuarrie contacted his uncle, Alistair. With Fergus dead, how long would it take Alistair to realise something was amiss? Ian had hoped Fergus had a way of getting word to Alistair, yet the old man had died months ago, and no one had come to check on either of them.

He shoved aside the thought that his uncle had abandoned him on Skye. Ian had to believe someone would come for him. His uncle would have some kind of plan in place in case something happened to him. Alistair *always* had a plan, and the treasure was important.

Ian could only hope luck was on their side. Or the magic surrounding Robbie and his curse worked for them, instead of against them. That harp wanted Robbie as much as Ian did. It had to realise it could lose the lad if Campbell got his hands on him.

Ach, no point in thinking the worst. It will be here soon enough.

Determination fuelling his need to act, Ian got to his feet, guilty he'd taken the time to rest. He had to keep going, to find help. He scanned the way ahead yet couldn't see anything apart from grass, buttercups, and sea birds. If MacQuarrie's men had any sense, they'd have kept their outpost well hidden—at least if they could find anything to hide it behind. With no trees or brush, it seemed just as likely they'd spot him first. He'd move cautiously, and be ready to surrender at the first sign of trouble, as he was more likely to get an audience with MacQuarrie that way. Depending on who was causing the trouble, of course, as he had no intention to giving himself up to Campbell, MacLeod, or anyone working for them.

Nevertheless, Ian drew his dirk. No harm in being prepared, aye, and despite Robbie's certainty they were where they should be, Ian wasn't so convinced. From what he'd seen, magic was complicated, and he suspected it could be leading them straight into a trap in order to reclaim its own.

As he turned to start walking, a flash of colour caught his eye. He spun on his heel. Even at this distance, he recognised the familiar tartan immediately. The plaidie he'd lost to the wind waved at him like a flag, caught fast by a pillar of rock.

He swore under his breath. If he'd seen it, it wouldn't be long before someone else— Too late! Not far from the flag, two ships anchored close to shore. Small rowboats were already heading towards the traitorous plaidie.

Why hadn't he seen them before?

The answer came quickly. Because he'd focused on what might happened instead of watching for what already had. He'd allowed himself to be distracted, something he'd promised himself he'd never do. His mind went instantly to what—or rather who—was most important to him.

Robbie.

Ian had left Robbie alone and too weak to defend himself, and Campbell knew his prey was here. He wouldn't rest until he found them.

Ian didn't have to imagine what Campbell might do to the lad. Campbell wouldn't care that Robbie didn't know where Ian had hidden the jewels. He'd take delight in hurting Robbie anyway.

To hell with finding MacQuarrie.

Ian headed back the way he'd come, praying the way back to Robbie was faster than the time he'd wasted climbing up.

*

By the time Ian reached the cave entrance, his heart was beating fast and sweat was pouring down his face. He didn't dare take time to rest when it could mean the difference between reaching Robbie in time or not.

He forced himself to slow his pace when he reached the uneven stone path. If he lost his footing and hurt himself, he'd be no use to Robbie. Trusting the sea to swallow the sound of loose rock crashing into it wasn't a good idea either. Not with the way the wind had taken his plaidie and given it to the sea to do with it what it wanted.

Listen to me. I'm treating both of them as though they're people with their own agendas, rather than nature, which does what it wants anyway.

The boats were moored at the east of the island. They still had to make their way south, as he and Robbie had. That gave them a small advantage, at least, although he'd already wasted too much time climbing back down from the headland.

The sound of his breathing, heavy with exertion, echoed through the cave. Pausing to take several deep breaths slowed it a little, but not enough.

What if Campbell was already here? What if Ian was too late?

He approached the wee sea cave cautiously, dirk in hand, pushing away thoughts of Robbie being held at knifepoint, unable to shout a warning.

Robbie could take care of himself.

But he'd looked so weak, almost a ghost.

Ian glanced around yet couldn't see anyone else. Surely if he could hear his own breathing, he'd hear someone else's as well?

He peered into the cave, his heart hammering in his chest. *Robbie, please be all right.* What if the sea had reclaimed Robbie while Ian was gone?

The sack of supplies stood in the corner.

Robbie was gone.

No sign of a struggle. Nothing else amiss.

Ian bit his lip. Stay calm. He could be…

"Robbie!" Ian whispered as loud as he dared. "Robbie, where are ye?"

No reply, but then Ian hadn't expected there would be. Perhaps Robbie had felt better and left the cave for some reason. Aye, that had to be it.

Forcing himself to calm, Ian methodically examined the cave. At the entrance, he found the edge of a footprint. Exactly the size and shape of the sole of Robbie's brogan.

If Ian hadn't passed him on the way, Robbie must have left by another route.

A narrow shelf of rock led to an alternate way down to the sea. Ian followed it as quickly as he dared, stopping in places to hug the side of the rock and jump to the next part of the path. He followed the trail across the beach— now a wet, sandy strip exposed by the ebbing tide. It led to the entrance of An Uaimh Bhinn. A sudden prickle of fear tightened Ian's scalp. He didn't *know* what would have drawn Robbie into this cave. But he could hear the music of the place even from where he stood, and it spoke of ghosts and magic.

Of a sudden, he was keenly aware of danger—not from anything dwelling in the cave, but dangers that must surely be on their way by sea. His first concern was Robbie and a long future filled with love, but that future might depend on victory for the Jacobite cause, or at least on the battle well fought. Robbie's harp and its strange key was only half the solution to their troubles. The treasure Ian carried in his sporran might well hold the other half, for his future with Rob, perhaps even for all Scotland.

He stepped over the uneven pillar-tops further into the cave.

"Ach!" Ian spit the word out just to hear something solid and familiar over the cave's humming tones, which seemed to drown him as if he'd walked into the sea itself. Struggling to keep his thoughts clear, he fought the urge to run to find Robbie, creeping so as to spy out a hiding place. He found one in a place where the cave wall curved back from the sea channel, widening the stone path. Close to the wall, a series of taller stones guarded a hollow niche.

"Aye, and there ye go, wee precious stones. Ye can abide here 'til I come for ye." *Or until someone does.*

He found a trio of loose stones without too much searching and laid them to hide the niche better, coming away satisfied that they looked haphazard, as if deposited by a rockfall.

Feeling much lighter on his feet, he made the sign of the cross. "Saints," he muttered and followed the stepped stones into the depths of An Uaimh Bhinn.

He was struck for a moment by the ethereal beauty of the place, but it didn't hold his attention for long. He came to where the cave ended in a black backsplash of basalt, spreading short arms to either side, and rounded the bend to the right.

Robbie stood on the stones in the furthest reach of the cave, his attention focused on something in the not quite still water at the end of the channel's reach. Ian felt his spirits lift at the sight of Robbie, but it didn't dispel his unease.

Why had Robbie left his safe, hidden place, and what had drawn him once more to the sea?

Chapter Seventeen

Robbie heard only the lap of the waves on the cave's rocks, and the more distant rush of the ever-moving sea. He smelled only the salt and mineral of stone and ocean, tinged perhaps with the sharp scent of hidden sea life. He saw only the clear waters in the almost still pool before him and the small, dark rectangle hovering over its sandy bottom. Yet something, some other sense he couldn't name alerted him when Ian rounded the curve of the sea channel into the deepest part of An Uaimh Bhinn. He wanted to speak, to call Ian's name, but when he tried, only breath rushed past his lips.

He closed his eyes like prayer, perhaps, and tried again. "Ian." Though he'd expected it, worked at it even, the sound of his voice and its distorted echo shocked him from his reverie, and he turned half around to face his lover.

"Robbie," Ian said on a rush of breath almost like a sob. "I thought I'd lost ye! What made ye clamber over the rocks to this place?"

Before Robbie could answer, Ian stepped closer and gazed into the eddy. His voice shook as if he had some sort of premonition when he asked, "Is it... Have ye found your key, then, lad?"

The smile Robbie gave Ian was small and gentle, and it calmed his own heart. "Aye. I believe I have. It's the box of ironwood, at the least, and I can't imagine the key would have escaped it."

When Ian gazed back at him, though, his brows were drawn together and his lips pursed. "How long have ye been standing here, then?"

Robbie shook his head and shrugged his shoulders for answer.

"Because, Rob, I don't understand why the key is still there in the water instead of in your hand."

The trepidation—the fear that had haunted Robbie until the smile he'd made for Ian had soothed it—returned like a hammer blow, starting his heart pounding fast and cruel. Short on breath, he croaked, "Because, Ian, look! It's deep, and the channel is open to the sea. I'm afraid if I go in, it will take me."

"Ach! I see. And nae, that's not a chance I'd take." Ian stood a moment, scratching at his chin as if he could pull his thoughts together by doing it. "I'll go in after it. The current isn't so strong."

He stepped in, finding a rock for purchase just inside the lip of the pool. Looking down to be sure of a safe path, he lifted his other foot, but before he completed the step, a wave came in and swished back out, clouding the pool with foam and sand. When it cleared, the box had moved further out in the channel.

"No!" Robbie's shout was panicked.

Ian turned to soothe him. "No worries, now. It's still within reach."

He took another step, and again the shadowy shape dragging the seabed—the ironwood box that contained the key to Robbie's harp and his only chance at a future— shot forward away from Ian and Robbie and towards the deeper, churning waters.

"No," Robbie repeated, this time not in panic but denial. "Ian, you can't. The magic won't let you near the key. I'll do it." He stopped, assessing the depth and distance. "If you'll hold my hand, I think I can reach it with my feet, drag it closer, then pick it up."

Instead of waiting for Ian to respond, he stepped off the lip of the pool directly into water up to his thighs, in a hurry now. He'd lifted his hand as he made his move, and Ian grasped it firmly. But when Robbie reached the end of his tether and stretched out a foot, he lacked more than a hand's breadth in reach. Straining made little difference. He turned back to Ian, who looked worried, or maybe heartbroken.

That's it. Ian needs me as much as I need him. So, for Ian...

Not giving Ian a chance to register what was happening, Robbie twisted free of his grip and dropped into a shallow dive, chasing the slow-moving box, determined to get it before it was out of reach forever. He had to swim, kicking hard to go deeper as the box dropped off the shelf where the quieter, pooling waters of the little eddy met the crazed, splashing waves of the main channel.

Deeper.

He latched on to the rock at the side of the channel, both to pull himself down and to keep from being dashed hard against it.

Deeper.

He released half the air in his lungs and resisted the urge to breathe. In the depths, the waves grew quiet, but a current—perhaps the tide—tugged at him, trying to pull him towards the sea. He fought it.

Deeper. Darker. His eyes assaulted by salt and moving sand, he could barely force them to stay open, barely make out the box that held all his hopes—and Ian's too. And he wanted so badly to surface, to breathe, to escape the ocean, but he *couldn't* let himself rise, couldn't give up.

And then all of a sudden it didn't matter so much. Time, a slow whirlpool somewhere above him, couldn't be measured. The box ceased moving away, floated towards him even, but it had lost its importance.

Why am I fighting the sea? I am *the sea, am I not?*

"Robbie!"

He heard the sound, a name, called from far above the cradling waters. It nagged at the peace he'd so recently found. Perhaps it was important? The moving black rectangle caught his eye, and he reached a hand out to caress the smooth, sea-polished wood. His fingers convulsed around the box, gripping it hard, and without meaning to, he pulled it close, suddenly aware of himself again and of a brilliant light shining into the water from above. He tilted his head back to look, and his body began to rise towards the light.

A familiar shape floated on the surface—his harp.

"Robbie!"

This time he knew the voice, knew the man who'd called his name—*his* name—and loved him. Loved Ian.

He would have spoken that name, it would have been sweet on his lips, but he had no breath. He was drowning.

A big, strong hand descended, pushing aside the floating harp, reaching for Robbie. He had no idea where he got the strength or the will or even the idea, but feebly, he raised his right hand, clutching the box close to his heart with his left. It was heavy, that ironwood box, as if it had absorbed all the weight of the vast ocean. Robbie *knew* that if he let his will to bring it up out of the water falter for even a second, the box would plunge to the bottom and take him with it. That's all he had to fight with: will. And will was forged and fired by the love he'd found with Ian.

He held on, and Ian found his wrist, clasped it, and pulled.

As Robbie broke the surface, Ian turned him onto his back, pulling him towards the uneven, flat-topped checkerboard palisades that lined the side of the cave. He came up underneath the harp, and for the barest moment, he felt the weight of the instrument as if the magic had been stolen from it, then the weight dissolved. A second later, perhaps less, black spiralled in and blocked out everything.

It couldn't have been much later when he woke, because he was still lying on the unforgiving stone, soaked and retching while Ian turned his head and shoulders to keep him from choking on the seawater and bile he expelled. Nothing about the moment was romantic or peaceful, but Robbie *felt* life coursing through him as he'd never done before, and it was sweet indeed. When he could, he gazed into Ian's blue, blue eyes, and they sparked like crystal. Robbie realised those eyes of Ian's— or perhaps the love he poured through them—had been the source of the amazing light that had shone down into the water.

Of course, he also realised that was nonsense, except...magic. He smiled.

"Ach, Robbie! How can ye smile? You were gone, faded away. I dinna even ken how you're here wi' me now."

Robbie could only shake his head, because words would be useless even if he could speak without coughing, which he didn't think he could do, anyway. Ian sat cross-legged, lifted Robbie until he sat in his lap, and held him tight, quiet for a long time. Eventually, Robbie became aware of the sharp-cornered wooden box pressed between them, and he pulled away.

Ian looked down at the box Robbie still held with one hand. "So...is it done, then, lad? Are ye free of the magic?"

Robbie thought he knew the answer, but he didn't speak right away. He contemplated the harp which lay nearby on its side as if catching its own breath after Robbie's near drowning. He met Ian's eyes for a moment, then stood on shaky legs and took the two short strides necessary to bring him to the harp.

He picked it up. It was weightless.

"Nay, Ian. It's not done. Not yet." He smiled to ease the impact of the words, having seen Ian's hopeful face fall. He glanced around and found they'd come near the open front of the cave, and now he took note of the choir of stony, watery voices singing their wordless song all around. *A marvel, truly.* But he and Ian weren't safe there—it was too open, and though night would soon fall, until it did, they could be seen from the mouth of the cave.

He said, "Come back with me to where I was before. I need to bring the harp and the key together, I think, and this isn't a good place to do it." As tired as he was, he started to walk, carrying the weightless harp and the heavy key, stumbling now and then on the crazy-quilt pillars of basalt. It was slow-going, but it wasn't far, and Ian kept with him, holding his arm, keeping them both from stumbling back into the drink.

At the back of the cave, the channel flowing in and out of An Uaimh Bhinn parted, the busy waters eddying at the end of either fork. Robbie followed the left branch and knelt near the edge with the harp before him.

He touched a finger to the latch on the ironwood box.

Something like small lightning travelled through him, and the lid creaked open.

At that moment, all sound in the cave ceased—or at least it did for Robbie. Hearing only his breath and beating heart, he pushed the lid up all the way and inside found the harp key lying solitary on its velvet bed, still slung on its leather cord, dry and perfect. Untouched since the day the witch had laid it there.

He dared touch it now, and laughed nervously when nothing happened.

"Rob?"

Robbie turned to meet Ian's gaze and found clear worry in his countenance—brows drawn down, squinting, frowning. He wanted to smile to ease Ian's mind, but he didn't have it in him. He answered simply.

"I'll tune the harp."

Incredulity apparently overtook the anxiety Ian had been suffering. "But...but it's broken."

"Yes," Robbie said, but he wasn't paying much attention anymore.

He set the key to the peg of a string near the middle of the harp—a C note, it should sound, but all he needed to do was get close to that, then tune the octaves and go from there. He heard the harp in his memory as it should sound and twisted the key to tighten the string until it resembled the sound in his mind. It seemed then that a light coursed from the peg, all along the wire, to the bray pin, and over the soundboard.

"That thing you're holding doesn't look like a key," Ian said.

Robbie smiled slightly but didn't answer. Ian was a little behind the course of things, but he was right, if it was a chatelain's key or some such that he compared it to. The key was a *T*, a bar of wood with a metal tube made to fit over the wooden pegs and turn them. But Robbie knew, somehow, that tuning the harp *now* was essential to defeating the witch, breaking the long-held spell, and—for him—staying alive, so he kept his focus on his task. He did, however, wonder in the back of his mind about how the strings had survived at all. They were of brass wire. Some were green crusted and broken, but one would think after nearly a century and a half there would be naught left but stubs, if anything. He supposed they, and the harp itself, had survived because, like him, during the long stretches between landings, they didn't really exist except as ghost things. Yet clearly, washing up on a beach every so many decades and then drowning again had taken a toll.

Now I think of it, perhaps that's why my chances to break the curse are finite—the necessary hardware can't last!

He'd worked through the octaves, found an easy-to-hear open fifth, and worked octaves up and down from that note. By the time he had two of those fairly well-tuned, he began to hear the music of the cavern again. He finished the last of the fifths and moved on to the flat, churchy sound of a fourth from the first C he'd touched, and then the doubled the F's at the octaves up and down. Now the cave's music grew louder, and its sound changed. It was reaching, Robbie thought, for the harp's tones.

By the time he'd tuned all of the strings that had survived, the harp had begun to sound its own complex music. The last time Robbie had come ashore—decades past—he heard a harp played with gut strings. The sound had been lullaby sweet, hardly resembling the almost military strength of the brass strings he was used to. Now that fervent, metallic sound marched out by its own volition, a song never composed, chords and snips of melody playing and sparring amidst the insistent harmonies and dissonances voiced by ancient An Uaimh Bhinn, the whole of it a campaign song for a devil's army.

And light shone everywhere from the glowing, flaming harp strings, flashing over the waters, glancing and glimmering over the wet stones, blinding Robbie's eyes. But he didn't know if it was real, and he started to turn to ask Ian if he saw it too, except just then an unmusical sound, a clatter and stomp foreign to both the harp and the sea, interrupted his thoughts.

Ian's hand landed on Robbie's shoulder for just an instant as he passed, probably going to spy out the source of the new commotion.

Then Robbie turned his attention back to the problem of the harp. Problem because there was one more string to tune, and it wasn't there at all. In his mind, he made something like a wordless prayer—to God or to gods and goddesses or perhaps to the old witch Melisandre, and then he touched the key to the missing string's pin and twisted.

Light shot wire thin and flaming white from the pin to the soundboard, an ethereal string, and it sounded the note—a bright E, lifting the entire cacophony of sound into agreement. The devil's army gave way to a band of angels.

*

Ian crept cautiously from their hiding place, dirk in his hand. One glance behind him to check on Robbie confirmed the lad was still focused on tuning the harp.

The light that had come from the thing, bathing everything in a strange glow, hadn't scared him as much as it once might have done. Robbie's limp body as he'd pulled him from the water after he'd retrieved the key had scared him far more. Not just scared, but terrified. He'd spent a terrible moment, convinced Robbie wasn't breathing before he coughed and spluttered up seawater.

But everything they'd been through so far would be worth naught if Robbie lost the chance to tune that final string and finally be free of the old witch's curse. Aye, Ian would leave Robbie to do what he knew while he went to find the source of the commotion.

Hope stirred, then was quickly dashed. Whoever the intruders were, they weren't taking the time to hide. That ruled out Ian's hope that his uncle's men might have found them. More like, it was Campbell or his men. Or both.

If it was Campbell, the man's arrogance might be used against him. Only an overconfident opponent didn't take the time to survey the lay of the land and any advantage his prey might have before closing in for the kill.

Ian growled silently. Someone might die today, but it wasn't going to be himself or Robbie. Ian would fight for their future together, a real future without the curse trying to reclaim Robbie's as its own at every turn. Robbie would too—Ian had no doubt of it.

"There's nowhere for them to hide." Niall's voice was little more than a whisper, yet it echoed as though he stood a foot away instead of by the entrance.

Ian pressed himself against the wall, edged along a bit, then ducked behind a boulder, and peered around it. Niall had half a dozen men with him. Ian recognised

James and Donnell, but the others he hadn't seen before wore the MacLeod tartan. It didn't take much of a guess to figure out that MacLeod would have sent some of his men along with Campbell to make sure their alliance favoured his needs rather than Campbell's. MacLeod had always been a canny one. It wouldn't have taken him long to realise that although he'd employed Campbell to work for him, the only loyalty Campbell had was to himself. Once he found the jewels, he'd try to take them—he'd already made an attempt, and the opportunity to kill Ian, who had thwarted him more than once, would be an opportunity he wouldn't pass up.

"I'm not going in there!" One of MacLeod's men glanced around nervously. "Did ye nae see the ghosties? White light, coming from where ye want us to go! They'll kill us."

"I'll kill ye if ye don't go in there," Campbell muttered, bringing up the rear. "This is some trick of MacDonald's. It has to be."

A loud noise reverberated around the cave, causing several loose rocks to wobble. Ian nearly lost his balance but luckily managed to regain it before he lost his footing. Another crash quickly followed, this time with the light glancing over the rocks so bright, Ian held his hand over his eyes just in time.

Before some of the smaller rocks settled, he kicked them with his boot, sending them into the water with a loud plop.

Even Campbell glanced around nervously at the noise. Ian picked up a smooth stone, weighted it in his hand, and sent it skimming across the water. The acoustics of the cave not only amplified any sound but made it difficult to figure out its source, so he'd use that to his advantage.

Another explosion, or at least the noise of one, resulted in several of the men diving for cover. One poked his head up, only to cover his head with his hands when the noise grew to mimic thunder. Ian crouched in the middle of a storm, magical thunder and lightning all around him, yet not touching him.

Ian grinned. If he hadn't known the source of the noise, he'd been reacting the same way.

Maybe magic could be useful after all.

But only up to a point. Once Robbie finished tuning the harp, and its magic was gone, they'd be two men relying on their wits and their ability to fight their way out against overwhelming odds.

Campbell scrambled to his feet. His men might be ruled by superstition, but Campbell never had been. Once he figured out the storm wasn't real, and only light and sound effects that couldn't hurt him, he'd quickly remind his men he was paying them to be there.

Or threaten to kill them himself.

Whatever worked. Campbell wouldn't care, and the lives of his men wouldn't mean much in the shadow of the temptation of the jewels.

Ian couldn't let him get his hands on those jewels either. He had to find a way to save himself and Robbie, and get out alive with the treasure. He'd vowed when he'd arrived on Skye that he'd keep it safe for the prince, and he intended to do just that.

*

Ian quietly crept away, heading further back into the cave. A quick check verified the jewels were where he'd hidden them, but something—instinct or intuition, or maybe it was the damnable magic—told him they were not as safe there as he'd first supposed. Perhaps it was simply that if he could spot the hiding place that easily, so could the enemy.

He reached behind the taller basalt pillars and pulled out the small bag of jewels. He put it down, surveyed the formation in front of him, and stepped carefully onto a drowned pillar so he could reach a large rock he saw there. He grunted as he retrieved the heavy rock, loosening the sandy dirt holding it in place, but finally, he held it in his hands. He then placed it where the jewels had sat, making sure the arrangement of stones was slightly askew so it was more obvious there was something hiding there. Hopefully, it would distract Campbell for at least a few moments.

Ian had hoped to find another way out of the cave at the rear, but he'd seen earlier that a solid wall of rock stretched out for a short distance in either direction, creating a *T* where the sea channel ended. Robbie was with the harp in the branch that ran a bit north. It was a fair hiding place as it couldn't be seen from the cave entrance, and even some distance in, it was impossible to know the shape of the cave at the rear.

But, while it might take a while for Campbell to find their hiding place, Ian didn't like the idea of waiting to be caught. A good hiding place—especially one that was only a curve in an otherwise straight line—also had the potential to become a trap. Not only that, but with the wee storm the harp had conjured up, he wasn't sure how stable the stone ceiling was. The cave itself seemed solid and would probably still be there long after he and Robbie had left this world, but it would only take a good rock fall to bury them, or worse.

The conversation he'd heard echoing from the cave entrance had gone quiet again. Ian dared sneak back that way only to find Campbell had retreated to a good distance away. He couldn't hear the words, but the tone and the way Campbell held himself with his shoulders and back taut suggested he was in the middle of an argument.

Probably trying to convince his men to venture into the cave. Two of MacLeod's men were shaking their heads, and one of them glanced at the sky, then turned to leave. Dusk wasn't far off, so they wouldn't be happy entering a cave they thought haunted in the dark. Not that Ian believed ghosts preferred one time of the day over another, but he'd discovered his imagination tended to be more active when he couldn't see clearly in front of him. He hoped it would be the same for other men.

Campbell knew they were close by but hopefully not their exact whereabouts. With the hope of a back door dashed, Ian and Robbie were left with one way out. They'd have to lay low and wait until the cover of darkness.

As far as he could see, the cave didn't offer any truly secure hiding place for the jewels, so they'd have to take them with them. Escaping under the enemy's nose, hidden only by the dark, was a risky plan, but he couldn't see any other options.

With the jewels once again in his sporran, Ian headed back to where he'd left Robbie. Surely he'd finished tuning the harp by now. Maybe he'd see their situation in another light, and together they could come up with a plan that had a better chance of seeing them safe.

Ian set his mouth in a grim, determined line. They'd not come this far only to lose everything to the likes of Campbell.

Chapter Eighteen

Just as he finished tuning that ethereal last string, Robbie saw Ian coming towards him. The big man staggered slightly, held his hands over his ears, and hunched his shoulders. When the noise created by the harp and the sea together in the cave smoothed from a cacophony of demon howls and clashing metals to a mighty sound of angels in an angry, determined march, Ian stopped, straightened, and—looking relieved but worried—walked more steadily towards Robbie.

As he came close enough to be heard, he said, "That noise your harp was making in cahoots with the sea and the cave—it was enough to drive a man past sanity. Better now, though."

"Aye," Robbie said, but that was all. He felt oddly empty, and he suspected the magic had all but spent itself now. A peculiar feeling—not a bad one, but it left him at loose ends. Not sure why he did it, Robbie dropped the cord of the harp key over his head so that it lay strangely warm against his chest. Then, woodenly, as if guided by some unseen puppeteer, he stood and carried the harp to the uneven ledge of stone at the side of the cave and set it there gently. He stroked the uncannily smooth wood of the forepillar once, then stepped back and turned to meet Ian's eyes.

"Is it done, then?" Ian asked, but he didn't seem to want an answer. He peered squint-eyed at the harp, then brought his gaze back to Robbie's as if remembering something. "The jewels, Rob. I have them. We need to hide them well, outside the cave, I think. The only place to secret them in here is behind a stone or two, but I can see no way to conceal them well enough."

Robbie thought for only an instant, then picked up the now empty ironwood box and opened it. "Put them here, Ian."

Ian looked as if he was about to argue, and Robbie understood. How could putting them in a box help?

"Trust me."

"Aye." Ian dropped the cloth sack of jewels onto the dark velvet. As he did, the knot at the closure loosened and a few of the jewels slipped out—bloodred rubies, white diamonds, emeralds the green of summer, and sapphires like the blue of distant hills. Catching the glimmer of faded daylight, they seemed to burn against the dark.

Surveying the pool, Robbie found a corner where odd things—shells, stones, small bits of driftwood, even glass from some faraway broken pane—remained caught against the stone sides. Without hesitating or asking, he lowered the box into it, allowing water to get in before closing the lid completely and securing the hasp. It sank to the bottom, heavier with jewels and water inside than it had been when sealed airtight with only the harp key enclosed. He and Ian surveyed the eddy from every angle they could reach. The box could be seen, but only barely so, and it looked like it had been there for ages, nothing more than a piece of waterlogged, sea-worn flotsam.

Robbie smiled, and Ian clapped him on the back with a laugh before pulling him into a hug.

Though the sounds in the cave remained undiminished, something about the harp's sound changed and both men turned to look at it.

"Oh," Robbie said, breathless. The instrument was fading! The harp's form could still be seen, but it had gone translucent, as if melding with the stones of An Uaimh Bhinn.

Ian let out a choked sort of cough, shook his head, and said, "Aye, then. It's magic. It's all been magic. Quite real." Suddenly turning angry or perhaps afraid, he swung Robbie to face him. "Are ye free of that bloody curse, then, man? Is it gone from ye?"

"I hope so… Or rather, I hope it's *leaving* me—I feel its absence. But truly, I also hope there may be enough of it left to help us escape and complete your task—for your cause and your promise." He stopped, but took Ian's hand in his and held him with his eyes. "And then, one more thing. To help us gain the life we want to live. Together, aye?"

"Ach aye," Ian said with a great rush of breath. "And I suppose if we hope to get any of that done, we need to move."

But before Ian told Robbie his plans or led him away, he took the few seconds needed to lay his lips, sweet and urgent, on Robbie's. Neither said anything of love, but it was all there in that kiss, and it was enough for Robbie to hold on to for hope's sake.

"We need to get out of here, Robbie, and there's only one door. Campbell's men are out there—scared of the cave, it seems. Magic and ghosties and strange noises and such. But I don't know how long they'll be more scared of that than Campbell's wrath. We've got to get past them, get out and pray to find MacQuarrie for help, or at least sanctuary. I came back in just as dusk began to come rollin' o'er the water, making everything grey and shadowed. Now's our best chance to slip past. Are ye up to it? Your leg is all right, and ye've recovered from your...drowning?"

"Oh...well, yes. I'm more than tired but otherwise fine. I think the water helped my leg—the magic was still working then, it seems. It doesn't hurt, and the wound's closed over again. And as for the rest...I can't explain it. I feel empty and made whole all at once."

"Good, then. Or at least I think so? But...what about the harp?"

Robbie looked back to the cave wall where the instrument seemed to have become one with the stone. "I think it isn't mine anymore, Ian. Mayhap it will belong to the sea, but for now it belongs to An Uaimh Bhinn."

They set out across the back of the cave and then out towards its front. As they neared the entrance, the sounds—the harp's chords, the sea against the rocks— seemed louder, rather than more distant and faint. Robbie said a small prayer to whatever gods or saints watched over harpists and Highlanders, asking that the wild, uncaged music keep the enemy distracted until he and Ian could sneak out and climb the headland.

At the entrance, in the deep gloaming with neither the light of the sun nor the moon flashing on the waves, it was easy to fade into shadow. They crouched low and took stock of the scene outside. A ship was anchored offshore far enough to avoid the treacherous rocks—an old-style birlinn. Though someone might spot Ian and Robbie from that distance with a glass, that wasn't the greatest risk. On shore, beached in the tide zone, were two small boats, and men stood about sullenly while Campbell himself railed at them to move their "pathetic arses" or he'd give them something solid to fear. And out on the waters, drawing swiftly closer to Staffa, a much larger craft proudly flew MacLeod's colours—plain enough out on the water even in the dusk—and it certainly brought more men to the fight.

Robbie broke the silence with an obvious question. "Why do ye think they brought so many just to face the two of us?"

"Now there is a question, to be sure. But we've nae time to learn the bloody answer. If we're going to get by unseen, this is our moment. Let's go."

Robbie had brief seconds to be thankful they'd come out on the left-hand side of the cave. The path out would have to be that one, though leading over the uneven tops of the rock pillars as it did, they'd find it tricky to speed along in the poor light. To their right, the way would have been over exposed beach with the tide partly out, but they couldn't have gone that way. They'd have had to cross the rough water at the entrance to An Uaimh Bhinn, and then—if they survived and got away—in that direction lay two more sea caves requiring a hard swim before they'd get to a place they could climb. And if all the swimming in the chop didn't kill them, it would be capture at the end of it, for not far away, Campbell's landing craft lay beached, and his men ashore stood deciding whether to fear the cave and its ghosts or Campbell's wrath more.

Ian grunted and indicated the path before them with his chin, then whispered, "Stay low when you can, and try not to make sudden moves. Slow, smooth progress might be torture when all we want to do is get away, but it's less likely the movement will catch someone's eye."

The path was tricky, and the light worse than uncertain—the latter both a blessing and a hazard for Robbie and Ian. Both were sure-footed, but they were worn out from the hardships of the last few days, and they slipped and stumbled from time to time. Robbie considered it good fortune that Campbell was such a showman; his blathering and posturing kept the attention of the others on him, and not on who or what might be picking their way over the rocks.

"Maybe gods and saints listen to prayers after all," Robbie mused at a whisper.

"What?"

Robbie might have answered, but just then the dying sun moved far enough in its arc for a corner of it to clear the rocky outcrop in the water across from the cave's entrance. A beam of light hit the rocks immediately below them, as if a mighty red finger wanted to point them out. Ian stopped dead, and Robbie halted behind him, but as the sun sank, the light fragmented and angled slowly upwards from the sinking sun, reflecting off the water.

Robbie watched it creep closer to his foot and then drew in an alarmed breath, certain he was about to be put on display for their enemies. He whispered harshly, "Ian!"

But Ian had seen and stepped forward and down onto the next pillar, and the next, moving out of the way. Robbie followed and stepped away just before the light would have found him. They took a scant moment to breathe, then continued to steal cautiously forward towards the curve in the headland. Once they were around that, they'd be out of the line of sight of Campbell and his men, and near the trail Robbie had climbed down earlier that day—or perhaps a lifetime ago.

Please, Robbie silently begged, once again addressing gods and saints unknown. *Please.*

In a few seconds that seemed a month long, the weak light brightened to moonglow, but it was all right. They'd rounded the bend. They embraced briefly as they caught their breath, preparing for the climb, and then started up over the rugged path.

Once they got into the higher places, loose stones knocked by a foot fell noisily, threatening to give them away to the enemy. Still, luck held, and they made it safely to the top. Not wanting to make silhouettes in the rising moonlight, they slithered on their bellies until they found a screen of stone outcrops, loose rocks, and clumps of taller grass, which they could hide behind while they again surveyed the action at the cave entrance.

"Campbell's got those men well and truly whipped," Ian said under his breath.

Robbie, who was lying slightly closer to the ridgeline than Ian, turned his head back to get a look at him, but the moonlight was blocked by shadows. He could see nothing, but the tone of Ian's voice revealed much. For the first time, Robbie understood the depth of Ian's hatred of this man. It was personal, and though jewels and promises and causes held great importance, Ian's cold rage at Campbell had little to do with them. It ran deep, like the cut of betrayal.

"I hope you have your triumph over him, Ian, just as I hope your cause will win out. But have a care, if ye will. Our love and a chance at a life are the two things of greatest importance in all of it, to me."

Ian turned to meet his eyes then, and his expression softened. "Aye," he said. "Also to me."

After a moment's silence unreachable by anything but moonlight and breath, he looked again down at the shore, where the tide had continued to ebb. Campbell's threats had held sway, and his men were preparing to storm the cave. But Ian was looking past that.

Jolly boats from McLeod's ship were making way to shore.

"Those men will be better disciplined than Campbell's. We need to find MacQuarrie and hope for support—including more people. MacLeod won't find the jewels in the cave, but when they fail, they'll overrun the entire island if need be to capture us again."

Robbie took his cue from Ian and snaked downslope away from the summit until they could be certain they wouldn't be seen from below. Then they rose and hurried towards the northern part of the tiny island, where Ian said he expected to find MacQuarrie's outpost. If he didn't already have people on the isle, Ian gambled he would have a presence here now for the sake of loyalty to his MacDonald friends and perhaps the Jacobite cause—at least to help with the transfer of the Bonnie Prince's treasure. But before they reached any sort of encampment, they dropped down off a low bluff to find what Robbie decided to think of as a welcoming party.

Half a dozen burly, kilted men were gathered there, concealed by the curving bluff in either direction. Before either Ian or Robbie could fight or speak, they were knocked from their feet and held face down in the dirt. Robbie felt a blade at his throat, so close he was afraid to swallow.

And then, even more disturbing, someone laughed.

"Stop bloody laughing, John MacDonald," Ian said, then paused to noisily spit, apparently having collected some dirt on an indrawn breath. "Tell them to let us up."

"Ach, aye. Let the bloody fools up." As the other men moved to obey, the man who'd spoken—apparently John MacDonald—went on. "My apologies to ye, Ian. Ye'll no doubt know about the doings on the south point of the island around the big caves. We thought ye might be McLeod or Campbell men."

After Ian had regained his feet and brushed himself off as best he could, he looked up to find John staring at him with an oddly probing gaze.

"I see ye've brought a friend, Ian."

"You'll mind ye're tongue, cousin. This man is Robbie Elliott, a Lowlander, but well met, and standing wi' us in the Jacobite cause. He can be trusted."

"Ah, yes, the cause. Well now...*cousin*." The smirk on John's face matched the sarcasm he put into that last word perfectly. "It seems you're thought less than trustworthy yourself, having been banished from home by your uncle the laird for shifty deeds. So keep your peace 'til I get ye back to the camp. After that, ye'll be out of my hands. Meanwhile, ye and the laddie here best be careful of your moves, if ye don't want to get taken down rough. I'll take your word on it...for now."

"Ye have it," Ian said.

Robbie read in Ian's voice and stance how hard it was for him to take such abuse. Knowing as he did that Ian's banishment was only a cover for his purpose in the Isles, he sent Ian a look encouraging patience, hoping Ian could read his intent but John couldn't.

They surmounted a hillock and on the other side found a bubbling spring. Perhaps John wasn't as cold a man as he'd sounded, because he stopped and offered them the chance to drink. The fresh water went down sweet, and an all-over ache Robbie hadn't known was there faded away. His mind cleared too. As they neared the encampment, which was closer than he'd expected and centred around a half-ruined structure that must once have been a cot of sod and thatch, he began to think on how he might help in the battle to come.

Two things he observed as soon as he saw the camp. First, he believed several MacDonald men were there along with John. Though some wore trews, two wore the same tartan as John, and also the men seemed to divide into two groups. Presumably, the second group was MacQuarrie's, a few of those men wearing a plaid as bright with red as the MacDonald, but of a different pattern. The second important observation Robbie made: regardless of what clan anybody belonged to, the whole group remained badly outnumbered by MacLeod and Campbell.

Ian was greeted with hand clasps by a man wearing MacDonald tartan, a long, gleaming sword, and a brace of flintlock pistols. He appeared to be in charge.

"Ian MacDonald. Your uncle became aware of the trouble brewing here in the Treshnish, and he figured Staffa with its caves might be an important sight for the rendezvous with the ships from France. Ye'll understand, I'm certain, as a thing he tasked ye with revolves around that expected meeting. Coming here, I was to gather MacQuarrie's support from Mull, and make a stand on this isle, if need be." He stopped for a moment, looking around at the men standing together in small groups, all listening. "As well as tellin' me about your mission," he said with a little more force, "he let me know I should trust ye regardless of rumoured events."

Ian took in a breath before answering, his nostrils flaring with what might have been quelled anger at the reference to his past. Robbie thought he understood, at least in part. After all, the love of one man for another was as pure as any love. Why should it be the subject of foul rumours and disdain?

Ian spoke firmly. "I'm relieved, then, sir. And as to the task ye spoke of, it's well in hand. We need to clear out MacLeod and his Campbell rabble, make the passage safe for the one who's coming."

"Aye, and let's talk about a plan to do that while you and your friend here take some food and drink. It's rough fare, but I'll wager it's welcome."

From Robbie's viewpoint, it was more than welcome. Bread, sausage, cheese, dried fruit—a feast as far as Robbie was concerned, and he had to keep himself from eating too much and ending up cramped and sick.

He wasn't really part of the discussion—trusting Ian didn't extend to trusting him—but he listened. The plan it seemed was a simple one, but they had to put it in motion quickly. They needed to get in position to watch MacDonald's landing and then come behind them from either side as they headed into An Uaimh Bhinn. They'd need to deal with any sentries or accidental encounters, but scouts could be sent ahead to take those out quietly. If they could ambush the enemy near the entrance to the cave, come at them from all sides including above while they were stuck in a narrow and dangerous passage, the MacDonald group could take the win. First, reduce enemy numbers, then hold the remainder under siege in the cave if needed. There was no way out for MacLeod except the front door, where they'd emerge right into the grip of MacDonald.

A few men would be staying behind to keep the outpost secure and, if things should go awry, carry a message back to the mainland. Ian wanted Robbie to stay.

They argued, but Ian had what he thought would be the final word.

"Robbie, you're my captive. I ne'er said you were not. Despite everything, ye'll need to do as I say."

Robbie watched as Ian walked away to join the men heading back up the hill to the summit. It might have been just luck that his eye was caught by the piper MacDonald had brought with him. He thought about the pipes, and he thought about music, and he thought about the noise of the harp and the sea. And then he thought about what a demon-spawned racket would be made if one were to add pipes to that cacophony.

The plan for a sneak attack left the pipes out of the main thrust, of course. Hard to sneak and pipe the fighters to battle at the same time. But pipers such as this one—a brawny man of thirty or so—came armed for battle as well. He laid his pipes aside and hefted an axe Robbie would not want to run afoul of—a thought which made him cringe. The man was not going to like the plan Robbie had simmering.

Would it be worth the piper's wrath?

Yes. MacLeod and Campbell were not *playing* at war. They had strength and grim, grizzled men. Cornered in the cave, those men would fight like demons to avoid death and the hell they'd been taught to fear. Swords, fists, and axes would be bloodied on both sides. Ian and the MacDonald clan might think their Catholic God would bring them favour in battle, but Robbie had never been sworn to any Christian God.

The only gods that will be watching here are those that rule death, the deeps, and the underworld. And those gods wouldn't skip over Ian if he stood in their path.

Robbie felt a tickle at his chest where the harp key—all but forgotten over the last hour—still lay suspended on its leather cord. Then a wave of magic like falling into the sea itself washed over him.

I still have the magic on me. Perhaps it will favour me one last time.

The piper tucked his instrument away under the crude lean-to that held supplies before he stepped off to join the others mustering for the attack. The fire had grown dim, the moon and stars were cloistered behind a screen of clouds, *and no one was watching Robbie.*

*

Robbie stole a glance around the camp. Ian was leaving with the main group of MacDonald men, moving at a fast trot towards the eastern coast of the island. From what Robbie had heard, they would attempt to come down beyond where the Campbell and MacLeod boats had unloaded. In the dim light, Robbie could just see the glint of Ian's eyes as he turned around once, still moving away. Robbie met his gaze. He couldn't be sure Ian didn't suspect he had a plan other than following orders. But Ian had no choice but to keep going as he was, keeping up with his cohort, so Robbie didn't worry about his suspicions.

A quartet of crossbowmen were already making their way straight to the southern summit, and a few MacQuarrie archers headed west. As the enemy entered the cave, MacDonald warriors would come at them from the east, with bolts from the crossbows raining down from above, and arrows flying across the channels from the west—a three-pronged pincer. The few men designated as scouts had left ahead of the others, and they'd attempt to head off runners, should there be any, as well as deal with sentries.

Robbie had seen the fear on the enemy faces when they contemplated entering the cave. Campbell was cruel, and fear of his well-known wrath must have beat out the fear of unknown magic—but it didn't mean that fear was gone. And though MacLeod's own men would have greater discipline—being largely closer kin and better paid, Ian had said—Robbie suspected their hearts would race and their heads spin just the same once they heard the noise of harp and sea.

And then there will be the pipes. Robbie smiled—he'd always loved a devious surprise, and as a Reiver son, he'd learned the art from the best. He reached up and clutched the harp key, thinking the witch Melisandre had never had the least idea what a gift she'd given him, wrapped in the coils of a curse.

Seeing all eyes elsewhere, Robbie muttered an apology to the absent piper, lifted the pipes to his shoulder, and began his run. He made his way over uneven ground and scattered rocks to a place just east of An Uaimh Bhinn's mouth. He'd chosen to make his descent closer to the cave than where the main body of MacDonald fighters would come out on the coast, yet the spot was still fairly hidden from the enemy. He could likely remain concealed, at least until he made his dash for the water.

The sea would be cold, and Robbie suspected it wouldn't harbour any love for him now that the harp had been taken from its embrace. But he hoped...nay, he felt certain a bridge still existed between himself and the deep, a bridge balanced on a fulcrum—the harp's key.

Muscles sore, scratched in a hundred places, old wound throbbing, Robbie panted by the time he reached the edge of the cliff to the east of the cave. He dropped to the ground behind an upthrust of stone and drew the key's leather cord over his head. For luck or for a reason he couldn't guess, he brought the glinting metal key to his lips, then wrapped the cord around the pipes' chanter, making sure to tie it securely. Then, with the bagpipes slung over his shoulder once more, he started his descent.

He was almost to the beach when he stopped to survey the action. Most of the MacLeod and Campbell men were either in the cave or heading that way, picking a careful path over the stones. Their backs to Robbie, their attention focused on placing their feet safely. MacDonald's men, with Ian near the lead, were coming in close by the headland, still unseen by the enemy. As they neared, a man pointed at Robbie, and someone drew a bow, probably thinking him an enemy sentry who may have spotted them. Robbie hoped someone would recognise him, and nobody would think he was either an enemy or a traitor helping them. He needed to make it to the incoming tide without being pierced by an arrow.

No time to wait, though, and no way to make his fate more certain. He dropped the last four feet to the level ground in a leap and ran right across their path for all he was worth, splashing into the waves when he reached them, stepping right off into deep water.

The pipes wanted to float to the top, but Robbie held them under long enough to be sure they were taken by the tide heading into An Uaimh Bhinn. As he saw to that task, it became clear the sea wanted him back. Its oblivion beckoned, opening before him like a broad, bright doorway.

And he *wanted* to go through. Wanted the blessed peace on the other side of that gateway. No struggling, no fighting. No hope, but also no despair. An eternity of rest and peace. But the voice of Melisandre, sweet and low and close even though a long time gone, ghosted through Robbie's mind.

"You have more magic than I thought," she'd said. And then, as she prepared to curse him, she'd called upon her goddess, she of the deep water and the underworld. "So that Clíodhna will bless you, and you indeed may live."

Live. Not an easy thing to do, but as a tide within him turned, he became certain he wanted it. Because in life lies love. *Ian.*

A light filtered to him from above—the moon, perhaps—and he raised his face to bathe in it, and watched the shadow of a great seabird cross, then return, circle, and cross again. Suddenly he knew that love mattered more than eternity.

He would live for Ian and love. He *had* his own magic; the witch had affirmed it. And he knew from lessons at her hand that magic was made of mind and heart, word and will. His mind and heart united, he thrust his will upon the harp key now bound to the pipes, felt it pull at his soul, tearing the old spell magic from him at seams long ago made by the weaving words of the witch's curse.

I bind you, he thought, firmly affixing the freed magic to the pipes. *I bind you to harp and sea, from now until moonset.*

As the pipes raced into the channel towed by the harp key, Robbie rose, broke the surface, and breathed deeply, bobbing in the moon-frosted waves. All that had just happened seemed like a dream. Remembering where he was and the fight that was to be taking place, he turned towards the shore to see that little time, if any, had passed since he'd run into the sea.

MacDonald's men came in perhaps a beat later than planned, but they came at a run, brandishing swords and axes, the sneak abandoned as there was no need. Most of MacLeod's men had entered the cave, though a few stragglers and perhaps sentries remained out on the rocks or with the boats. They cringed at the clamour of Jacobite shouts and battle cries. Robbie picked out Ian's blood-curdling, wordless roar among them. But that ferocity was not enough to cow the enemy. They raised swords and met the attack. *Bravely*, Robbie admitted.

Or desperately.

Now that Robbie was free of enchantment, the sea felt frigid, and it sapped his strength. He knew he had only a short window of time or all he'd done for the sake of life and love and Ian would be for naught; he would succumb first to cold and then to drowning. He turned his eyes shorewards and concentrated on making his way to an upraised rock formation. If he could make the rocks, get high enough to be out of the water but still to the seawards side, he could lay low until an opportunity arose to go further.

As he kicked and paddled the short distance through the waves, he listened, waiting for a noise, waiting to hear his magic take hold. He reached the rocks and as quietly as he could, pulled himself up out of the water, and lay half on his back, half on his side facing the sea. It was far from comfortable, the squared off tops of basalt rising unevenly and putting pressure on ribs and knees and skull. But at least it was warmer, or so it seemed for a moment. But then a blast of wind rose from over the waves and shot its chill straight through Robbie's skin to his core. He struggled to shiver silently, and then to turn quietly, thinking if he could curl in on himself away from the wind, he'd remain warm.

Once he'd made the change, he found he had a view of the battle engaged only yards away—three rocks he lay against came together, leaving a triangle of space between them which made a perfect window on the action. There wasn't much—isolated fights between MacLeod's rear guard and MacDonald's van. When a blast of noise shook the island down to the deep-rooted basalt on which the whole of Staffa seemed planted, even that fighting stopped, all motion suspended for a long instant while, it seemed to Robbie, people slowly comprehended that the noise heralded neither Ragnarök nor any apocalypse.

Robbie reasoned the great sound had been the result of the pipes passing the mouth of An Uaimh Bhinn, and it quieted as it continued inwards. It hadn't been quelled, though, merely muffled to those outside. It went on, echoing from within, blended with the strains of harp and sea already reverberating in the cave.

Demonic.

Perhaps it should have scared Robbie, but he was glad for it, for even though the sounds crawled over his spine and set his nerves alight, the more terrifying they were, the better chance they would confound the enemy.

And they did. It must have been very loud indeed, within the cave. Men who'd gone in thinking to find a worthy treasure now poured out holding their heads against pain. Staggering, some missed their steps on the treacherous basalt columns and fell into the sea. Others ran straight onto the swords of MacDonald's men. Some found their feet and ran across the narrow beach through a screen of crossbow bolts shot at close range. A few of those runners went down, but some made it to the boats and, apparently forgetting all loyalties and duties, began to row—only to be shot before they could get away.

In the midst of it, unarmed except for a single slender dirk, Robbie could only lay still and watch, wait, and pray to whatever deity might hear: *Let Ian come through safe.*

After a moment, he found Ian in the dim light, the spun red-gold of his hair flashing silver in strands of the moonlight reaching through massing clouds. Ian raged with battle lust, standing like a conquering giant on a high platform of stone, slashing any enemy who came on fighting. But he hadn't lost his mind or heart in the heat of battle, for when a ragged-looking warrior—no doubt one of Campbell's—came pleading mercy instead of brandishing steel, Ian disarmed the man and knocked him down, but didn't strike a killing blow.

Robbie's heart tattooed hard and fast against his breastbone, a feeling of awe bordering fear burning through him as he watched Ian in action. *That such a man as this loves me.* But couldn't finish the thought. It was beyond his belief or even his imagining, and close on the heels of awe came a cooling wave of love.

Then a man came running straight at his hiding place. Just as he stepped up onto the top of the rock formation, directly above Robbie, he shook as he was struck with something, probably a bolt, and pitched forward. His body came down hard on Robbie.

With his breath knocked away, Robbie struggled through blinding pain to draw breath. When finally he did, the air came thick with the stench of sweat, filthy leather, blood, and piss. He had turned to look up at the enemy falling down on him, so now he couldn't see what was happening beyond the rocks on which he lay. The man's body weighed heavy over Robbie's head and upper body, and even the sounds of the battle—and the devil's music coming from the cave—were lost to him.

Once he could breathe, Robbie tried to move and discovered a dozen sharp pains where the fallen man's heft pinned him to stone corners and edges. One arm lay beneath him, the other free, and with that hand he pushed, trying to dislodge the crushing weight. But the felled enemy soldier in wet leather armour was heavy, and Robbie was tired, weakened from cold and pain, and he could accomplish nothing.

In the end, he pushed from his mind the horror of lying beneath the carcass of a slain warrior and forced himself to relax. He struggled now only to expand his lungs against the weight, to keep breathing, to keep believing the tickle of water against his legs didn't mean the tide would soon cover him.

To keep faith that Ian would find him. Somehow. Soon.

Chapter Nineteen

Most of MacLeod's men had entered the cave, although Ian couldn't see any sign of Campbell. The pent-up excitement of his clansmen rose thick around him, all of them eager to do battle with their enemy. Ian had almost forgotten what it felt like to be a part of the clan, with being on his own for so long before he and Robbie had found each other. He couldn't help but exchange a grin with the man next to him, although it looked more half-grin, half-sombre on his clansman, a mirror of his own emotions. Not every man would survive the day, on either side.

Keep safe, Robbie. Although he'd told the Robbie to keep well away from the battle, he knew the lad well enough that he wouldn't sit idle if he thought there was something he could do to help them win.

John gave the signal, and the MacDonalds moved forward as one man.

"For the cause!" Ian yelled, brandishing his sword. One of MacLeod's men lunged at him. Ian parried with his broadsword, sidestepped, and plunged his blade into the man's side. The man took a step back, the hand on his side sticky with blood. Ian pushed him down, ducking to narrowly avoid a blow from another man who stepped over his fallen comrade.

"Ach, fight fair, man." Andrew MacDonald hit the man on the side of the head with the hilt of his sword. "Watch ye back, young Ian."

"Thank you, cousin." Ian thanked Andrew with a curt nod. He recognised many of his kin in this battle, several of whom had come from villages surrounding his own.

Andrew shouted something unintelligible and ran enthusiastically into the fray, deflecting one blow while knocking another man out with a quick jab of his elbow.

It felt good to hold a sword again, although it didn't take long for the reality of its weight to remind Ian how out of practice he was. Perspiration ran down his face. He shook his head, hair flying like an unruly dog shaking itself free of the water. Ian ducked and thrust. Pulled his sword from one man's gut. Held back a hiss when an arrow whizzed past him, grazing his sword arm as it hit its MacLeod target.

"Thank ye," he muttered, "but not so close next time, aye."

A cacophony of noise filled the air. Men on both sides stopped fighting, confusion written over their faces. Ian recognised the music—if it could be called that—immediately for what it was, and smiled. "I knew ye would do what ye could, however ye did it," he murmured. A final farewell from Robbie to the harp, and fitting that he would add a Highlander's pipes to the mix.

The MacLeod in front of him recovered quickly. He lunged for Ian. Ian stepped back, bringing his sword up to parry, but not soon enough. He hissed in pain, blood dripping from the same arm that had been grazed by the arrow. His opponent grinned and moved in for the kill. Ian reached under their locked swords and jabbed the man in the upper arm with his dirk.

He screamed and dropped his sword. Ian kicked him to the ground. The man crawled to his knees. Ian kicked him again. This time he lay still.

Men streamed out of the cave, holding their heads, their faces twisted in pain. Ian winced in a half-remembered ghost of the pain he'd felt when the harp had loaned its voice to that of the cave.

"They'll nae have their wits," Ian yelled to John, but John was already taking action. The retreating men found themselves facing a wall of swords. Some had the presence of mind to skid to a halt; those that didn't died quickly, skewered on a sharp blade.

Ian ripped the sleeve from his shirt and wound it around his arm. Just a flesh wound, so the makeshift bandage would do for now.

Half a dozen men escaped MacDonald blades only to lose their footing on the basalt steps already slippery with the blood of their clansmen. They hit the water with a loud splash, some connecting with corners of sharp rock on their way down. If they weren't already dead, they soon would be.

Campbell followed his men from the cave, keeping a safe distance behind. He grimaced, staggered, yet still kept upright. He gestured urgently to the man immediately in front of him, his eyes scanning the beach. The man took off at a run, diving through the gap in the MacDonald line. Other men followed his lead, heading for the beached jolly boats, but one man came straight for Ian. Did he think he would push his way through? Ian raised his sword, ignoring the pain in his arm, and growled.

The man whimpered. He stumbled and looked up at Ian, fear in his eyes. Now they were close, Ian recognised Niall immediately. His shirt was ripped, and his knees scraped raw, most likely from his attempt to flee. A bruise formed, purple and ugly, under one eye, spreading across his cheek. "Demons! Have mercy. The cave is full of demons!"

"Nae, the only demons I see are the men who just abandoned it." Ian grabbed Niall's hand, twisting it until he dropped his sword with a grunt of pain.

Niall closed his eyes and clasped his hands together, a pathetic attempt to plead for mercy.

Ian leaned closer. "Where's Campbell?"

Niall shivered. "Boats," he moaned.

Ian didn't waste time answering. He knocked Niall down, left him for John and his men, and headed for the beach. Campbell wouldn't escape justice. Not this time.

By the time Ian reached the narrow stretch of beach, many of MacLeod's men lay face down in the water, arrows and bolts having felled them as they tried to escape. One of the jolly boats bobbed on the water close to shore, half-launched, taunting the would-be crew. A man lay slumped half-in and half-out of the water, killed while he was trying to climb into the boat. Another—Ian was sure it was Campbell—waded out towards a second boat, which had raised anchor but not made much headway.

"Campbell!" Ian strode out into the water. "Give it up, man. You'll nae escape now. It's too late. You've nowhere to go. Your boat is leaving without ye."

Campbell turned towards Ian. One push and his dead companion fell into the water, only to come up alongside the small boat, a bloated corpse staring sightlessly at the sky above.

"MacDonald." He spat Ian's name. "I'd hoped you'd died, after watching your lad perish in front of ye."

Ian ignored him, not about to confirm or deny Robbie's whereabouts. Let Campbell think what he wanted about the two of them. He wouldn't be thinking anything for long. The waves lapped against his bare thighs, his kilt sodden with water. Each step felt like walking through mud with the tide pushing against him, determined to force him back to shore.

"You'll no try to take anyone else from me," Ian muttered. He dived into the water, coming up for air at the stern of the boat. His muscles straining and his arm screaming in pain, he heaved himself up into it. "Face me like a man, rather than the coward I know ye to be, Campbell."

Campbell drew his sword. "And once I've finished with you, I'll take the lad for myself." He grinned when Ian glared at him. "Then, once he's served his purpose, perhaps I'll seek out your cousin. Pretty lassie, if I remember rightly."

"You'll nae touch either of them." Ian raised his sword, blood trickling down his wet bandage. He spread his feet, steadying himself in the boat.

Campbell lunged at him. Ian sidestepped quickly, his leg hitting the side of the boat with a thump. Campbell turned to have another go at Ian, his face twisted in rage, his eyes wild.

Ian took a deep breath. If he could keep calm, he would win this fight. Campbell fought on pure instinct, his anger his undoing as it always had been. Ian drew his dirk, a weapon in each hand. He gestured to Campbell.

"Come get me, if ye want me," he taunted.

Campbell lunged again. Ian sidestepped, slower this time. His waterlogged clothes weighed heavy against his skin, as the wind whipped like ice against him.

The waves heaved, and the boat lurched. Campbell sprawled on the deck, landing on his arse. Ian stood over him, sword against his throat.

"The sea owes me," he muttered. "One last parting gift, it looks like."

"Ye don't have the nerve." Campbell met Ian's gaze for a moment, then looked away.

Ian kept his sword at Campbell's throat and crouched down beside him. "Aye, I do, but I'm thinking it will better if I deliver you into the laird's hands instead. Ye can tell him what ye just told me, about your intentions to seek out his daughter."

Campbell's eyes showed real fear then. "Kill me now. Show me you're no coward."

Ian grabbed a handful of Campbell's hair and pulled his head closer so his face was only an inch away. He scraped the sharp point of his dirk across Campbell's throat, not enough to seriously wound, but enough to hurt and leave a trail of blood.

"I'm no coward," he said evenly, then let go of Campbell who hit the deck with a thump, unconscious. "It's going to be far more satisfying to let my uncle deal with you."

He lay back in the boat, allowing himself a moment to shut his eyes. Exhaustion shook his body, but he wasn't done yet.

On the beach, a couple of men had collected one of the other jolly boats and dragged it up the narrow beach. John waded out to Ian's boat. "You should get that arm seen to."

"It's fine." Ian climbed out of the boat. "There's still—" He looked past John to the beach, and beyond. "Where's Robbie?" Surely the lad would be helping with the boats? Ian frowned. Surely he hadn't been caught by the caves.

"You should get that—"

Ian didn't wait for John to finish something he'd already heard. He ran for the shore, heading for the bottom of the cliff face, pushing his body to keep going. Robbie must have got those pipes into the cave somehow. Surely he wouldn't have dared sneak past the men already in there. Ian scanned the shore frantically. He was a canny one, was Robbie. He'd use something that no one would look at twice, the same way he'd hidden the jewels. The sea flowed into the cave. They'd take the pipes in with it.

"Ye can't have him." Ian saw a hint of something that didn't fit. Leather amongst rocks half submerged in the risen tide. "He's paid your price, and more." He sprinted towards the rocks, offering up a silent prayer, hoping he wasn't already too late.

"Robbie!" Ian waded into the water. The lad would be fine. He could... The spell was broken. He'd die like a mortal man and drown, if the cold didn't get him first.

Ian's heart raced, his breath rasping. He grunted and put his weight behind the enemy soldier wedged between the rocks, trapping Robbie underneath. One shove. The man rolled forward, then back. Ian cursed under his breath and tried again. The only part of Robbie he could see lay too still.

With one final shove, Ian managed to free Robbie from his dead captor. He pulled Robbie into his arms and held him tightly.

"Don't leave me." Tears streamed down his cheeks. "The sea won't have ye. Not now." He kissed Robbie's forehead, strained to feel breath on his cheek. "He's paid your price. The magic's gone. Give him up! He's mine."

"I'm yours," Robbie whispered weakly. He opened his eyes. "You came for me."

"I'll always come for ye." Ian kissed Robbie again, this time on the lips, and hard. "I love ye, Robbie Elliott."

Robbie smiled, colour already returning to his cheeks. He hugged Ian fiercely. "I love you, too, Ian."

*

"You're bleeding." Robbie frowned when he noticed Ian's bloodied bandage.

"Ach, it's nothing." Ian kissed Robbie's forehead again. "We should retrieve the jewels and return to Skye." Although this battle was over, they'd soon have a much bigger war to fight and win.

"You're exhausted." Robbie didn't waver in his concern.

"Dinna fash. I'll be fine. Nothing some rest won't mend." Ian stumbled, nearly losing his footing. His vision swam, yet he managed to stay upright.

Robbie put his arm around Ian's waist, steadying him.

"I'll be fine," Ian repeated. "Ye nearly drowned, and you've had that oaf on ye. Ye need to save your strength. It's a long journey back to Skye."

"Stubbornness isn't always a virtue." Robbie didn't remove his arm. "And I'm not the one wounded. You're paler than I've ever seen you, Ian. Let me help you." He rolled his eyes when Ian let loose a frustrated sigh. "I'm going to help you, whether you want me to or not." Robbie removed his arm. "Or you can walk a few steps and fall over."

Ian put one foot in front of the other and closed his eyes when the ground shifted under him. "I'm nae going to fall over."

"Stubborn," Robbie said, yet there was affection in his words. "What if we help each other? Would that sit better with you?"

"Aye. Maybe." Ian could justify that a wee bit better. He put his arm around Robbie this time and tried not to notice that Robbie took more of his weight than he did of Robbie's.

A familiar figure strode over to meet them as they approached the cave.

"Douglas!" Ian freed himself of Robbie's embrace. His arm hurt something bad now, although there was no fresh blood on the bandage. He reached for Douglas's arm, then grit his teeth against the pain.

"You've managed to injure yourself, I see." Douglas frowned. "It wouldn't have been while you were leaving us that arse in the boat, would it?" He held Ian's arm gently and examined it. "Jamie was sure that was you, though I dinna ken why."

"Jamie taught me how to fight," Ian reminded him.

"Aye, that would be it." Douglas grinned. "He was always proud of your fighting and wasn't afraid to take credit for it either."

Ahead of them, MacDonald men stood around talking in groups. Bodies covered a section of the beach, laid out to be identified. MacLeod's men on one side, MacDonald's on the other. Ian said a silent prayer for his fallen clansmen.

MacLeod's ship limped away from the isle, another moored in its place.

"The laird is here?" Ian felt foolish for asking the question as soon as it left his lips. Douglas and Jamie's presence should have alerted him to that immediately. Alistair's personal guard rarely left his side. They'd hardly come to the aftermath of a battle and leave their laird unprotected.

"Aye." Douglas eyed up Robbie, who had stood back as soon as Ian and Douglas started talking. "Who's this with ye, Ian?"

"Robbie Elliott, this is my clansman Douglas. Douglas, Robbie is a good friend, and fought by our side." Ian wanted to tell Douglas that Robbie's action had turned the tide in the battle for them, but that would bring with it a long explanation about enchantment and magic, which he doubted Douglas would believe, so he decided not to.

Alistair looked up from his conversation with Jamie when they approached. His smile faded when his gazed fixed on Ian's injury. "Ye should get that arm looked at, lad." Worry creased his brow for a moment, then he shook his head and continued. "Truth, I'm verra pleased that you're still with us. When MacQuarrie's men reported seeing a MacDonald plaid caught on the rocks, I feared the worse. I sent the nearest of our clan to find you, and then followed as soon as I could. It appears we arrived just in time."

He motioned Robbie forward. "John tells me ye've been a good friend to my nephew."

"I've tried to be, sir." Robbie inclined his head towards Alistair.

"This is Robbie Elliott, Uncle," Ian said. "Robbie, this is my uncle and my laird, Alistair MacDonald. Robbie's been a verra good friend to me, and to the cause."

John strode up the beach towards them. When he saw Alistair, he hastened his step. Ian started to leave but Alistair motioned him to stay.

"I haven't finished our conversation yet, Ian," Alistair continued, "and John's news will have bearing on it, if I'm not mistaken."

"I have confirmation, sir." John glanced at Robbie and hesitated.

"He can be trusted," Ian said quickly. "I'll vouch for him with my life, and already have."

Alistair raised an eyebrow, yet didn't question Ian's comment. "You may speak, John. We are all friends of the cause here."

Ian wished he could reach for Robbie's hand and squeeze it. Robbie gave him a small smile, a silent reassurance that he understood, and stood his ground in front of the laird, only taking a step back to stand with Ian.

"The prince's ship has been seen, sir. He is heading up the coast, and it will only be a few hours before he is in Scottish waters."

"Then the time to fight is almost here," Alistair said softly. He smiled, although it was grim. "Ian, ye still have what I entrusted to ye." He said it as a statement, not a question, as though he knew Ian wouldn't have failed him.

"I do, sir." Ian couldn't help the pride in his voice. "Although if it wasn't for Robbie here, it might have been lost. I couldn't have kept it safe without him."

"I didn't—" Robbie started to protest, but Alistair held up his hand to stop him. "They're well hidden, sir," he said instead.

"Good." Alistair grew silent for a moment, his brow creased in thought. "Robbie, lad, would you show John where they are? Ian has done his duty, and it is now time for John to relieve him of it, and ensure it reaches the prince and serves the purpose for which it was intended."

Robbie hesitated. "Ian should—"

"My uncle wishes a word with me, Rob." Ian knew his uncle well enough to see the transparency of his request. "Show John the hiding place. I will wait for ye here."

Douglas and Jamie glanced at each other and walked a short distance away, out of earshot but still watchful as ever. The brothers had always had a way of communicating without having to use much in the way of words.

Alistair gestured to a rock. "I suggest we sit while we talk, before ye fall over. You're verra unsteady on your feet, and nae hiding it as well as I suspect you think you are."

"I'm..." The word died on Ian's lips when Alistair shook his head. Truth be told, he felt relieved to be off his feet as he was more than a wee bit lightheaded. "What did you wish to talk to me about?"

"To the point as usual." Alistair smiled. "So I will do the same." Nevertheless, he paused for a moment before continuing.

"I'm verra proud of ye. I know it wouldn't have been easy on Skye all these months." He lowered his voice. "I'm pleased you found someone to share your burden. I've despaired of you finding someone who can make you happy."

"We're not—" At the bemused expression on Alistair's face, Ian met his gaze head on. He'd not deny his feelings towards Robbie. "How did ye know?"

"I've known you since you were a bairn. I'm your laird, but I'm also your uncle. It pained me to have to send Angus away, but it needed to be done. There is a tenderness in the way you look at Robbie, although I doubt anyone else would have noticed."

"Thank ye." Ian felt relief that his uncle knew and approved. If he hadn't, Ian would have taken Robbie and left, rather than risk being parted from him.

"That wound of yours isn't just a scratch. Come back to the clan hall and recuperate."

Ian glanced at Robbie in the distance. He and John had reached the entrance to the cave. "Thank ye for your kind offer, but I think I'll be staying with Robbie." He added hurriedly before Alistair could protest. "I will, of course, pledge my service to the clan when it is time to fight. I will be well healed by then, and able bodied."

"I would expect no less." Alistair scratched at his chin. "I have a proposition for you. You have given to the cause already, and you do need time to rest and recover. Therefore, I gift you the cottage on Skye. Ye have no need to worry about the lad either. He can stay with you for as long as ye both wish, and once the time comes to fight, we will adopt him into the clan in return for his pledge to fight by our side."

"Thank ye!" Relief rushed through Ian. Alistair had given his blessing to him and Robbie, although he hadn't said it directly. "It will be Robbie's decision as to whether he wishes to fight, but I suspect I know what his answer will be."

"Aye, lad." Alistair smiled. "So do I."

Epilogue

To Robbie, the journey back to Skye—with an injured Ian—seemed somehow both more arduous and more restful than their flight south to Staffa. At Alistair's behest, they sailed their boat—one of McLeod's launces taken as spoils—alongside the laird's own ship. The little MacDonald fleet wound through the innermost of the islands until they reached the southern tip of Skye. There, Robbie and Ian bid the larger ship—and the protection it offered—farewell, beached the boat, and began a trek up the island on foot. They didn't think McLeod or Campbell would be seeking them out—they too had larger worries now that the Bonnie Prince had arrived. Still, Ian thought they'd be safer going overland—or maybe he just wanted to be away from the sea and heading for home.

Home. Robbie smiled to himself as he trudged along behind. *How about that, James Stuart? How about me going home to a cottage on the Isle of Skye a hundred years and on after ye died, and me a young man still, with a good man to love and a lifetime still ahead of me? Mayhap I should thank ye for sentencing me to hang, and thank Melisandre too. Never before, I'd wager, has a witch's curse turned out so well for its victim.*

He was excited to get back to the cosy blackstone cottage on the hill, with its single window that could be shuttered against the island wind or thrown wide to let in the sun. It was home in a way no other place had ever been for him, and that had nothing to do with the overlarge stove or the overcrowded bed. It was Robbie's home because it was Ian's.

He watched Ian carefully for signs he was tiring. Ian kept his injured arm bound to his middle and protected it, but it obviously still hurt. And he'd apparently given in to an urge to look pitiful about the pain, a behaviour Robbie had seen in big, strapping men before. It had bothered him when his brother-in-law had done it, but somehow, watching Ian, all he wanted to do was hug him and sing him a lullaby. And maybe kiss it and make it better. Or not kiss *it* per se, but... Anyway, Ian seemed strong enough now. As they came to the place by the stream where—was it only days ago?—Robbie had washed out their clothes and sung of being in his own country tending ewes, Ian turned and shot Robbie a smile as glorious as the daystar before adding a little skip to his step and picking up the pace.

"We're close, now, Robbie. And I admit I'm happier than I ever thought I'd be, coming back to our little house."

Robbie smiled too, glad that Ian's spirits had lifted. Robbie's wounded leg didn't bother him at all except for an occasional twinge. It had healed fast as they sailed, causing Robbie to wonder if perhaps the sea would always favour him, a little remnant of Melisandre's magic. He stepped nimbly over the stony path, now, and kept up easily with Ian's long-legged stride.

Almost there!

They trod the familiar last rise to the cottage and then forded the seasonal stream, shallow and wide, that crossed just down the hill from home. Stepping through the chill waters, Robbie began to hum an almost forgotten song from the Borders. After a moment, snatches of words about the lads around the Gala River came back, and he sang them low, his fingers playing against his thighs as if sounding invisible harp strings.

> *"I'll kilt my coats aboon my knee,*
> *And follow my love through the water."*

Ian turned and gave him a half-smile. "What's that you're singing, lad?"

Robbie smiled back. "It's just an old song you're not likely to ken."

"Sing it out, then," Ian said.

Robbie might have done, though he couldn't remember much more of the verse, but by the time he'd whistled once through the tune, they were at the cottage. Ian paused for a deep breath, opened the door, and stepped in, with Robbie close at his heels.

They stood in the dim light as if frozen in place, feeling the homecoming like a shock. It occurred to Robbie he'd thought all the time they might never make it back, and he'd wager Ian had thought the same. The cottage smelled only slightly musty—they'd not been gone as long as it seemed—and the air still held its hints of woodsmoke and herbs, sweat and sex.

It was beautiful, and when Ian stepped to the window and pushed the shutters wide, the familiar sights of the small room seemed a gift. The kettle on the stove gleamed dully in the late afternoon sunlight, and the wood of the table—polished with use—gently shone. Robbie breathed deep and cast his eyes around, wondering how a place he'd known for such a short time could be so dear.

Then Ian stepped away from the window, and the sun's beam lanced across the room to the milking stool, which Robbie had set by the door just as he was on his hurried way out.

There was a harp on the stool.

Familiar and fine and in perfect repair.

Is it...?

It was *the* harp, the one that had been with him all the long seasons of storms and tides which he, Robbie, had spent oblivious, wrapped in the watery silk and hidden thorns of Melisandre's curse.

"Ian," he said.

But Ian had already caught sight of the instrument, and he stared, slack-jawed. When he spoke, his voice trembled with trepidation. "Ach, sweet man, you don't think..."

His mouth worked for a moment as if trying to shape words to end the question, and Robbie's heart bled to think that fear—fear for him, for them, the future they were counting on—could twist Ian's heart so painfully.

"No, Ian! Look—the harp is *restored*. It's as if the curse had not happened, as if our lives—the harp's and mine—have begun anew. My wounds are healed. All the decay the harp was showing before? Gone. It's a gift, Ian. A gift flying to us through the long century and more since the spell was spoken against me. I don't know—can't know—If Melisandre meant to wrap this sweet inside the bitter shell of her curse, or if perhaps it's Clíodhna—the old sea goddess herself—who's taken pity over my long travail and blest us here, you and I. But make no mistake. Troubles we will have, but they will not be born of an old curse by Lady Talwyn, Melisandre, the Witch of the Hermitage."

Ian nodded, but he didn't meet Robbie's eyes. Was there a glisten of tears on his cheek? Perhaps, Robbie thought. He went to the harp and picked it up—its weight a surprise, now that the magic was gone from it. He sat on the stool to keep silent watch as Ian moved mechanically in and out of the cottage, bringing in wood and water.

"I found the cow," Ian said. "She didn't go far. And I think heard chickens just down the hill on the inland side."

He laid the fire and lit it with flint and tinder, then put the water on. "For tea," he said. And then finally, it seemed the truth came home to him that the danger of the curse had passed. He looked at Robbie and smiled. Reached out a hand to caress his cheek. Ran his thumb over Robbie's lip. "I fancy a song whilst I drink my tea. Will ye play?"

Robbie put his fingers to the harp's strings and glissed over them, but stopped short at the disturbing dissonance at the third string. "Ach! But that's an awful sound." He opened the small compartment in the base of the harp where the tuning key was kept, but found it empty. He told Ian of the problem and cast his gaze around the cluttered room, looking for something that would suffice to grasp the peg and turn it.

Ian looked around too, then opened his sporran and began rummaging through it, muttering a low curse when he poked his finger on a pin. He moved to the washstand and began emptying the contents. Robbie couldn't help but watch the amazing process. *How can so much fit in a single pouch the size of a double fist?* There was a wooden spoon, what looked like a lump of bark, a forked stick, a teasel such as one used for cleaning teeth, leather bands, something that might once have been cheese, and the familiar packet of whale fat—which Robbie was unexpectedly happy to see.

Suddenly, Ian exclaimed, "Ach," and pulled a last item out of the sporran.

Lying small in Ian's great palm, polished metal gleaming softly, it somehow conveyed an air of innocence, as if to say, *I've been here all along, have I not?*

"The key," Robbie said flatly.

"Yes."

"How...?"

"I don't..." Ian looked up from the key to meet Robbie's gaze and shrugged.

"Never mind." Robbie held out his hand for it.

When Ian passed it to him, their fingers brushed against each other—and *sparked*.

Robbie looked at Ian and smiled, then used the key to set the errant string right.

He played, and once the cottage room had been thoroughly soaked in a cascade of gambolling notes and stately chords, he sang the words, smiling impishly at the weighty melody and mock-serious lyrics.

> *Westron wynde when wilt thou blow*
> *The small rain down can raine*
> *Cryst if my love were in my armes*
> *and I in my bedde again.*

Ian listened through the verse once, through Robbie's playful, dancing instrumental embellishment, and almost all the way through the verse once more. Then he laughed and shook his head, advanced on Robbie and stole the harp from his hands. He placed the instrument securely on the floor, picked Robbie up and slung him, laughing, over his shoulder.

He carried him to bed, laid him down, and lay over him, bringing a thousand kisses.

A dull sound, off in the distance. *Cannon fire.*

For a moment they stopped and searched each other's eyes. Then Robbie pulled Ian's lips down to his again and kissed them with the kind of fervour one only finds when facing the truth that both time and life might be short.

He whispered against the shell of Ian's ear, "The battles will come, Ian. And we'll fight them then. But now, the day is ours. My love is in my arms, I'm in my bed, and I shall do my very best to love every care and worry away."

Ian frowned, as if he were about to argue. Then his eyebrows arched up over twinkling eyes, and a mischievous smile played over his lips.

"Well, then, lad. Ye'd best start by kissin' me again, before the wind blows the other damned way."

Acknowledgements

LOU

I have to start by pouring out some thanks to my co-author, Anne. Writing this book was a wild and wonderful ride, and it was a joy to take every step of it in her fine company. I'm grateful too to our editor Elizabetta, who attacked...er, edited our manuscript with skill, care, kindness, and passion. Of course, my thanks go to Raevyn and all the folks at NineStar who've played a part in turning our story of dreamy Scots into an actual book! I so appreciate our beta readers, who provided thoughtful and useful feedback as well as encouragement. To friends who never stop believing in me, and readers who never stop amazing me, and of course, my family, who never stop surprising me: thank you all. And if I didn't name you, but I should have? You know who you are, and you know I'm forgetful. Forgive me, and merci beaucoup!

ANNE

A huge thanks to my co-author, Lou, for sharing her love for our Scots lads, and all the time, conversations, and work she's put in with me so we can share their story with you. I'd also like to add my thanks to our editor, Elizabetta, and to Raevyn and everyone at NineStar for giving our story a home. To our beta readers Angela, Heather, Patricia, and Moira for their enthusiasm for the story, and commenting on the historical and Scottish elements of it. To my family. Love you guys. And to my writing and reading communities for your support and friendship, in particular the NZ Rainbow Romance Writers, RWNZ, and my Facebook groups Anne's Books and Brews, and Kiwi Authors Rainbow Readers. And last, but in no way least my friends at Upper Hutt Science Fiction Club, and Hutt City Libraries.

About Lou Sylvre

Lou Sylvre loves romance with all its ups and downs, and likes to conjure it into books. The sweethearts on her pages are men who end up loving each other—and usually saving each other from unspeakable danger. It's all pretty crazy and very, very sexy. As if you'd want to know more, she'll happily tell you that she is a proudly bisexual woman—a mother, grandmother, lover of languages, and cat-herder—of mixed cultural heritage. She works closely with lead cat and writing assistant, the (male) Queen of Budapest, Boudreau St. Clair. She lives in the rainy part of the Pacific Northwest, and hearing from a reader unfailingly brightens the dreary weather.

Email: lou.sylvre@gmail.com.

Facebook page: www.facebook.com/AuthorLouSylvre

Facebook Authors page:
www.facebook.com/sylvrebarwellhoffmann

Twitter: @Sylvre

Instagram: www.instagram.com/sylvre

MeWe: www.mewe.com/i/lousylvre

Website: www.sylvre.rainbow-gate.com

About Anne Barwell

Anne Barwell lives in Wellington, New Zealand. She shares her home with Kaylee: a cat with "tortitude" who is convinced that the house is run to suit her; this is an ongoing "discussion," and to date, it appears as though Kaylee may be winning.

In 2008, Anne completed her conjoint BA in English Literature and Music/Bachelor of Teaching. She has worked as a music teacher, a primary school teacher, and now works in a library. She is a member of the Upper Hutt Science Fiction Club and plays violin for Hutt Valley Orchestra.

She is an avid reader across a wide range of genres and a watcher of far too many TV series and movies, although it can be argued that there is no such thing as "too many." These, of course, are best enjoyed with a decent cup of tea and further the continuing argument that the concept of "spare time" is really just a myth. She also hosts and reviews for other authors, and writes monthly blog posts for Love Bytes. She is the co-founder of the New Zealand Rainbow Romance Writers, and a member of RWNZ.

Anne's books have received honourable mentions five times, reached the finals four times—one of which was for best gay book—and been a runner up in the Rainbow Awards. She has also been nominated twice in the Goodreads M/M Romance Reader's Choice Awards—once for Best Fantasy and once for Best Historical.

Website & Blog: www.annebarwell.wordpress.com

Facebook: www.facebook.com/anne.barwell.1

Facebook page: www.facebook.com/annebarwellauthor

Facebook Authors page:
www.facebook.com/sylvrebarwellhoffmann

Facebook group:
facebook.com/groups/annesbooksandbrews

Joint FB group:
facebook.com/groups/KiwiAuthorsRainbowReaders

Instagram: www.instagram.com/anne.barwell

Twitter: @annebarwell

Sign Up For My Newsletter:
www.mailchi.mp/39edaba3e3ad/annebarwellauthor

Also Available from NineStar Press

Connect with NineStar Press

www.ninestarpress.com

www.facebook.com/ninestarpress

www.facebook.com/groups/NineStarNiche

www.twitter.com/ninestarpress

In 1605, Robbie Elliot—a Reiver and musician from the Scottish borders—nearly went to the gallows. The Witch of the Hermitage saved him with a ruse, but weeks later, she cursed him to an ethereal existence in the sea. He has seven chances to come alive, come ashore, and find true love. For over a century, Robbie's been lost to that magic; six times love has failed. When he washes ashore on the Isle of Skye in 1745, he's arrived at his last chance at love, his last chance at life.

Highland warrior Ian MacDonald came to Skye for loyalty and rebellion. He's lost once at love, and stands as an outsider in his own clan. When Ian's uncle and laird sends him to lonely Skye to hide and protect treasure meant for Bonnie Prince Charlie's coffers, he resigns himself to a solitary life—his only companion the eternal sea. Lonely doldrums transform into romance and mystery when the tide brings beautiful Robbie Elliot and his broken harp ashore.

A curse dogs them, enemies hunt them, and war looms over their lives. Robbie and Ian will fight with love, will, and the sword. But without the help of magic and ancient gods, will it be enough to win them a future together?